THE EXILED

(English translation of Odia novel BIBASINI)

THE EXILED

Ramshankar Ray

Translated by
Snehaprava Das

Foreword by
Jatin Nayak

BLACK EAGLE BOOKS
Dublin, USA | Bhubaneswar, India

Black Eagle Books
USA address:
7464 Wisdom Lane
Dublin, OH 43016

India address:
E/312, Trident Galaxy, Kalinga Nagar,
Bhubaneswar-751003, Odisha, India

E-mail: info@blackeaglebooks.org
Website: www.blackeaglebooks.org

First International Edition Published by
Black Eagle Books, 2024

THE EXILED
by **Ramshankar Ray**
Translated by **Snehaprava Das**

Translation Copyright © Snehaprava Das

Cover & Interior Design: Ezy's Publication

ISBN- 978-1-64560-518-8 (Paperback)
Library of Congress Control Number: 2024932904

Printed in the United States of America

DEDICATION

In the Hands of my Beloved Parents

Foreword to The Exiled, A Historical Romance

Jatin. K. Nayak

The period during which Odisha was under Maratha rule has been, generally speaking, neglected by historians, who tend to focus Odisha under Muslim and British rule. Only one book-length study of this period was undertaken long ago by eminent historian B.C. Ray but is out of print and not easily available. Information about this period available in accounts left by British travellers such as Leckie and Thomas Motte who passed through the province in the later part of the 19th century presents Marathas in rather a poor light. this is the spectacle that awaits Motte when he crosses river Kharasuan on his way to Sambalpur. Now it is the custom of the Maratha troops to plunder as much in the Zamindaries tributary to them, as in any enemy's country; the tenants of such Zamindaries, therefore, desert their villages at the approach of an army, while the Fouzdar meeting the commander with a present, obtains an order to be exempted from pillage, the execution of which he attends to himself, and if any inferior officer commits violence, fails not to repel force. The Fouzdary also having continued sometime in the same family, contributes to render the country populous. Jagoo Pundit has secured the succession to his son-in-law Incoojee, who came to see me. He praised Sehoo Butt, the Late Governor of Odisha when I asked him, 'Why, people in general preferred him so much to the present governor?' He answered in the style of a baron-bold: 'Sehoo Butt supported the national troops with the plunder of foreign countries; Bowanee Pundit, with the plunder of his own.' Leckie, who travelled through Cuttack on his way to Nagpur in the last decade of the 18th century, feels disgusted by the picture of dirt, disorder and decay that confronted him in the city which was the headquarters of the Maratha rulers. Piles of skulls and bones scattered in and near the town: A miserable spectacle! At which humanity shudders; and the streets are crowded with beggars starved almost to death. They frequently surrounded my tent, and I could not shut my ears to the cries of wretchedness. I could not help drawing comparison between the wretched state of these people and those under the protection of the British Government; and only wish that Mr. B. could be a spectator of what I have seen.'

From all appearances, curiosity about this period in history has been minimal and one wonders if if some young historian is hard at work in the archives of Maharashtra to throw light on what many consider a very unpleasant era in Odishan history. Muslim rule has left behind a few impressive monuments and the interaction with Islamic culture had interesting cultural outcomes such as Mogul Bibashi consent ushered in modernity, that magic word. but five decades of Maratha rule find few, if any, apologists or enthusiasts among historians. Except words like 'marahatti' meaning someone terribly old fashioned and hopelessly out of date very little reminds one of Maratha presence in Odisha, which was once so awesome and terrifying.

However, the world neglected by historians has been explored by creative writers in their novels and autobiographies. The abbot of the monastery in *Padmamali* (1888) is a Maratha soldier who chooses to stay in Odisha even after the Marathas cede the province to the British. The central action of *Bibasini* (1891) unfolds against the background of resistance against Maratha misrule. It keeps shifting between Paradeep, where Robin Hood figures rob the agents of Maratha rule to bring succor to the oppressed subjects, and Cuttack, the seat of Maratha power. In this unusual endeavour they have the support of the king of Paradeep and the blessings of two hermits. One can easily detect the influence of Bankim Chandra Chatterjee's *Ananda Matha* here but there the resemblance ends. Regeneration of Hinduism is no part of the agenda of the author of *Bibasini*. The scene of dacoity brings the two strands of narrative together: the story of resistance to Maratha rule gets intertwined with a love story. The dacoit-rebels abduct the widowed daughter of the agent of Marathas and her young companion. Their leader falls hopelessly in love with the young widow but is persuaded by the king and the widow herself to marry her young companion instead. The representative of the victims of the Maratha misrule, a pitiable man called Dasa Khadanga, is falsely implicated in the robbery and is sentenced to death by the cruel Subedar. He, his wife and his mother die before the sentence is carried out. When a famine strikes the province, an irate mob set fire to the Subedars fort and he saves his life by swimming across river Kathjuri and escaping into a forest. He interesting thing about Bibasini is that its story of life under the Maratha rule is embedded by the narrator in the context of British rule. The moralizing, intrusive narrator informs the reader that the word dacoit originated in

Burma under British rule. He constantly sets up a contrast between the British and their immediate predecessors, not always to the former's advantage. The rise of selfish individualistic young men and women shaped by a new education system are made objects of censure and ridicule. Although Bibsini depicts scenes of devastation caused by a famine and human indifference and cruelty and shows a young woman committing suicide to escape her utterly hopeless situation it nevertheless ends on a note of subdued optimism. The scene of a community feast which closes the novel leaves this impression on the reader's mind even if his joy is tempered by the young widow's suicide.

Written about three decades after *Bibasini*, Fakir Mohan Senapati's *Lacchama* offers no such consolation. It chooses for its setting the conflict declining Mogul power and ascendant Marathas and shows how an Odia chieftain finds itself caught in this conflict and gets destroyed. Fakir Mohan vividly depicts how the anarchy let loose by Marathas in Odisha affects everyday life and ordinary characters in the narrative like Jaga Fateh Singh's mother embody this suffering. *Lacchama* is remarkable in the sense that the Hindu chieftain chooses to side with the Muslim antagonists of the Marathas in their battle for supremacy and lays down his life for his heroic defiance. When the emissary of Marathas urge him to side with Marathas his court priest presents a stirring version of a future world where the Muslims and Marathas would be superseded and amore humane order represented by the British would be established. The story of revenge which is embedded in the narrative of the larger conflict finds its resolution in the assassination of the oppressive Maratha chief, Bhasker Pandit. But the note which the narrative ends, remains a melancholy one. The couple after being reunited inherit a kingdom but remain childless, and the novel closes with the narrator pensively reflecting upon the transience and futility of all human initiatives.

Years of Maratha rule can never simply fade away. Memories of this period must be lurking somewhere in records, oral narratives and other forms of collective memory. The opening chapter of Fakir Mohan's autobiography and his short story 'Dhulia Baba' provide fascinating glimpses of this period. It is time we tried to bring this forgotten period of our history to life.

Introduction by the translator

Why does a work of literature need to be translated? Does translating a fiction, essay or a poem or a play enhance its quality or aesthetic appeal or actually gain it an expanded readership? Does translation help the original to grow out of a limiting frame to reach out to a wider space or a greater height? Does it assign a new and extended life to the original that would otherwise have faded out of the literary scenario in course of time? and the most vital issue relating to translation that still remains an unsolved riddle is whether a translated replication could be trusted as the as the original text written in another language. These are confounding questions that are difficult to be answered conclusively. But still, translation, since ancient times, has survived its questionable status and thrived on as a legitimate literary activity.

It is believed by many that the same text cannot be written in two or more languages. There is some truth in it but at the same time it is also true that a translated text in almost all cases is another text aiming to be received by a larger segment of readers with greater and renewed interest. It must not be misconstrued as the translator's arrogance but an honest admission that a translator by no means can write the same text in another language. The language and narratology used in the translated version demands certain shifts and alterations without which the translated text would lose its own originality. A text, if transferred with competence could help not only in elevating the literary status of the original but also gain it a much broader and healthy exposure.

Several texts all over the world are written in vernaculars of particular provinces or regions which, in spite of their tremendous appeal and popularity, remain confined to a limited and narrowed readership. It happens in case of Odia texts too. Works like *Padmamali* and *Bibasini* which marked the inception and growth of a new genre of writing in Odia literature face the threat of relapsing into oblivion for want of such exposures. Such works do have a justifiable claim over a global identity and they can assume that identity only through translation, especially in English translation, which would enable them to reach beyond the language frontier and mark out a space for themselves in the ambit of world literature.

'Without translation, I would be limited to the borders of my own country. The translator is my most important ally. He introduces me to the world,' says Italo Calvino, the renowned journalist and fictionist. A work of art written in a marginalised vernacular, however great, may die a premature death unless it is introduced to the world through a translation in a widely spoken and understood language.

Ramshankar Ray's *Bibasini* (1891), believed to be the second full length novel in Odia, the first being Umesh Chandra Sarkar's *Padmamali* (1888), is a novel with an intricately woven plot structure written in style that is at once descriptive, informative, and lyrical. Viewed mostly as a work of fiction delicately poised between a historical romance and a socio-political narrative, Bibasini relates to the period of Maratha hegemony over Odisha spanning from 1751 till the British occupation of the province in 1803. It holds out a panoramic view of Odisha reeling under the tyranny of the Maratha ruler Shambhuji Ganesh Rao during 1769 to 1771, and of the native resistance offered in terms of sporadic but organised assaults launched on the oppressors and collaborators by the Bhuyan dacoits acting at the instances and with the support of the king of Kujanga, Paradip.

The plot that seemingly centres round a tragic love story is actually a complex one, knitting many strands of random episodes into an attractive and coherent tale of unmerited suffering, of crime and vengeance, of sin and retribution. The novel is thronged with characters from different socio-cultural backgrounds, portraying multiple contours of Odisha, the social, cultural, economic and religious ones being the most pronounced amongst them. The novel chronicles the agrarian crisis in Odisha during the Maratha rule and the debacle of the famine that threatened to bring the peasantry of Odisha down to a state of collapse. It narrates the hardship and the misery of the common man especially those who earned their living through farming, had to pass through under the repressive measures of a tyrannous governance and the selfishness and all-devouring avarice of the moneyed local landowners or zamindars.

'Shambhuji Ganesh was the subedar of Odisha during the period in which the incidents mentioned in the earlier chapter occurred. He had assumed office about a year before. the fellow had proved himself to be a tyrant as soon as he came to power. Immediately after becoming the subedar, he imposed various new taxes on his subjects. Tax was levied on the lands which were earlier rent-free. This offered a golden opportunity to the accounts-managers for pilfering the revenue of the state.'

(The Village of Navagram, chapter 6, The Exiled, A Historical Romance)

It is also a gripping tale of a band of burglars, motivated by a romanticised ideal of plundering the rich to sustain the poor, assuming the role of the vindicators of socio-economic equality. They declare themselves as the god's chosen moral agents for delivering violent justice to the wrongdoers. At the same time the novel camouflages a satire on the hollow morals of a socio-cultural system that compels a Hindu widow to practice religious austerity and denies her the right of living the life of a normal woman.

The novel also details the spread of a new religious cult, Vaishnavism, in Odisha that advocated the worship of Lord Hari(Vishnu) and pleaded against a discriminatory caste system that deprived the people of the lesser caste and poor economic status of their legitimate rights. The preachings of the Vaishnava monks Hanuman Dasa and Giridhari Dasa, appears to reflect a semblance of the mystique.

'It would be ridiculous to question the widespread influence of Vaishnavism on Odisha after witnessing how people of all castes beginning from the brahmins to the untouchables eat the *Mahaprasad* (the food offering made to Lord Jagannath, Lord Balabhadra and goddess Subhadra in the temple at Puri) from one another's hands inside the temple. It was the influence of Vaishnavism that inspired the people of Navagram to partake in the ceremonial feast that day and eat together forgetting their social differences. Readers, I must admit that the caste system prevailed in Odisha as it did in many other provinces. And it was rather more rigid here......... But while eating the *prasad* , people ignored it completely. The merit of such a gesture, in my opinion, need not be elaborated on. Alas! Had every Indian been initiated to the doctrines of Vaishnavism in this manner, a new life-force would have been generated in our country. Would a time ever come when we would see the entire nation pulsating with such a spirit of brotherhood?' (The Grand Feast at the Mound of Jatia, Chapter 24, The Exiled, A Historical Romance)

One of the significant elements that lift the novel to almost a sublime plane is the metaphysical concepts underlying the surface narrative. The author reveals a Thomas Hardy like belief in the invincibility and inexorability of destiny and attributes the turns and twists of events taking place in the lives of human beings to the inscrutable ways and wills of Providence. That is why sometimes the innocent characters suffer and perish while the unscrupulous ones flourish.

'Life is strange! The intentions of Lord Almighty are still more so! It is beyond man's power of comprehension why He brings why he brings two different human beings from totally different walks of life together. These two young women, living in utterly dissimilar circumstances lay together on the carelessly spread bed sharing one pillow, like two playing balls set to rolling by some invisible hand had dribbled along the intricate paths of life and come to stop at one particular spot…..'

(Two Friends, Chapter 13, The Exiled: A Historical Romance)

However, the author had a strong, unshakable faith in the divine justice that metes out adequate and the deserved punishment to the evil ones at the appropriate time. There are several instances of unmerited suffering but in the end every sinner is led to his inevitable nemesis.

'Finally, the ruined house that had once been his dear home, came into view. The terrible picture that he had thought would be awaiting his eyes since he had heard the news of the burglary rose vividly before him. The sight of the wreckage filled him with an emptiness that paralysed his senses for a few moments. As soon as his mind could register the immense impact of the reality his last breath was emptied out of his body. The next moment, his lifeless body fell on the ground.'

(The Judgment, Chapter 25, The Exiled: A Historical Romance)

'Before leaving the palace they fixed the severed heads of the villains to the top of a bamboo-post following the orders of Sardar Singh and pitched it in front of the ransacked house. It looked like a flag holding aloft the symbol of sin to teach a lesson to the world!'

(Sardar Singh, Chapter 16, The Exiled: A Historical Romance)

Translating *Bibasini*, is by no means, an easy task. Being an early prose work in Odia authored by a Bengali writer, the language and style both pose considerable impediments to the to the task of the English rendering of the novel. If at one stage the sentences are crisp and brittle, they are long and lyrically evocative in the next. The poetic descriptions the novel abounds in offer quite a challenge to the translator's competence and craftmanship. The scene of the boat approaching the land narrated in the in chapter three of the novel has a unique beauty that is difficult to be captured in its exactitude in another language.

'The outlines of the boat became dimly visible as

it made its way towards the shore. In the still air of that desolate isle the rhythmic rowing sounded musical. The boat came into sight. Bathed in moonlight the river glittered like liquid silver and splashed water along both sides of the boat when the oars struck it the brilliantly lit foamy spray gave an impression as if the boat was spitting fire as it moved forward....'

(The Passengers Aboard Chapter 3, The Exiled: A Historical Romance)

A more or less similar waterscape is delineated in chapter 16.

'It was a noiseless chilly night. Silence reigned everywhere. No one was in sight. The moon and a few stars, shivering in the ice-cold air blinked at the earth from the sky. The blue waters of the river Mahanadi caught the reflection of the moon and the dimly twinkling stars, and made an impression as if there were two skies, one above and the other below. The firebugs that circled the trees on both sides of the river were like the eyes of those trees with which they witnessed the twin images. This beautiful moon blanched landscape glimpsed through the icy film of mist brought some sort of relief to the earth that writhed under the tyranny of the winter...'

(Sardar Singh, Chapter 16 The Exiled: A Historical Romance)

The text abounds in dialects and colloquial expressions. In spite of the odd it involves, translating texts like *Bibasini* sometimes turns out to be quite an engaging and interesting occupation. Translation 'is a creative work', says Subodh Sarkar, 'to be restricted within the boundary of a given text which has as its agenda the task of decoding from one language to another. (Editor's Note Indian

Literature vol. 263, May-June 2011) Quoting from an essay on translation by Professor Salawu Adewuni (Department of European Studies, University of Ibadan, Nigeria) he adds, 'In translation, it is a question of satisfaction rather than perfection. Satisfaction in translation lies in the ability to minimize the gap between the theory and practice.' Hence, while translating such texts a translator has to be more concerned how satisfactorily s/he has transferred the original into the translated version and to what extent it would be able to satisfy the readers who do not know the original language, and in all probability live in another time-segment. Every translation is conditioned not only by the need of fidelity to the original text but also by the demands of creativity of the new writing. A translated text, as often supposed to be an interpreted text and the act of interpretation instead of confining itself to the act of explaining the surface meaning and replicating the ostentatious, travels further to explore the sub-textual aspects since in the opinion of Paul Valery 'Fidelity to the meaning alone in translation is a kind of betrayal...' While on the job, the translator can succeed in manoeuvring the readers to newly discovered areas of richer experiences that actually exist in the original text but somehow get missed. That is one of the reasons why early texts like *Bibasini* are in need of being hauled out of the depth of anonymity and introduced to the new-generation readers in a new light.

Snehaprava Das

Chapter-1

The Conspiracy

It was a full moon night in the month of Pausha. The night marked the end of the month. The moon had covered almost one-sixth of its journey across the sky and was sending down its cool light everywhere. The esoteric landscape might have been rendered oppressive by the cold of the winter, and appeared solemn. But the soft moonlight lent it a picturesque charm.

Patches of cloud had clustered in the sky for the last few days. This had mitigated the cold considerably. But the clouds had gone away that night perhaps to watch the coronation ceremony of Lord Indra, and the cold had come back. The chilly wind, having vanquished the breeze from the south that was wafting in a few days ago, had again started blowing. It had heightened the intensity of the cold. The unhappiness caused by the presence of the clouds that prevented it from exercising its absolute power had dulled the moon, but now that the clouds had beat in a retreat, the moon was overwhelmed with joy and penetrating the net of icy air that wrapped the earth, bathed it in the exotic beauty of its own soft white beams.

How lovely! It was as if the Nature-Goddess as it were had draped herself in a white robe to keep away the cold after taking a bath, and was drinking the nectar of the moon- light in a serene mood. It seemed as though the moon-god, otherwise named Sudhakar or the carrier of nectar-sweet beams, had increased its brilliance two times more in joy having realized that his name had justified itself. It is true that now and then the winter conjures up such beautiful pictures unexpectedly which, no wonder, arouse a mood of ecstasy in a sensitive heart.

Dear Readers, in a lovely hour like this, I would invite you to the islet of Nandikeswari lying in the bed of the deep and far-flowing, melodious river Mahanadi. The islet is a part of the landscape spoken of earlier and to describe the luxurious bliss that is reflected over it too, will be a repetition. The islet is devoid of human habitation. Only the thick growth of shrubl-ike plants and a number of huge dense trees that grew at random, made the place appear wild and scary. To the west there stood a tomb made of stones. An idol of lord Mahavira installed on a platform close to it seemed to rule over the place.

Having heard of the presence of the lord Mahavira in that riverine islet, the readers might expect to find a priest be dwelling nearby to perform the religious rites. But this hope, like all other hopes in this world, is a vain one. The tomb of princess Nandika that stood as a testament of her betrayed hopes and made the somber-looking place even more so affirms this truth. The idol of the deity installed at a place uninhabited by human beings,teaches that that nothing other than the glory of noble deeds endures in this illusory and transient world.

There was no one to offer worship to the god. Some driven by their devotion visit the place now and then to worship him and later having been initiated into Faith pursue spiritual truth. Once these devotees depart, the deity stands there alone, unattended and unworshiped. Such is the manner in which short-term events come to occur in this transient world. Lord Mahavira is worshipped on this earth because of his noble deeds. He is deathless. Only the ones who do not attain any such glory are subject to death ; the virtuous ones, if not acknowledged in the present, are sure to be worshiped by posterity. They are never forgotten. It is true that they conquer death. The poet, therefore, says: "The glorious ones live for ever."

The readers might be wondering why they are asked to visit this deserted islet in a winter night. The place should be visited in summer and spring when people can enjoy the fresh air here and engage in sport and merry- making. It might be sensible to come here during those seasons when the landscape, acquiring almost an incredible loveliness, welcomes people to enjoy its beauty. But what is the use of coming to such a place in winter- when it is lashed by chilly winds?

True ! Such a visit is not of much use. But in this world created by God Almighty all sorts of events come to take place at his playful direction. The holy water of the deep Mahanadi that hemmed the islet, shone brightly in the moonlight. But you are not asked here to witness the simmering river,nor are you invited to see how the dense vegetation on the islet, looking somber during winter, sipped the nectar of moonlight in a calm, resigned mood. The gruff howls of wild animals like the jackals and wolves shattered the blissful tranquillity of the place time and again. You are not called upon here to listen to their noise, too.

I have invited you here to draw your attention to a couple of hefty men sittting on the platform on which the image of lord Mahavira stood. These two, without being bothered in the least by the chill that spread over the river, are engaged in a deep conspiracy.

Chapter-2

What Conspiracy ?

What conspiracy were those two men hatching? Were they the only ones involved in the plan or were there others, too? The answer is simple – The plan is a dangerous one and, if successful, was sure to destroy someone. About fifty men, including the two mentioned above, were involved in it.

One of these two men was Bahubalindra and the other was known as Baliarsingh. Like all others in the group, these two were devotees of lord Mahavira and were dacoits by profession.

The manner in which the sight of ferocious animals makes the heart beat faster, the menacing look of these two is sure to scare people unless they are relieved of their fear and are convinced that they will not be the targeted by these awesome characters. Their height, enormous torsos, powerful thighs , rock-hard biceps , flowing unkempt beard, lofty brows, and the grim , broad foreheads are enough to strike fear in anyone. They were physically so strong that they could make large stone- built houses shake with a powerful blow. They were very fond of wine and meat.They did not approve of the traditional method of cooking – and would even eat raw meat if the occasion demanded. They had the instincts of brutes. The only thing that told them apart from brutes was their human form. What other instances can be given to illustrate the ferocity of their nature? From the above description the readers can figure out for themselves how fierce they must be. Further elaboration shall be nothing but exaggeration.

"I swear before lord Mahavira that I will clip my mustache unless I carry out the job single handed." Bahubalindra declared ; he stroked his mustache, flexed his muscular biceps and let out a raucous laughter expressing an animal delight. Baliarsingh, who, sitting cross-legged, was listening to the bravado of his companion in silence, slapped his own thigh and said: " Bahabalindra, am I too not one of the wrestlers patronized by the Sandha-King of Kujanga ? If Bahubalindra can smash a boundary wall and open a road straight through, Baliarsingh can scale such a wall with one leap. O Friend! Could anyone on earth to defeat our combined force?"

Bahubalindra was pleased with this remark ; " Come, let us play the game of arm-wrestling. The cold can do nothing to deter us", he said and stood up, then rubbed his palm on the ground before the image of lord Mahavira, touched the dust to his forehead and jumped down. Baliarsingh repeated the act. The two remained engaged in the arm-wresting sport for some time, then came back to the platform and sat down.

"Have you seen it yourself?" Baliarsingh inquired.

"Yes, I have seen it with my own eyes", replied the other.

"We have never come across such a tempting prey. When there are plenty of birds perching in a tree, one gunshot of the hunter brings many of them down at a time. Similarly , this time we can plunder much with a single stroke."

"Very well ! What could be more exciting than being able to snatch a large prize in a single attempt?" Baliarsingh remarked happily.

"Baliarsingh, the booty will be so large that even if our chief takes half of it as his share, the rest cannot be spent easily even if we gave away a large part of it in charity." Bahubalindra assured his companion.

Baliarsingh roared with laughter. When Bahubalindra joined him, the air reverberated with the sound.

Just then they heard the sound of a boat sailing towards the shore. " Hail Lord Mahavira !!!" shouted Bahubalindra and came out to the open space. Baliarsingh followed him. Hand in hand, they strode towards the place where the sound came from and stood at the edge of the isle.

***

Chapter- 3

The Passengers Aboard

The outlines of the boat became dimly visible as it made its way towards the shore. In the still air of that desolate isle, the rhythmic beat of rowing sounded musical. Slowly the boat came into sight. Bathed in the moonlight, the river sparkled like liquid silver and splashed water on both the sides of the boat as the oars struck it. The brilliantly lit foamy spouts of water gave an impression as if the boat was spitting fire as it moved forward. The grandeur of the picture thus created, blended with the music produced by the oars hitting the water, was a treat for the eyes as well as the ears. The hearts of Bahabalindra and Baliarsingh overflowed with excitement as they watched the approaching vessel.

The readers might think that some wealthy pleasure-monger, accompanied by friends, was on a visit to the islet intending to spend a few hours enjoying nature's enchanting beauty. Indeed, the isle was such an ideal spot for picnics as well as private amusement, it would not appear strange if it lured some fun-loving person on a cool moonlit night in winter. Such people, rather, prefer to come to this un-inhabited place in search of a temporary diversion from the cares of the worldly life and engage in fun-fare and musical entertainment. Had there been some such men aboard and by ill-luck they fell victims to robbers like Bahabalindra and Baliarsingh , it would never be easy for them to go back home. But, let us wait and see if the passengers in the boat were friends to the two dacoits or if they were their enemies?

The vessel was not too long nor too wide. It was shaped like a rowing- boat but its width was comparatively less. Its small size allowed it to negotiate the treacherous currents of narrow and perilous mountain streams. But its concave bottom was not narrowl. In fact, it was larger than that of a Malangi boat. The entire length of the boat was canopied over, but it was open on all sides. Excluding the four oarsmen there were ten others on board.

From the sound of the oars, it appeared that the boat was moving fast. During the time the vessel was being described, it had sailed closer to the isle. It was only a few feet away from the isle's western border. The rowing stopped.

"Victory to Lord Mahaveer!!" A voice cried loudly from the boat.

"Victory to Mahaveer!" Bahabalindra and Baliarsingh shouted in reply and leapt into the water. The cry came again from the boat as it cruised towards the land. The oarsmen threw a rope down. Bahabalindra and Baliarsingh caught hold of it, pulled the boat along the edge of the isle towards the north and fastened it to a large Banyan tree there.

By now, the readers might not be having any more doubt that the men on the boat were of the same group to which Bahabalindra, and Baliarsingh belonged. Eight out of the ten were musclemen like the two mentioned earlier. Their appearances were more or less similar to that of Bahabalindra and his companion. Though they were not Bahabalindra and Baliarsingh's equals in muscle power they were strong enough to resist them for at least an hour. Some of them perhaps would grow to be as strong as Bahabalindra and Baliarsingh in six months or so.

Let us turn our attention to the oarsmen! They were sturdily built and stood guard like silent sentinels. Dear readers, you pursue knowledge at the cost of your health. Sometimes your ill health lands you on a sick bed. You suffer from poor appetite, and when invited by friends to attend a ceremonial feast, you ask them in advance to be excused on grounds of your ill health. You can't take a long walk and will not be able to pay a visit to a dying friend without a vehicle even if he lives only a mile away or so from your home. On the advice of your physician you stroll in a flower garden or along the river-bank. Even such small exercises demand a lot of effort. You go for boating in a lake and make a few strokes with an oar; the effort become so taxing that you keep confined to bed for a few days. But the oarsmen were made of different stuff. Readers ! here you can notice the difference between physical and mental labour. Can the schoolboys of these days who spend about eighteen hours a day studying books and devote only an hour or so to playing games like cricket in the fields adjacent to schools, possess such vigour and energy ? Similarly, will the persons who eat fine rice and roam in smart outfits have such strength ? The boatmen, in contrast, were so strong that they could row to make the boat move on still waters at the speed of a steamer, wielding only a couple of oars. They had derived this energy and vitality from a simple lifestyle and were enjoying a long and healthy life. It need not be debated whether or not such a life is desirable.

Among the the passengers was the chief. Ranghunath was his name. He hailed from a Mohanty family of the Karana caste. The title 'Pattnaik' was conferred upon him by the wrestling maestro and was chosen as the leader of the gang. The man was handsome to look at. He had the complexion of the champak flower; his forehead was broad, his cheek-bones were high and the tip of his sharp nose, as is often found in poetic descriptions, was like the beak of a parrot. His eyes were drawn a little towards the ears on both sides and this lent his face a celestial charm. His long arms, not too broad chest and the attractive shape of his beard added to this charm. In short, the fairness of his skin was a perfect match to his physical features. At a guess, he would be about thirty years. He had decent manners, and a good-humoured nature that reflected itself in his eyes and made him look more attractive. He had lost his wife five years ago; and his face bore the mark of this grief in the form of a grim line on his otherwise handsome forehead. It might seem strange that such a person was the chief men who were engaged in a deplorable profession life robbery.

But, as it is said, the course that Destiny takes is not always straight. One can't have a hold over fate.

The last of the passengers was Mayadhara ; he was an associate of Raghunath. Even though he was not honoured with any title, he could undoubtedly be declared a swindler par excellence. The maestro addressed him 'Uncle', perhaps because the man's nature resembled that of 'Shakuni' , the uncle of the Kaurava prince, Duryodhana. The colour of his skin was pitch black. But since he too hailed from a karana family , the black colour had a grace of its own. There is no need to dwell upon his facial features; his face faithfully mirrored his shrewd mind. God shapes the face of a man in such a way that it bears the imprint of his inner nature. Exceptions, however, are there- but they are but few in number.

The readers might be getting impatient. A full chapter has been devoted to description and the suspense still stands unresolved. But there was no other alternative. The purpose of the elaborate description was not to increase the length of the narrative, but to make the events, which would come to pass later, intelligible to the readers.

******

Chapter-4

Exchange Of Greetings

One might wonder whether it was customary amongst the dacoits to greet each other when they met. It was, however, not the conventional ways of greeting the readers are familiar with. But it is believed that the thieves are tied in strong bonds of mutual loyalty. So why wouldn't their heart-to-heart talk be described as a form of greeting? All the same, it is understood that the sentiments the readers attach to the word would not permit them to use it for the aforesaid conversation among the robbers.

The passengers alighted from the boat after it was roped to the tree. Coming down Raghunath took the hand of Bahabalindra and the two walked ahead of the others towards the temple of Lord Mahaveer. As they walked hand in hand, the following exchange took place between them:

Raghu: I reckon you to be very efficient. You have proven your efficiency on all occasions. Have today's arrangements been made as planned? Is everything taken care of?

Baha: Everything has been arranged according to plan. We have made necessary preparations at Harito and Raghunathpur. I am sure that things would be ready by the time we reached there.

Raghu: When did you leave Raghunathpur?

Baha:	In the afternoon. Chanchana Singh assured us that all arrangements would be complete much before your arrival there. He said that he would clip his mustache if he could not make you admit that you were late in reaching there.
Ranghu:	Very well . Chanchana Singh is an able man. You must have passed Harito'.
Baha:	Could we disobey your orders? We were there."
Raghu:	What did Sardar Singh tell you?
Baha:	Sardar Singh is a loyal man . He was pleased with your plan. He jumped in joy when he saw us and said 'No one can give us better ideas than Raghu-babu, or else the Maestro would not have chosen him for such an important job'. He had promised to get the things he had been in charge of collecting at the appointed place some time around the early part of the night.
Raghu:	How about more help?
Baha:	I had inquired about that, too. Sardar Singh asked us not to worry on that count. He himself would meet Chanchana Singh and get everything organized.
Raghu:	So, we need not make any extra arrangements from our side?
Baha:	No. Both of them asked us not to worry. They said that, since the ceremony would take place in their area, it was their responsibility to put things in order. ' We shall cut off our own hands if Raghubabu found even a minor flaw in the arrangements.', they said.

Raghu: Good ; when did you reach here?

Baha: Late in the evening.

Raghu: Did you take a careful look at the place where the raid is going to be executed? Did you find anything amiss?

Baha: We could not resist the temptation to have a look at the place. We had gone there on our way back from Raghunathpur. The preparations are ful-proof.

Raghu: Have you told everything to Baliarsingh. What is his opinion?

Baha: Can anyone find fault with your plan ? I have told everything to Baliarsingh. He flailed his arms in excitement. He is eager to pounce upon the prey.

Had they taken the straight path that led to the temple, they would not have had time enough to hav a long discussion. But they took the round-about way along the western border of the islet. Raghunath and Bahabalindra were the first to arrive at the temple; others in the group followed them at a distance. After all of them reached the temple, Raghunath told them,

"We do not have much time on our hands. Have your food quickly. Everything has been taken care of by our friends there. Delay on our parts may cause problems."

There was no dearth of food in the boat. Plenty of rice, beaten rice and salt, chilli and other food items were kept in the boat. It was decided earlier that they would not eat cooked meal that night since it was a full-moon night of Pausha. Therefore, all of them helped themselves to uncooked uncooked food.

Sitting together they ate in a jestful mood, cutting jokes with one another and exchanging pleasantries, and enjoyed that simple meal immensely even though they had to eat in the insufficient light of the moon. The want of a lamp or the solitude of the place could not mar their enjoyment. Could the rich ones, feasting in spacious double-storied mansions illumined with many lamps, experience such pleasure? A rare kind of contentment is obtained from eating when the food satisfies real hunger. Rich people are deprived of such precious joy.

Our earth, a treasure-house, stores in abundance a variety of things to fulfil man's craving for pleasure. Man too has discovered with the help of his imagination ways of utilizing these things for the purpose of comfort and enjoyment. But an attitude of indifference renders those otherwise precious things meaningless. A man who defines happiness only in terms of sheer physical comfort can't savour such unblemished joy. The laws of existence are not that simple. There would not have been any problem in a man's life had happiness been so easy to find. All happiness springs from hard labour. No one can obtain pure pleasure without hard work. These men might be dacoits, but a rich man can not derive even a small portion of joy from eating the delicious food cooked and served by the beautiful hands of his beloved wife which these men got from eating the simple meal of coarse beaten rice.

Eating over, they all walked down to the rocky part at the edge of the isle, washed their hands and drank water from the river. Thereafter they returned to the place where the image of Lord Mahaveera stood. "HailLlord Mahaveer!" They cried in unison and bowed before the Lord. Taking the dust from near the image's feet they touched it to their foreheads, and playing the game of mock-wrestling with one another, headed towards the boat. After boarding the boat the dacoits chewed 'paan' or smoked tobacco. The chief asked the oarsmen to unmoor the boat and proceed. The oarsmen untied the boat as soon as they received his orders. "Hail Lord Mahaveer!" the dacoits shouted lushly and the air reverberated with the sound. The oarsmen pushed the boat a little away from the isle and, singing songs as they did so, began rowing the boat. The boat shot forward with the speed of a flying arrow.

***

Chapter -5

Two Sisters

"*Apa*, do you know that the procession shall pass this way."

"Yes , I know."

"Father said that the procession will pass along this road in front of our house. There will be lot of fireworks and musical entertainment. But tell me Apa, who is getting married in the month of *Pausha*?"

"Why , won't your bridegroom come?"

"Don't joke; doesn't it seem odd?"

"No dear! Neither will any groom come nor the procession is a bridal one. A royal ceremony is going to be celebrated tonight."

"What ceremony?"

"It is the full-moon night of '*Pausha*'. Don't you remember that in royal families a ceremony is celebrated on this occasion ? There will be a lot of festivities and display of decorated lights ; plays will be enacted."

"Is there a Subedar here?"

"I don't know all the details and therefore can't explain things to you. Had the Subedar been here, he would have attended the procession in person. But he is not here at present. A letter has come from him instead. Hence the

Naib will ride the palanquin as his representative and accompany the procession.. You will see for yourself how handsome the man is. You will want to marry him."

"Apa, don't be funny. What time in the night will the procession start?"

"Around midnight."

"Then I shall eat my supper and come to sleep in your room. You will wake me, won't you?"

"All right"

Two young women talked in this manner in an unfrequented part of the house of Radhagovinda Choudhury who lived in Navagrama, about the same time the boat carrying the bandits sailed rapidly away from the isle of Nandikeshwari at the command of Raghunath Pattnaik.

The village-folk, during those days, usually ate their supper in the evening and go to bed. By early night the atmosphere became absolutely still, and the village wore the look of a scary, lonely graveyard where only uninhabited houses stood in silence as though through a spell cast by some sorceress every one lay numb. Nature, by the wave of a magic wand as it were, rendered everyone motionless. In those silent hours of the night everything that came into sight--- the alleys, the streets, the houses, and the forest-- appeared inert and lifeless. Had anyone by some chance been awake, he would be visualizing horrible forms of ghouls and monsters in his imagination and praying desperately the Sleep-Goddess for her blessings. If more than one person were attending to any urgent work that could not be postponed till morning, they would be talking in a voice so low as not to be audible even from a short distance. The only sounds that could be heard were the dreadful howls of the nocturnal animals like wolves, jackals, and dogs, which came bounding back from different parts of the village and resonated across the sky like the merciless command of an inexorable fate. People residing in urban areas would not be able to sense this fear the villagers experienced in the depths of lonely nights. The villages looked desolate and abandoned in the early hours of the night. Occasions of festivity, however, were exceptions. The village remains active late into the night on those special occasions. The night spoken of here was the full-moon night of the month of *Pausha*; the deities of the village temple were offered worship at auspicious hours of this night. This was the reason why people in the village of Navgram, including the members of the Choudhury family, were still awake. The two ladies wouldn't be talking to each other at this time of the night had the occasion not been so special.

The readers by now must have reckoned that one of the girls was a little younger than the other; she was sixteen. Each of them was hauntingly beautiful like the nymph Tilottama of the mythologies. A man, who had the power to exercise maximum control over his desires, wouldn't be able to take his eyes off them. The picture of their beauty would get deeply imprinted forever in his heart, and would flash in his imagination again and again despite strong attempts to wave it aside. So beautiful were these two young women that all their body parts seemed to give an inferiority complex to those beautiful objects of nature usually chosen by poets to provide parallels for them. A poet would prefer to describe their beauty using figures of speech in the following manner:

'The moon, seeing the brightness of her skin began slimming each day and just in a fortnight disappeared from the sky; at the sight of her sleek, black hair the dark cloud burnt itself in the fire of lightning born of its own body, and looked lusterless like smoke; her sharp nose mocked at the beak of Garuda, and the great bird in utter distress swallowed snakes; the mountain peak of Mandara, ashamed of its own height in comparison to her bosom, held its head down; envy pricked at the heart of the lotus-stem when it witnessed the smooth roundness of her arms and it sprouted thorns; the red berry smeared itself with ash when it noticed the lush pink of her chin; the hibiscus paled at the sight of her crimson lips; the banana tree loaded itself with fruit in order to lower its head to overcome the humiliation caused by watching the shapeliness of her thighs; her body was cooler than sandalwood; in utter shame, therefore, the sandalwood chose to be used as fuel; the row of her small white teeth forced the pearl to hide itself in the oyster-shell; the *veena* sang in distress a melancholic note when it heard the melody in her voice; her slim waistline seemed to ridicule the narrowness of the lion's waist and his wounded pride drove the beast into the thick forest where he could not be traced; unable to face the challenge her graceful gait offered to the swan, the bird wished to bring an end to its life and desperately ate the lotus-stem which is otherwise called *visha*, meaning poison.' The poet may add: 'The doe, seeing the beauty of her long, large eyes, escaped into the forest in shame. Her slanting, bow-shaped eyebrows hurt the self-esteem of Lord *Shiva*'s bow and therefore it gave in quite easily when Lord *Rama* lifted it to break it. The white column of her delicate throat compelled the conch to seek seclusion in the ocean-bed.'

Even without these elaborate comparisons it could be put more simply that each of the young woman's body-parts that supplemented one another flawlessly fitted to appropriate places in her body to create an image of absolute beauty. Each excelled in its own way any other beautiful object of nature that could have been thought of as a proper simile to describe it. Watching them one must be compelled to presume what meticulous care Lord Almighty would have taken in designing their shape, which exhibited the finest form of artistic craftsmanship. There was, however, one little imperfection in this picture of absolute beauty. She was neither gaudily attired nor wore precious jewellry; but the absence of expensive clothing and ornaments did not mar her looks in the least. It is true that expensive costumes and jewellry add but a little to real beauty.

The other girl was a couple of years younger. She had, as poets say, arrived at the crucial juncture of childhood and youth; her youthful charm, therefore, was not yet manifest in its full bloom. Do the readers mind my saying so? I sincerely believe that they will forgive the flaw, if there is any, in the statement. While narrating the beauty of a woman, a novelist stands perilously poised between a strict adherence to the accepted moral code, and an honest depiction of the grandeur of the beauty. He had to maintain a perfect balance between the two in order to prove his eminence as a writer. On the one hand, a rigid moral stance on his part might mar the beauty of the description, while a little liberty would amount to exaggeration, on the other. I, therefore, seek the learned readers' forgiveness for any slip I might have made in any way.

Great poets might say that King Youth accompanied by his queen Blush had just invaded the curves of her body, and after being crowned as the sovereign ruler of her body on the altar of her heart, had bestowed bountiful gifts on all her body-parts and gratified them. I can only take the liberty of saying that at the onset of youth, her beautiful body having attained a fullness of growth that had a blossoming freshness about it, was nothing less than a snare that would unfailingly captivate the hearts of men. She had had a beautifully proportioned figure; though not identical with that of the elder one, there was a likeness between the physical build of the two ladies. People around presumed that God had shaped both of them in the same mould effecting only a few alterations here and there. Youth, arriving freshly, had multiplied the loveliness nature had gifted her with. The girl, urged on by the natural desire that youth arouses in the minds of women, had decked herself with ornaments and wore expensive clothes and they added to her attractiveness. The splendour of the beauty of the young girl, with the hardly traceable lacunae easily compensated with these, was capable of robbing a saint of his peace of mind. Both the girls were well mannered and decent. They were shy by nature, soft-spoken, and adept at household work. They were hardly seen roaming outdoors. The invasion of western civilization has prompted the women of these days to undervalue these essential feminine qualities. The less their inclination towards these virtues the more they are admired by their husbands. Today's woman believes in sending out the radiance of her beauty everywhere like the moon in the sky does instead of keeping her face concealed under a veil. A woman is not considered fit to be called so if she wastes her beauty keeping herself confined to the four walls of the house and hiding her face behind a veil. Can any woman, who, instead of occupying herself with fine crafts like embroidery and needle work, prefers to ruin her life toiling in the kitchen day in and day out in order to cook and serve delicious dishes to her parents or parents-in law, be called decent and refined according to the standards of modern civilization? Can a wife that fails to launch a verbal attack on her husband given the slightest opportunity, by any means deserve as a modern women? A woman that shies away from displaying a fiery outspokenness in the midst of a social gathering can never be accepted as civilized. Blind emulation of western culture has resulted in a rapid transformation of traditional values; the age-old social norms cast in the mould of this new civilization, have assumed fascinating shapes. Coming under their influence, the youth of the present time are attracted towards girls, who, even though bereft of nice looks and nice qualities, clad themselves in provocative costumes, and come riding horse-drawn carriages to stroll along the river bank. These educated young men, representatives of the new civilization, deride theirvirtuous wives because of their incompetence in appraising and appreciating novels or plays, and their lack of expertise in the art of singing and dancing. They are oppressed by a feeling of shame at the conduct of their wives who refuse to touch meat or wine, and silently admire modern girls without moral scruples.

It might seem unusual to expect that the picture of the two young women portrayed here would evoke admiration in the hearts of the readers at a time when the impact of the western civilization is so widespread and so strong on our society. But they had the virtues that lend charm to a woman's character. The blinding flash of lightning or the ear-splitting crack of thunder may take our minds briefly away from the rain-clouds that actually generate them; but those are temporary digressions and cannot leave a lasting impression on our minds. Only the qualities concordant with the nature of an individual or an object get permanently etched in the heart. Disagreeable diversions from accepted social norms, tempting though they may appear, do not have an enduring value. Hence the wise ones must discreetly desist from emulating such wanton and irresponsible manners.

It is the reader's choice and prerogative whether to appreciate or not the virtues these two young women were endowed with; I, nevertheless, have presented a true picture of the girls. If it fails to arouse interest in the readers, the fault lies with the characters and not the author who has portrayed them with all honesty and sincerity.

We can recall that the younger girl had sought the elder one's permission to sleep in her room, and the later had agreed.

A voice called from outside: 'Rasa, you are sitting here till so late; won't you eat?

'Your mother is calling you', the older girl said, ' go and have your supper'.

The other one rose to her feet. ' I shall be through with supper in a few minutes and come back here.' She stepped briskly out of the room. The older girl got up too and walked slowly to the kitchen located in the inner wing of the house.

***

CHAPTER-6

The Village of Navagram

The village of Navagram was located at the south bank of the river Mahanadi, some twenty miles down the island of Nandikeshwari. This beautiful village that stood on the lee bank of the river, was precariously exposed to its fury during the flood seasons. But perhaps, by the grace of the god whom the villagers worshipped, or because the river had been kind to it, floods had never caused any great damage to Navagram . The large, thick-foliaged trees and the colourful houses on the upland, and the blue river that spread just below the village, lent it a picturesque profile. The barrages that are constructed over the river at present to hold its water in check, are symbols of the British architectural excellence. But there were no such barrages those days. The huge volume of water that remained confined to the river instead of flowing out in canals conferred great benefits on the village. People could conveniently travel to different places by the water-route, which was neither very expensive, nor too difficult. But after the barrages were built here as in many other parts of the river, the water level became lower, these new structures have not only marred the lovely look of the village but deprived its people of the privileges they were enjoying earlier.

On the eastern as well as the western bounds of the village were two old banyan trees; it was believed that Goddess Bhagavati had made one her abode and the other was home to Goddess Sarala. No one can find any image of the goddesses there. Unlike other villages, there was neither an image nor a stone representing the goddesses installed under the trees. Only the large vermilion mark on the tree trunks testified to the presence of the omnipotent goddesses. The villagers would never dare to pass by the trees without paying respects to the goddesses. People offered worship at the trees if an epidemic broke out. They firmly believed that the village would not be saved unless and until the goddesses were pleased to save it. The villagers would probably venture to tell a lie swearing by the Lord Almighty, but they would fear to swear by these goddesses even while speaking unblemished truth. They beg for her mercy in hard times; and celebrate the birth of a male child or other festive occasions by offering homage to her. Some seek her blessings to beget a son while some others pray to the goddess requesting her to eliminate their rivals. Presumably, the goddesses held everything that transpired in the village under their supreme control. The two goddesses, it was said, stood on guard on the two ends of the village to protect its inhabitants.

Man is peace-loving by nature; every human being, in the end, yearns for peace. Eternal peace lies only with Lord Almighty who regulates everything that takes place in the world. Barring a few blessed ones, the minds of all human beings are shrouded in ignorance, which prevents them from attaining it. Only the great sages, through spiritual illumination are able to enjoy this supreme bliss. These spiritually enlightened ones, to help the common, unwise people attain peace, have attributed god-head to certain things. There is no fixed law to determine the nature of the things that should represent divinity since God is omnipresent, and every object in nature, animate or inanimate, is permeated with a divine presence. It is 'Faith' only that inspires man to imagine the presence of a supreme power in different objects at different places. Therefore, in different villages these objects are worshipped as the dwelling places of the tutelary gods or goddesses who are believed to be the embodiments of Lord Almighty. It is believed that these deities, by regulating man's conduct and action, condition his present life, and pre-ordain the next one.

The village Navagram mentioned above actually comprised three separate villages: Navgram, Ragpur, and Sirilo Nuagaon. The local people called it Sirlo Nuagaon; but people outside knew it as village Navagram, one and undivided. Civilization flourished faster in the provinces that were located on riverbanks since such places were conducive to the growth of trade and commerce. People in those provinces, therefore, were more illumined with knowledge and more refined in their mannerisms in comparison to those dwelling in the interior regions. This was the reason why quite a large number of people in the village of Navgram were educated; the Choudhury family was the most well known amongst them. Radha Govinda Choudhury was a famous personality in the village, but most of the villagers did not know his first name. Those who knew his real name which was Radha Govinda Choudhury, did not address him using it. He was simply known as Choudhury in the village.

Radha Govinda Choudhury was fifty-five. He was a handsome man. Though old age and the ailments associated with it had spoiled his looks to a some degree, it was obvious from his present appearance that he must have been a quite handsome man in the prime of his life. His grandfather and his father had taken care to make him receive a little education in his boy hood. His father was in charge of maintain the accounts at the court of the Subedar. Radha Govinda worked under his father as an apprentice and acquired expertise in keeping accounts- Later, after the death of his father, Radha Govinda appointed to his father's post and discharged his duties with skill and sincerity. Since he did the job of a Choudhury for a long period, his actual surname 'Mohanty' was forgotten and he became popularly known as 'The Choudhuy' everywhere. In most places during those days reputed persons were given surnames in accordance to their official status.

Long years of apprenticeship had helped him acquire expertise in accounts management. The Subedar, therefore, was very fond of him. Nevertheless, the Choudhury did not hesitate to misappropriate the revenue and the taxes received from other sources, which was actually the Subedar's due, whenever he got an opportunity. A person having access to the royal treasury commanded great respect in those days. Radha Govinda Choudhury was, therefore, treated as a privileged man. His grandfather was a learned man, well-versed in literature as well as the scriptures of the Hindu religion. Unfortunately, he was not a happy man; his wisdom did not help him much much in enjoying material prosperity. It is said that goddess Lakshmi,{the goddess of wealth and goddess Saraswathi, the goddess of learning, do not pull on well and therefore cannot reside at one place. The wise but poor grandfather of Radha Govinda was a perfect illustration of this saying. Yet, his wisdom could bring him to the notice of Sibabhatta Samantaray Marahatta. After Samantaray took over as the Subedar of Orissa, the old man brought his son to his court. His own extensive studies in literature and religion could not help him in acquiring material prosperity. He, therefore, with the aid of generous and experienced persons, made his son study accounts management, and subjects related to administrative work. Sibabhatta Samantaray knew the old man but had never met his son; the Subedar took an instant liking towards the boy in the first meeting. Inspired by a strange affection for the young man, the Subedar immediately appointed him the accounts-manager of his province. The old father was overwhelmed with joy. His heart was filled with gratitude for the Subedar and he showered his blessings on him. Leaving his son with the Subedar, the old man started his journey back home. But perhaps he was not destined to enjoy the happiness; he suffered from some serious ailment in his return journey. Some benevolent people made arrangements to send the sick man to his village on a rope-cot. But he breathed his last on his way home. Fate had played a cruel joke with his family. The joy at the good news of the son being appointed the Choudhury by the Subedar, instantly turned into bitter grief.

After a few day, Radha Govinda's father, having obtained the official orders from the Subedar, came to work at Navagram. His appointment to the prestigious post of a Choudhury made people look upon him with awe and reverence. Soon he came to be known as the Choudhury of Navagrama. But the man was extremely parsimonious, and that perhaps was the reason why he could not enjoy the worldly life for long. Within a period of seven years he passed away. Radha Govinda was a young man at the time of his father's death.

Shortly after his father was appointed the accounts-manager of Sivaram Samantaray's province, Radha Govinda had come to stay with him; the young boy assisted his father with his work, and dutifully obeyed his instructions. He learned fast, and Siva Samantaray was quite impressed with the way young Radha Govinda carried out his father's responsibilities. The Subedar had a mind to offer young RadhaGovind a position at the court at the court, but he could not do so owing to certain constraints. When he received the news of his father's death, the Subedar immediately appointed Radha Govinda as the Choudhury in the place of his father. After he had performed the death rites of his father, Radha Govinda went to meet Subedar Samantaray, and received the official charter from him and assumed the office of Choudhury.

There are numerous instances of the sons squandering away the wealth amassed by their miserly fathers. But Radha Govinda did not follow their example. He proved worthy of his father. Instead of indulging in extravagance, he, by dint of his perseverance and resourcefulness added to the property his father had acquired. Soon he managed to own a huge property, and came to be regarded as one of the richest men in the area. Fate had given him many opportunities to accumulate wealth by various means. Orissa had come under the Maratha rule just a little before, and the Maratha rulers had not had enough time to organize the administrative system of theprovince properly. Narayan Dev, the king of Khimidi claimed to be the legitimate heir of the king of Khurdha, declared war against Virakishore Dev, who was the king of Khurdha at that time in 1761 A.D, and defeated him. King Virakishore sought the aid of the Marathas and Sibavatta Samantaray agreed to support him in the battle against the king of Khimidi. He instructed Radha Govinda's father to take necessary steps in this connection. Radha Govinda's father made the maximum use of this unexpected opportunity that came his way. Virakishore Dev won the battle and lavished gifts on Radha Govinda's father as a token of appreciation of the services rendered by him. Events had taken such a lucky turn during the tenure of Radha Govinda's father as the Choudhury. Fortune favoured the son, too, opportunity came knocking at Radha Govinda's door. Samantaray was dismissed from his post, and four other Subedars, in quick succession, took charge of the province of Orissa. Because of these frequent changes at the level of higher administration, sheer anarchy prevailed in the province and the officers in charge of collecting the revenue and other taxes conveniently used this state of affairs to their own advantage. Radha Govinda produced fake account sheets and false reports before the Subedar with such cunning, and explained matters so convincingly that he continued to remain as one of his most favoured employees despite his embezzlement of funds.

Sambhuji Ganesh was the subedar of Orissa during the period in which the incidents mentioned in the earlier chapters occured. He had taken up the office about a year before. The fellow had proved himself to be a tyrant as soon as he came to power. Immediately after becoming the Subedar, he imposed various kinds of taxes on his subjects. Tax was also levied on the lands which were earlier rent-free. This offered a golden opportunity to the accounts-managers for pilfering the revenue of the state. Radha Govinda thanked his stars and strove tirelessely to amass more and more wealth.

Nowadays, people prefer to buy shares of companies, or deposit cash in the bank. They have no alternative other than silently cursing their fate in case the price of the shares goes down or the bank fails. But things were different in the past. Moneyed people, those days, invested in land, or easily convertible assets which would be of immense help at the time of need. Following this usual pattern, Radha Govinda bought landed property at various places, and built large granaries where huge amounts of grain were stored. Many avenues for acquiring property open up for the man favoured by Lakshmi, the goddess of wealth. Radha Govinda was one of these blessed men. By the grace of goddess Lakshmi, he was able to store tonnes and tonness of paddy in his granaries within just five years after his father's death. Radha Govinda was a miser and had no inclination to show charity. He would not lend money to anyone, even to a man of repute, without obtaining either his signature or thumb impression on a promisory note. Once a man fell into the clutches of Radha Govinda by taking a loan from him, he would find it extremely difficult to escape. Radha-Govinda would keep a detailed account of what one owed to him, and nothing could stop him from squeezing out the last drop of the borrower's blood in order to get his money back. The borrower would not be excused a single pie even if he had paid back three times what he had originally taken. Radha Govinda was such a miserly man that he would rather let the leftover food rot than give it to some beggar. No beggar, therefore, would ever approach his house. Despite such hard-heartedness, RadhaGovinda was greatly favoured by Lakshmi, the goddess of wealth and prosperity. People said that the goddess was so fond of him that she never wanted to leave his house.

Radha Govinda married twice. His first marriage was issueless. He married for the second time in order to beget an heir to his property. But fate was against him; he remained childless even after the second marriage. His first wife had given shelter to an orphan girl of their own caste in their home after the child's parents had died during an outbreak of cholera in the village a few years before. The child was only six months old at that time. Though Radha Govinda's financial condition was not good at that time, he came to get attached to the little girl and reared her with much love and care. This was perhaps ordained by fate. He named her Kalavati. She was the older one of the two young women we have already met in the previous chapter.

***

CHAPTER-7

The Miser's Family

We know that RadhaGovinda was a miser like his father. Miserliness is a relative term. One cannot be called a miser unless he has enough money to spare for charity but is reluctant to do so. It is not wise to name the moderate parsimony often found in men of meagre resources as miserliness since the expenses of a man should always be proportionate to his income. Men of meager income must be careful and discreet while spending their hard-earned money. They can be called economical but never misers. But when an extraordinarily wealthy man who can afford to spend lavishly behaves in a niggardly manner no other appilation than a miser can be given him. Such an attitude usually degrades an individual's character. All the people in this world do not enjoy equal economic status. To be generous towards the poor and the needy becomes a moral duty for those who, by God's grace, enjoy material prosperity. It is of course not to be expected that they should squander their hard-earned money in the name of charity. One must be careful how he spends his money and at the same time try to donate a small part of it on pious activities if he can afford to do so. This is what is called a true religious temperament; it redeems a man's life in this world and ensures that his soul would rest in peace after death. But Radha Govinda and his father did not have this streak of generosity. A beggar would never receive a handful of rice from them; on the contrary, neither the father nor the son would have the slightest hesitation to ruin a creditor if the poor man failed to pay back his loan on time. As they walked along the village street sometimes some village urchins would clap loudly and jeer at them. They would run after them and sing:

'Long back to a poor man the Choudhury

Had loaned a little grain

And till today he is running after the man

Along the village lane.'

People acquainted with Radha Govinda's nature did not want to utter his name; therefore they referred to him as 'the Choudhury'. But this never bothered either Radha Govinda or his father. One who does not refrain from sucking people's blood to fulfil his own selfish desires never pays any heed to what the world thinks about him. 'People can only jeer at us but no one can take our wealth away', they thought to themselves.

It is true that an individual would not suffer from loss if he abides by certain moral principles. If one sows the seeds of discontent in others' hearts by trying to prosper at their cost, he must reap the fruit of his action in the form of disastrous consequences. No one can expect to live in peace and happiness without earning the goodwill and sympathy of his fellow men. Radha Govinda's father was perhaps a little worried about not being able to incur people's goodwill and had a secret fear that some harm might be done to his property. So, to protect his ill-got wealth, he had decided to build high stone walls around his house, his barns and granaries, and his office. But he passed away shortly after the construction had started, and Radha Govinda took up the responsibility of completing his father's half-finished project.

We know that the desire to have an heir to his property had tempted Radha Govinda to marry for the second time. This desire did not arise in him as long as he was poor and had no opportunity for earning wealth. In fact, he was reluctant to have children because he thought that rearing children meant a lot of expenses. But when there was the sudden influx of wealth immediately after his father was posted as the choudhury in the Subedar's royal office, Radha Govinda was constantly haunted by a sense of loss. Both the father and the son were worried that the property amassed with so much hard labour, misery, and cunning would pass into the hands of outsiders in the absence of an heir. The old man, therefore, readily agreed to the idea of his son's second marriage. Hence, Radha Govinda married again at the age of forty. His first wife was alive at the time and the orphan girl, Kalavati she had brought home, was six years old. She was a cute girl and her mother showered all her filial love on her. It was not that Radha Govinda was not fond of her although it was not in his nature to love another's child. But his wife would push the baby-girl into her husband's lap on one or other pretext whenever he came to the inner wing of the house. Not wanting to hurt his wife's sentiments, Radha Govinda would feign a show of love towards the child; but he could not fool his wife with the ostentatious display of affection. The lady, however, would not give up her efforts to kindle a spark of true love for the girl in her husband's heart. The constant and untiring persuasions of his wife, and the power of love that exercises a hold on every earthling eventually worked their way into Radha Govinda's heart and he seemed to develop slowly a genuine fondness for the child. Life had fallen into a pattern as far as Radha Govinda's first wife was concerned when she learnt about the plans of her husband's second marriage. The frustration resulting from her own inability to become a mother was a constant source of sorrow; the shocking news of her husband's plan to marry again compounded her distress. She was utterly depressed at the unexpected turn of events. One day, when Radha Govinda was in her room, she asked him: 'I hear that you are going to marry again', she said.

'I have not made up my mind, that's why I haven't told you about it', Radha Govinda answered. 'The idea occurred to me because we do not have a son. I have discussed the matter with father; he has no objection.'

'These matters are preordained', his wife said. 'Were we destined to beget a son you would have one by this time. Five marriages cannot fulfill your wish if fate does not ordain it.'

'True. Who can say what fate has in store for me? Let us wait and see.'

'Don't you love Kalavati?' Overcome with a love that was pure and unblemished, Radha Govinda's wife took the little girl who huddled behind her mother in her arms and put her in her husband's lap. The girl was listening to her parents' conversation intently. It was not that she understood anything; but she kept watching them out of sheer childlike curiosity. When her mother put her in Radha Govinde's lap she curled her little arms round his neck and fixed her gaze on his face. Her face glowed with a divine joy as she fondly regarded her father.

'Look, how beautiful our daughter is! Don't you like her?'

'Why did you say that?' Radha Govinda asked in surprise. 'Of course I love her!' He said and kissed the child.

'What would happen to Kalavati if you married again? Will the new bride take proper care of the child?

No woman can bear the thought of living wih a co-wife. Radha Govinda's first wife was no exception. Moreover she feared that if the second wife begot him a son, not only she herself but the little girl Kala would be deprived of the little love Radha Govinda bestowed on them. It was a vain hope that the other wife would have any love for Kala; if at all she did develop a little attachment for the child it was bound to disappear after she herself bore a son. The heart of Radha Govinda's wife was in a turmoil.

Her husband did not reply.

'I think you would have had a son had fate willed so.' She tried her best to convince her husband. 'But why do you worry? Isn't Kala there? We shall get her married to a suitable boy and bequeath the property to our son-in-law.'

The suggestion did not appeal to Radha Govinda. 'Why should we do that?' He asked in a displeased tone. 'We must wait and see.' He said testily and pushing Kalavati into his wife's arms strode out of the room without paying heed to her entreaties

There were several such discussions on the topic between RadhaGovinda and his wife; on each such occasion his wife tried to dissuade him from a second marriage and every time Radha Govinda refused to listen to her. Finally his wife gave up and decided to reconcile herself to the inevitable. She was tormented with anger and frustration, but did not exhibit her sorrow either in her words or action.

Plans for the marriage were made and shortly afterwards RadhaGovinda wedded a young and beautiful woman from a nearby village. Four years passed one after another but the second wife did not bear any child. As the hope of begetting a son receded, RadhaGovinda's love for his second wife wore away in a proportionate measure. The first wife of Radha Govinda, from the very beginning, harboured hostile feelings for the new bride and had always looked upon her as her arch-enemy. The second wife, however, probably because of her decent upbringing did not seem to mind. Though the fear of the first wife that the new bride would ill-treat Kalavati proved unfounded in course of time, the former would never let the girl come close to her. The later, too, was afraid to show any affection to the girl in the presence of her foster-mother. It is a truth everyone knows that that when one marries a second time, he tends to ignore his first wife. Radha Govinda was no exception. The characteristic jealousy of a woman and the suffering born out of her husband's aloofness compelled Radha Govinda's first wife to constantly wish her co-wife ill. A shadow of unrest, in this manner, hung over Radha-Govinda's family as both his wives distrusted and disliked each other. The dreams the second wife had cherished at the time of her marriage, vanished soon. Her life became a sea of turbulence. The raging tides of discontentment hit her heart so hard that in a short span of just five years she suffered from a serious ailment; the frustration of failing her husband by not being able to bear his child and the undercurrent of hatred emanating from Radha Govinda's first wife that constantly aggrieved her eventually took their toll. Her husband was a miser by nature. It would have been foolish to expect that he would spend money on the proper treatment of his wife. The disease went untreated and the

patient's condition became critical. Finally, compelled by
the criticism and the reproofs of the friends and relatives,
Radha Govinda got hold of a village physician who moved
about hanging a medicine-pouch over his shoulder and
asked him to pay a visit to his house. Driven by some kind
of sympathy for the ailing woman rather than the temptation of earning fees, or the confidence in his own skills,
the physician accompanied Radha Govinda to his house to
have a look at his wife. He found the patient hovering on the
brink of death. Her hands and feet were cold. Her co-wife,
even at this hour of crisis, didn't throw a glance of sympathy at her, let alone take care of the dying woman. Rather
she was secretly happy that her arch-enemy was fast heading towards her end. Only an old maid, who was the patient's nanny when she was a child, came from her parental
home to attend the suffering woman. Day and night the old
woman sat by the patient's bedside and nursed her. But no
one can live beyond the time span allotted to him. The lack
of proper diet and medication hastened the patient's end.
The first wife, with a ruthless determination refused to ac-
ceept any help that came from the patient's parental home.
The poor woman, therefore, could not get any help from
her own relatives. Her father was posted at a far-off place
and was unable to get a few days' leave to pay a visit to his
ailing daughter. There was no other reliable person in the
house who could go to Radha Govinda's home and bring
news of the patient to her worrying mother. The old nanny
was very fond of the patient; she could guess that the lady
was going to succumb to her illness and wept silently. But
outwardly she tried to embolden the patient by kindling
false hopes in her. It was not that the patient was unaware
of her deteriorating condition. She realized that her end
had arrived and unburdened her heart to her trusted and

loyal nanny. The sight of the village physician aroused a hope in the old nanny's heart; she fell at his feet and begged to do something to save the dying woman. The physician knew that only a miracle could save her; but as a last resort he decided to administer to the patient the life-saving drug, the *Haritala Bhasma* (the ash of yellow orpiment). He took some of the powder, made a thin paste of it by adding to it a little juice of basil leaves and put it into the patient's mouth. The medicine got stuck at the patient's throat and did not go down. Her eyes rolled up. She breathed her last immediately after.

The physician did not receive his fees; nor did Radha Govinda did not bother to offer the formal, obligatory thanks to the man. He, instead, spread the news in the village that the physician had killed his wife. The physician had no alternative but to accept his fate and curse the ways of the world.

The loud wailing of the nanny filled the air. The first wife and her mother-in-law shed a few drops of false tear. Her miserly husband was relieved that the household expenses would come down now that onemember was gone. Yet his eyes became wet as he remembered the love he had felt for her in the early days of their marriage. He wiped his tears away and set about making arrangements for the funeral. Little Kalavati could never forget the love and affection her stepfather's second wife had showered on her. Her death came as a shock to the child. The pangs of loss agitated her heart; she went inside and wept miserably.

Kalavati was eleven at the time. Radha Govinda's first wife passed away after a couple of years. His parents had died earlier. Only Radha Govinda and young Kalavati lived in the big house.

RadhaGovinda reflected what his first wife had said years ago about Kalavati's marriage; it appeared to be a wise suggestion to him. He, therefore, chose a good looking, good-natured but homeless boy from his own village and married him to Kalavati. The son-in-law came to live in the house.

The expenses of the household had come down considerably as there were only three members to be fed. Instead of feeling sad at the loss of his two wives and parents, Radha Govinda seemed pleased with the state of affairs. He offered silent thanks to God for ridding him off the burden of extra expenses.

Days rolled into months, and a year passed. His son-in-law dutifully looked after the responsibilities Radha Govinda had entrusted him with. But one thing troubled him; his son-in-law was fond of good food and was getting delicious dishes prepared for himself whenever Radha Govinda was absent from home. Radha Govinda would get angry when he came to know of this. Though he his displeasure time and again the young man took no notice of it. At first, Radha Govinda thought to provide his daughter and son-in- law with as much as would take care of their food and clothing, and ask them to live in a separate establishment. But there was a problem—Kalavati cooked food and took care of the house. Who would do all this in her absence? Radha Govinda was unable to put his thoughts into action on account of that.

But destiny had some other plan. The son-in-law fell ill; he went down with fever for just one day and passed away. Words would fail to express how heart-broken young Kalavati became at her husband's untimely death. The tragedy that befell young Kalavati rent the heart of the villagers. The shock of the loss was so great that Klavati lost consciousness; the womenfolk of the village rushed in to take care of the bereaved wife. The girl came to sense after two hours of ceaseless effort. But for their care and nursing she would have followed her husband on that very day. That, perhaps, would have been better for her; but no one can leave this world unless and until he undergoes what fate has in store for him. So Kalavati survived the shock. She lived to experience the unbearable pangs of widowhood. She went on living because she had to go through a lot more.

The readers might think that Radha Govinda, in the face of such a sorrow, would have developed a feeling of resignation and detachment towards worldly matters. But such a mood could never find a way into the heart of a fellow like Radha Govinda. His passion for amassing wealth was least affected by these unfortunate incidents. He set about completing the construction of the stone walls around his estate.

During the period the incidents of this narrative took place, high stone-walls were erected all around the barns and the granaries of Radha Govinda's estate and at every entrance stood a huge, powerfully built man on guard. The highest walls surrounded the living quarters. The two entrances of the house, one in the east and the other in the west, were guarded by massively built, awe-inspiring sentries. Radha Govinda knew that the world belonged to God and it is He who owned all the wealth and splendour of this world; he, therefore, had great reverence for Him. But his passion to accumulate wealth from God's world had never worn itself out. He was also aware that all the wealth he had hoarded would be left behind when he left this world.

Yet the fear of someone plundering or stealing his wealth made him pass sleepless nights. The knowledge that he would not be able to carry a penny from his huge property to the world beyond could not dissuade him from the act of stowing away money. His nature was such that he would not dare spend money even though he had had enogh of it. Was he not an amazing creature?

****

CHAPTER-8

Kalavati's Widowhood

╱ What a beautiful woman you are! The name Kalavati suits you.'

He touched his lips ardently to her chin as both of them roamed under the vine of *Malati*. Who would say such sweet, loving words to her now? Kalavati was torn with grief as she nostalgically recollected the days she had spent with her husband. When spring visited the garden furling its flower-flag, Kalavati would stroll in the garden; she would flick the bees away that were busy in sucking the flower-nectar from fresh blossoms. She would pick the flowers and put them in her flower-basket. Her husband would take her into his arms as she did so. Who would charm her heart and soul saying, 'Which is sweeter? These flowers or Kalavati's sweet nature?' while she collected flowers from the garden she herself tended? Kalavati, sitting on the platform built in the arbour, would string the freshly picked flowers to make various kinds of garlands inventing designs using her own imagination, and her husband would lean on her back and say, 'Your good qualities which are like colourful flowers, are strung together to make a wonderful garland like yourself'. She would serve him dishes she cooked with loving care and her husband would not tire of showering compliments on her. 'The moon is also known as a container of nectar', he would say; 'but it is still not one hundred percent perfect. The gods might have tasted the nectar the moon contains. But they did not have the fortune to taste the food prepared by you. The one that tasted it would no more relish the nectar. He can never forget you all his life.'

Kalavati would make the bed; lying on the bed spread out by Kalavati which was as white and soft as foamy milk, her husband would rest his head on her bosom and say sweetly, 'You are born under a good star; that is why your heart is even more clean and spotless than this white bed.'

While Kalavati would be putting a vermilion mark on her forehead or adorning her feet with *lac-dye* her husband would say: 'My dear, in what way all this stuff can help enhance your matchless beauty?'

In autumn, when the full moon shone in the clear, cloudless sky, he would pull Kalavati lovingly to the door and, pointing at the moon, tell her: 'Look, the moon is ashamed of your perfect, flawless beauty and therefore carries a black spot on its face. You are my moon and there is no blemish in this moon of mine. Because you have come to illumine my life the earth looks more beautiful to me than the light of the moon in the sky could ever have made it.'

When she would adorn herself with expensive clothes and jewellry her husband would hold her chin and remark, 'Kalavati, it is not you that chose these adornments, but they have found the best places for themselves in you.'

Alas!! Kalavati, those days of poetic ecstasy are over. The joy that had filled your heart is a things of the past too. The wheel of time that brings sorrow and joy to man in turns, has long since stolen away your happy days. All your lamentations and your grievances against it can never make time change its course. No appeal against the action of time can be made before the Almighty because it is He who turns the wheel of fortune that determines the events that come to pass in every human being's life. The final judgment always rests with Him. You can only shed tears lamenting your misfortune. So weep; weep till you wear yourself away. But you can never get back the person whom you weep for. Poor Kalavati! You would no more wish to step into the flower-garden; it would wear the aspect of a forest of cactus and the garden path would seem impassable to you. For you spring would never return furling its flower-flag. Flowers would no more bloom in your garden and enchant your heart. The flower-basket which you are so fond of lay unused in some corner of the house; you would not carry it to the garden anymore for collecting flowers to string garlands. You would never enjoy cooking good food and would never have the fortune to feel gratified by your husband showering of praise on your culinary skills. You would no more care to spread a clean, soft bed--nor would you experience the divine ecstasy of lying on it your husband's head resting on your bosom. The earth might bathe in the soft light of the moon that would shine in the cloudless sky of the autumn and smile, but it would mean nothing to you. The red lac-dye would never kiss your feet and feel gratified. The auspicious vermilion mark would no more adorn the parting of your hair. They have parted with you forever and taken away with them your wish to deck yourself with jewellry and expensive clothes. They would never enjoy the happiness of having found themselves on your lovely body. Poor Kalavati!! You have forsaken so many things for one! You have given up combing your hair and using oil and cosmetics!

Why have you done this Kalavati? Why such a great sacrifice? Did you weep? Why did this question bring tears to your eyes? Nothing has changed on this earth. The sun and moon shine as ever and spread their radiant net of light over it. The animals, birds, and insects, large and small, still continue to live here; the mountains, the rivers, and the forests still make the earth look beautiful. The wheel of time spins on its axis as it has always done, and therefore days and nights unfailingly follow each other; picturesque seasons come and go as years pass. The waves in the blue ocean have not stopped dancing and singing solemnly the glory of God. This earth has not changed a bit. God Almighty still continues reign supreme over the universe. Then why do you grieve? The loss of your husband has not affected the world in the least. The suffering of a handful of people does not bring about any change in the state of affairs of the world. Such things happen every moment in this world. It is true that your loss has brought you immense pain, but you must go through it stoically. Does your mourning have the power to bring your husband back? Wherefore then do you lament? All your sacrifices will be of no use, Kalavati! You do not speak a word! Who will answer these questions?

Though the movement of the earth always follows a cosmic pattern, the behaviour and views of the people tend to change constantly. Once upon a time, here, the blue-blooded Aryans had led a decent, aristocratic life. But now the Western civilization has invaded our land and brought the Aryan values under its tidal sweep. Under its influence the chivalrous Aryans have forsaken their old values and encourage their fellow members to adopt new ones. Inspired by a modern outlook many are tempted to join their group.Western culture and its values greater appreciation and more and more people are beginning to believe in and accept them. These so-called westernized youth are happy to have experienced the change that has come over the traditional world. They preach in favour of the new wind that has begun to blow 'To oppose the changing order of life is nothing but foolishness' they declare holding their head high.

Kalavati! These advocates of modernity would look upon your austerity as narrow-minded orthodoxy. Besides, life and death are natural events that occur regularly in this world. The human body is perishable. Even the poets have said so; Lord Krishna says that the human body is like a piece of cloth that wraps the living soul and must wear away in course of time. Hence, you have no reason to lament. Those who believe in modern values of course would suggest that, instead of grieving over the past, one must learn to adapt oneself to the changes. Don't you think one should do so, Kalavati?

Yet, it is not always easy to find definite and conclusive solutions to certain problems of life. Dear readers! Widowhood at this tender age was undoubtedly an ordeal for poor Kalavati. Her plight was like that of a large-horned deer that had to move very cautiously through a dense forest to avoid getting caught in the tangled creepers. She had to conduct herself with rigid austerity in order to escape the temptations held out by the world that are all the while ready to trap her. The death of her husband had loosened her bond with the world; her woe-begone heart never stopped pining for him.

A year passed. Several changes came over the pattern of people's lives in course of time. But Kalavati's bereaved heart experienced no change. Sorrow continued to hold absolute sway over the domain of her heart. But there is a difference. Its loudness had died down. Earlier the tears that flooded her eyes helped carrying away at least a little of her sorrow. These days the tidal waves of sorrow surged soundlessly inside her. The villagers were genuinely sorry for her. When she wept at her loss, they wept with her. Even after the passage of one year the somber look she bore excited a deep sympathy in their hearts. They could nothold back their tears at the sight of Kalavati, who looked like a picture of misery.

***

Kalavati's deceased husband, Raghunath, was born in Radha Govinda's native village. He was *karan* by caste. The only child of rich parents, Raghunathhad been brought up in luxury and comfort. But nothing lasts forever. Misfortune befell Raghunath when he was just a boy of five. His father, while returning from his work-place, met with an accident. His boat capsized in the river and the fierce currents of the Ganges swallowed him. Overwhelmed with shock and grief, his mother decided to end her own life. But she was unable to put her plan into action since there was no one to take care of her little son. She, therefore, requested one of her own brothers to come and stay in the house and take care of her son as well as her property. At her request one of her brothers came to live with them.

It was the seventh day of her husband's death; the bereaved woman found it impossible to bear her sorrow. In the silent hours of the night, she came out of the house and walked down towards the river-bank. She glanced once at the moon and at the rushing waters of river Mahanadi. Tears rolled down her cheeks; she uttered the name of her husband and flung herself into the river.

These days suicide is considered a punishable offence by the law; even the modern people look upon it as sheer madness. But those days, a woman choosing to lay down her life when her husband died, was regarded as an act of great nobility. She was worshipped by people as a 'Sati'. It was also a custom to erect a monument in her memory to remind the world of her glorious death. Raghunath's mother desirous to be with her husband in the other world, did not allow her love for her son to leave the mortal world forever. The only thing she left was the glory of her *Sati-* hood.

Raghunath thus became an orphan.

There was no one except his uncle to look after him. The uncle took good care of the boy and looked after the family property. Initially, he performed his duty sincerely; but the huge property of his sister soon made him greedy. He came under the wicked influence of his brothers and began embezzling the money that came from various sources. He squandered his sister's money that lawfully belonged to his nephew. By the time Raghunath was eighteen he had become so poor that it was difficult for him to get even a square meal a day. But his uncle had done one good thing: he had sent Raghunath to good Sanskrit and Oriya teachers and the boy had acquired sound knowledge in both the subjects. He had attracted the attention of the wise men at a considerably young age on account of his mastery of Sanskrit and Oriya. Shortly afterwards, a rift occurred between the uncle and the nephew on some issue. The uncle was on the lookout for just a thing like that, and readily left the house. Dear readers, you must be aware that the world is full of trecherous uncles who never hesitate to exploit their own sisters and nephews and nieces for their own selfish interest.

Raghunath was left all alone. Survival became a problem for him. He resigned himself to the will of God. Luckily, the education he had received came handy; using it he somehow managed to arrange what he needed for his bare survival. For other things he depended on the charity of the people of his own village and in the neighbourhood.

As the house of Radha Govinda lay at ashort distance from that of Raghunath, the boy was a frequent visitor to it. When Radha Govinda's first wife was alive, she had one day brought Kalavati to Raghunath and said, 'Raghu, you come here so often; can't you spare a little time to help Kalavati with her studies? It would benefit her a lot.' Raghunath was fifteen years old at the time. Kalavati had become very fond of the boy and spent a lot of time in playing various games with him. 'I will do well if you teach me', said Kalavati eagerly when she heard her mother speak to Raghunath. Her mother fondly gathered her in her arms and kissed her. The request was made with such innocent sincerity that Raghunath could not bring himself to say no to it. 'All right, I will teach her', he said with a smile.

Women in families of the *karan* caste are now encouraged to receive education. The light of western civilization has started filtering through the veil of conventions and it has brought many changes in the earlier modes of education. There is, however, need to say whether the change is for the better or for the worse. People vary in their tastes; and these varied tastes lose their identity and uniqueness when put inside the machine of 'the changing times' that moves with great speed to mould the older values into new shapes.

Earlier, the village *avadhan* taught the girls the basics like an alphabet and addition and subtraction. Besides, the young girls were taught how to draw drawing various designs on the walls and the courtyards with a watery paste of rice, or prepare rice cakes and other delicacies. But Kalavati was an intelligent child; so her mother had wanted to give her better education. She had heard that Raghu was proficient in Sanskrit and Oriya. She therefore,

Decided to ask him to teach Kalavati.

After taking up the responsibility of teaching Kalavati, Raghunath had to spend more time than earlier at Radha Govinda's house. He eenjoyed teaching Kalavati. Kalavati was a sincere pupil; she did well in her studies and the people of the village admired her for this. Radha Govinda extracted various kinds of work from Raghunath as he was present in his house most of the time. The boy discharged all the duties assigned to him without complaint. The satisfied expression on the face of Radha Govinda was reward for him. Both the wives of Radha Govinda were fond of Raghunath. They, as well as Kalavati, helped the boy in several ways without the knowledge of Radha Govinda.

The togetherness Kalavati and Raghunath enjoyed intensified their love and affection for each other. When Raghunath was twenty two, Radha Govinda h asked him to marry Kalavati. Finally Kalavati and Raghunath were united and the fondness and affection of the childhood was eventually transmuted into a deep love that was priceless. The stream of poetry found its way into the dreary desert of Radha Govinda's home after the marriage of Kalavati with Raghunath took place. Radha Govinda could not spend much time at home since he had to stay at the Subedar's court most of the time for office work. On occasions he had to stay away from home overnight as he had to visit villages for collecting taxes.

So happy were Kalavati and Raghunath in each other's company that they forgot to keep track of the passage of time. Their married life was like the poetry of love that penned by the great poet *Kalidas*. Shortly after their marriage the flower garden and the fruit-orchard adjacent to the house were cleaned. New plants were planted in the garden and fresh blossoms filled the air with fragrance. Like two angels that have alighted on earth from heaven, the couple strolled in the garden, absorbed in a divine ecstasy. The earth appeared to them as a beautiful land of romance; they thought that the sun and the moon shine in the sky in order to shower the light of love and poetry on their love on them as they do on the lotus and the lily; the entire earth, exulted as it were with the love that bound God and the Nature-goddess together. Words fail to describe the bliss of love they enjoyed. The universe was nothing but an enthralling love-poem for the newly wed.

Nothing lasts forever; life does not always flow smoothly like a madrigal of love! It is beyond man's imagination what incidents will occur as the wheel of fortune turns.

Kalavati, perhaps, had hoped that her life would always remain beautiful like a poem. along; but she had no idea that to entertain such a hope was an exercise in futility. She was yet to realize the truth that the wishes of human beings are not always fulfilled. Only the creator of the universe can explain how and why different events take place in this world that is nothing but an illusion. Only He can explain according to what cosmic law joys and sorrows visit a man and confound him. Death, awesome and terrifying, came in the guise of high fever and took Raghunath away. And all poetry vanished from Kalavati's life at that very instant. The women of the neighbouring houses, who came to comfort the bereaved girl explained to her the strict rules a widow must abide by. From then on, the sixteen-year-old

Kalavati practiced the rigid austerities of widowhood. She was oppressed by thememories of her beloved husband. Life became a long waiting for death and she prayed to God to bring a quick end to her waiting. And time moved on. Kalavati cooked with care only when her father was at home. On other days she mostly went without food. Even the custom of eating once in the evening which a widow had to follow, was notfollowed by her. A child would perhaps have helped her forget her loss but destiny had not decreed it. Kalavati had passed through difficult times since she was a child; but widowhood at the prime age had created a vacuum in her life. She suffered the terrible pangs of loneliness. The only one who could lighten the burden of her sorrow to some extent was her friend, young Rasakala, her friend. For most part of the day Rasakala gave Kalavati company.

We recall that on thatt fullmoon night in the month of *Pausha*, Rasakala told Kalavati of the procession of lights and how she was called away by her mother to have supper. Kalavati, too, went to the inner wing of her house where the kitchen was. There, in that wing, was also the room where the tutelary deities were installed and worshipped. Kalavati went inside, ate a little *prasad*, and came back to her bedroom. She lay down on the carelessly spread-out bed. Sleep eluded her. It was not that she had kept awake to watch the procession of lights that was to pass by their house. Her heart had turned into an arid land; s no desires stirred in it. What joy could such a heart derive from watching a procession of lights? Memories of her deceased husband oppressed her grieving heart and tears streamed from her sleepless eyes.

Rasakala called from outside, 'Open the door.'

CHAPTER-9

On The Way

The boat sped across the river; the villages on both banks, the clumps of trees, the hills that stood askew, all reeled backwards with an equal speed. The small patches of land quickly receded from view as the boat raced on. Islands and trees that appeared to be far away from one point become clearly and in no time were the quickly left behind as the boat sped past them. The moon and its entourage, the stars, seemed to be sailing backwards in the sky. It was as thoughl the moon, the stars, the trees, scared at the sight of the dacoit's boat were fleeing in the opposite direction. The river that rippled as the gentle breeze swept over its surface seemed to tremble in fear, and the splashing sound that was produced as the keel of the speeding boat sliced its surface sounded like the river's cry for mercy.

Who would not be afraid of the dacoits? The chief, Raghunatha Pattanaik, pointed at the objects that speedily disappeared from their view and said to his aides: 'Look, the whole world is trying to escape you; everything is running away in the opposite direction. What place shall you raid, and whom shall you loot?'

'They run away because we are in the boat. Who can escape us when we are on the land?', someone boasted. 'Our quarry can never give us the slip even if we are in a boat', Bahabalindra remarked disapprovingly. 'Then how does it matter if thousands of others flee?'

It was true. Those whom these dacoits target can never escape. The moon-blanched green trees on both sides of the river, the dense forests in the land-patches amidst the water, the stars glittering like specks of gold-dust, the moon that shone like a huge diamond in the crown of the Nature-goddess, all appeared to be rushing in the reverse direction; but they were not the target of these dacoits. The way they receded into the far-off regions only enhanced the beauty of the fast-moving boat. The dacoits were not tempted in the least to plunder this treasure of beauty.

There was no other boat in the river. The Subedar had passed an order forbidding boat-journey during the night. One who risked night-journey in the river disobeying the order, and fell into the hands of the robbers would be solely responsible for the losses he incurred. His complaint would not be entertained. In those days people, for their part, dreaded a boat-journey in night and rarely ventured to embark on one. So the dacoit's boat sped along without any problem.

When Rasakala knocked at Kalavati's door, the dacoits' boat had long since moved past Tarito and the confluence of the three branches of the river. Their destination lay a short distance away. Suddenly, another boat came into sight far away in the river. The sight of the boat sent waves of excitement among the dacoits. They were on their way to accomplish one mission, and here was another quarry! The other boat seemed to be moving straight towards them and the robbers made up their mind to attack it. They sought the permission of their chief. When he said yes, the boat raced ahead.

It was impossible for any vessel to dodge the dacoits' boat. Still one must at least make a try. But how strange!! The other boat showed no sign of trying getting away.

Had the oarsmen of the other boat fallen asleep? It was not unusual for the oarsmen to do so, though. There were instances of boats meeting with serious accidents on account of such irresponsibility on the part of oarsmen. How could any human being of flesh and blood fall asleep while doing some physical labour? It was seen that the palanquin-bearers sometimes fall asleep while carrying the palanquin. The readers might find them incredibl but such instances do occur. We wonder how scientists would explain such strange behaviour on the part of human beings. The dacoits were encouraged when they noticed that the other boat was making no attempt to get away. The boat that appeared like a dot from the distance loomed larger as it drew closer. It had already come within a striking distance. But the men on board seemed to be still asleep. There was no sign of any activity on the other boat. Well, it did not matter to the bandits if the people in the boat did not wake up in the face of such a grave danger. The bandits were extremely happy at the prospect of laying hands on a prey that offered no resistance. Some of them gnashed their teeth, some tried to gather up strength by smacking their own arms and thighs, and the rest, in order to assess their strength wrestled with each other. But the absence of activity in the other boat seemed a little odd to Raghunath. Addressing Bahabalindra he said, ' Bahabalindra, have all the people in the boat fallen asleep? Bahabalindra was engaged in an arm-wrestling match with Baliyaarsingh and answered confidently, 'The oarsmen have fallen asleep.'

Well, let all of you call out once, 'Hail! Lord Mahaveer!!' Raghunath suggested.

The great sound of the loud call that rose from the first boat reverberated through the river and the forests on its banks, and its echo resonated in the air. Before the echo died the other boat responded to the call; a low sound of 'Hail, Lord Mahaveer' came from it.

This time there was no doubt that the other boat also carried dacoits. The realization that they have lost a golden chance of plundering an easy prey dampened the spirit of the robbers in the first boat. Most of the dacoits who had stood up, ready to pounce upon their victim, slumped into their seats in utter frustration. A wrathful snake that had raised its hood to strike, lay back in a coil, as if rendered powerless by the chanting of some mantra. The first boat lowered its speed, and both the boats drew closer to each other. Raghunath addressed the man who stood at the helm of the other boat, ' Hallo, Sardar Singh. Is everything ready?'

'Of course, it is', the man called back from the other boat.

The two boats were now floating abreast of each other; Raghunath stretched himself and caught hold of the hand extended by of Sardar Singh.

'We won't have to wait for any thing?' Raghunath inquired.

'Raghubabu, could your orders be ever disobeyed? All preparations have been made as per your instruction. In fact everything was ready by the early hours of the night. I myself had gone there to check if there was any problem. There was none. All must be waiting eagerly for you.'

The information he received from Sardar Singh made Raghunath very glad.

'So, Chhanchan Singh had been true to his promises,' he said.

'What promise?' Sardar Singh questioned.

'I heard from Bahabalindra that Chhanchan Singh had sworn that he would shave off his moustache if he failed to complete the arrangements much before our arrival there.'

Sardar Singh roared with laughter. 'This time', he said, 'Chhanchan Singh will win. From what I observed there I assured you have to admit that you are late in reaching the spot.'

This made Raghunath feel genuinely happy. He ordered his associates to take the name of Lord Mahaveera . The loud call rose from both the boats simultaneously and pierced the sky. It resounded in all directions; so loud was the echo that it seemed to have the power to smite the enemies..

'What about the other job you have been charged with?' Raghunath asked Sardar Singh. 'That has also been taken care of. By the time the ceremony starts there will be another commotion. Please have no worries about it. You will find out in due time how flawless my arrangements are.'

Raghunath shook Sardar Singh's hand warmly and expressed his satisfaction, 'Very good!! Raghunath has no reason to fear even death if clever people like you worked for him.'

At the order of the chief the dacoits in both the boats

again shouted the name of Mahaveera , and the boats moved away from each other. Thereafter, they sped off in opposite directions.

***

CHAPTER-10

The Statue Of Lord Shiva

A short distance away from village Navagram and to-wards the east, amidst the sandy stretch on the south bank of river Mahanadi, stood the statue of lord Mahadeva popularly known as the Budha Linga. The ash-smeared Lord Mahadeva, who is believed to frequent cremation grounds and is averse to all forms of luxury, does not care where he puts up. He does not discriminate between a place at the mountain top and one lying in the heart of a thick forest looped by a singing stream, or a vast sandy stretch completely devoid of greenery. Likewise an impassable wilderness infested by wild beasts and an endlessly stretch-ing arid land would be equally acceptable to the god. He is equally fond of residing in a big temple located in the middle of a beautiful, well-populated village, and of stay-ing in the eerie crematories scattered with human skulls and bones. This noble and generous god is quite indifferent as far as the choice of a dwelling place is concerned. Any one who has visited the different abodes of the Lord-----in the caves of the mountain Kapilash, or the temple of Maha Vinayak and of Sri Loknath, the shrine of Paramhans, the massive temple at Bhubaneswar, or the Budhalinga------can see this for himself. Readers! Can you find this attitude in human beings? This sinful world of ours would have been transformed into a Heaven if you could find it in human beings.

Since the deity had chosen a place near the riverbank for himself to settle, he could not avoid the river water bathing him every year during floods. A large tacoma tree that stood by the image was the only property the lord owned. According to a popular legend the tree was there since the time the lord had made his first appearance in that place. It cast its shadow over the deity. A little further away, almost at the edge of the river, there grew a patali tree. This tree too, was believed to be as old as the Tacoma tree, but the passage of time had not brought about any visible changes in them, who stood there like two silent worshippers of the Lord. The trees offered their own lovely flowers to the Lord. Both of them, one standing by the Lord's side and covered with white flowers, and the other standing in front of him bowing its head laden with red-pink blossoms created a picture of indescribable loveliness. The endless sky was spread over the entire expanse of the earth like a star-spangled canopy. The tacoma tree loaded with its fresh-white blossoms that looked like a star-studded umbrella over the Lord's head was a small replica of that vast, starry sky. Likewise the pink-blossomed patali tree appeared like a devotee standing in front of the Lord. The red petals falling at the feet of the deity created an impression of a devotee praying for salvation who had slit his throat and was offering a blood-homage to the Lord as a show of extreme gratitude. Such a sight could have enthralled even the most hard-hearted individual. Can the patali tree in your garden be ever able to charm the viewers with such messages of spiritualism? Can the tacoma tree that has grown in your garden ever look so lovely? The statue of the lord that stood at the bank of river Mahanadi that had started its journey since time immemorial, was a perfect picture of the self-created Lord Shiva who had the power to destroy the universe standing at the edge of the River of Eternity. The god seemed to be explaining to man that, in order to attain salvation, he had to forsake every earthly possession, even his own blood. Did the deity choose the sand-strewn riverbank as his dwelling-place with an intention of teaching this lesson to mankind? The bees flew about happily carrying on their wings the fragrance of the flowers that bloomed on both the trees and sent it out to fill the air around. Did the bees understand this spiritual truth and that was what made them flutter in excitement?

The saying went that no one had installed the statue there. According to a popular legend, the self-created god had risen from below piercing the earth. The statue was large in size; but there was a small crack on its top, and it stood a little tilted to one side. An interesting interesting, popular explaination has been offered. In earlier times the bandits of the Bhuyan clan of the kingdom of Kujang launched sporadic attacks on village Navagram and took away valuable possessions of the villagers. The dacoits had great faith in the Budhalinga Mahadev. They always offered worship to the Lord before they set out for their mission. They never failed in carrying out their raids and were never caught. They believed that it was the blessings of the god that always protected them. Their faith in the Lord grew stronger and stronger and finally they made up their mind to wrench the statue off the ground and take it away to their own village. Determined to pull out the statue from its place, they came carrying large crowbars one night and began digging the ground around the statue. But the statue had emerged from the fathomless depths of the earth. Despite all the efforts the dacoits put in they were not able to reach down the base of the statue. Perhaps the arrogance of the dacoits aroused the Lord's wrath and He decided to make them realise His power. He appeared in the dream of a washerman who lived nearby (the progeny of that washer man still lived at that place) and commanded him to come out with an axe and a torch. Waking up, the washerman rushed to the spot where the image was, carrying an axe in one hand and a torch in the other. But the bandits saw some thing else, something much more frightening. The god had, perhaps, deluded them to see a different picture. They saw hundreds and hundreds of men running towards them carrying flaming torches and weapons. The Bhuyans, scared out of their wits, ran away for their lives. But before leaving the place, in utter frustration, they struck violently at the top of the statue with a crowbar. Under the impact of that severe blow, the statue got tilted to one side and a small crack appeared where the crowbar had hit it. But one good thing came out of it: the Bhuyan dacoits never returned to Navagram.

Under the Patali tree flowed the Mahanadi; the depth of the river at that point was difficult to measure. The clear, blue water of the river that rippled along the bank appeared to have been sweetly chanting the Vedas fo the Lord. So captivating was nature's beauty at that place that it would cause no wonder if some of the passersby, after offering their salutations to the Lord, decided to sit down for a while and drink the nectar of the beauty of the tranquil landscape. But the barrage that had recently been constructed accross the river had disfigured it. Vast stretches of white sand had encroached upon the area earlier occupied by water. It was a scary place during the night. There was always the fear of the dacoits; besides, tigers and other nocturnal animals that came out of the forest prowled about the place. People, therefore, hardly visited the place at night. Moreover, there was no safe place in the vicinity where some one could take shelter for some time. A priest came in the daytime to offer worship to the Lord. At night, the place became fearfully lonely. But on that particular full-moon night of the month of Pausha, a man was sitting alone under the Patali tree. It was past midnight. The boat of Sardar Singh was tethered to the tree earlier. But it was no longer there. The man sat there, a piece of coarse cloth wound carelessly round his body, quite oblivious of the biting cold. The earth basked in the cool, white light of the moon; so did Lord Mahadev. The blue, sparkling waters of the fathomless Mahanadi danced in the soft breeze and sported with the moonlight. The mist from the dew-soaked sand dunes on the far side of the river rose into the air as if to merge with the moonlight. But the man was not at all interested in the picturesque beauty of nature. He seemed to be waiting for somebody, and with an intention that had something sinister about it. He was a hugely built man of pitch-black complexion and looked strong enough to fight a tiger. He held an iron rod in one hand, probably to use as a weapon in the time of need. Such a man would naturally have no fear of either the cold or wild animals. He gazed intently at the westerly direction of the river. Suddenly he heard the sound of soft footsteps and whipped round to see someone running away from near the statue of Lord Budhalinga.

'Who is that?' the man shouted. The other fellow was scared by the awe-inspiring appearance of the inquirer; the sound of the harsh, booming voice sent a chill through his spine.He trembled in fear. All strength was drained out of his body, and he stood there rooted to the spot unable to open his mouth to give an answer. The big man seemed quite satisfied to find the fellow in the grip of such mortal fear. He raised the iron rod and said threateningly, ' Look, you cannot get away from me. Come here if you want to remain alive, or I will smash your head with this rod.' There was no escape. The man moved towards the Patali tree like a puppet pulled by a string. Reaching the tree he addressed the scary looking man, 'My lord, you have the power to take lives. My life has already left my body. You can take away whatever is left if you want so.' The big man roared with laughter: 'Don't fear', he said. 'You seem to be very poor. Where are you going?' the latter had guessed from the villainous appearance the man that he must be a Bhuyan dacoit from Kujang. His doubts grew stronger as he apparised the man from close quarters. He carried no valuables with him which the dacoit could snatch away. Yet, fearing that his life would be in danger unless he spoke the truth, he decided to tell him everything honestly. ' The Naib has come. I am going to watch the procession of light.'

'Just now you told me that your life was about to leave your body. And yet you want to watch the procession of light?' the big man asked amusedly. The later was a little nonplussed. 'No, not only that; in fact I want to make an appeal to the Naib.'

'What kind of an appeal?'

'You know that we are passing through a hard time. Floods and famines have destroyed the seedlings we had planted in our cornfields. There is nothing to eat. People are forced to sell away their jewelry and other valuables because their fields did not yield much.'

'Not much crop?' the big man asked in feigned surprise. 'You people had never had any trouble earlier on account of poor harvest.'

'What do you say?' the second man exclaimed with even greater astonishment, 'You think our people have no problems? Have you learnt from some other source that this year we have reaped a good harvest? That our fields have yielded good crops? This is not true. As it is the Subadar taks our complaints lightly. If he comes to know that you too do not believe us, he will refuse outright to do anything about our problems."

The big man did not show any sign of anger at such a sarcastic remark. Rather he looked a little ill-at-ease. ' No, no, that was not my intention', he said in a placating tone. 'But the Choudhury family and the Dasa family are there. Why don't you borrow grains from them? You can give your thumbprint on a hand-note and take a loan. When things improve you can repay your debts. Simple.' The latter pressed his hands to his ears. 'Don't utter their names please', he said irritably. The two of them are misers of the first order. They will not lend even the water with which paddy is washed, let alone paddy. Neither of them will give you a drop of water if you sit at their door-step all day long' The other man did not show any surprise at this information.' The villagers are passing through a hard time, and they don't bother to lend them a handful from their granaries bursting with grains! Why don't all of you get united and rob their overflowing granaries? Thereafter you will not have any trouble; nor shall you have to toil in the field.' The villager replied in a voice full of misery, 'We are poor peasants. How can we dare commit such an act? The Subadar's men will arrest us the next day and sentence every one of us to death.' The helplessness that the poor man's voice expressed filled the other's heart with pride. ' How would you like it if the Bhuyans plundered the wealth of these misers?' he asked eagerly. The peasant did not saything in reply. He had realized that his suspicion was not baseless. The ugly looking villain was a Bhuyan from

Kujanga. But the Bhuyans had stopped coming to Nava-gram long since. How come they had returned there after so many years? It was already past midnight, and the man was alone. What could a single dacoit do? The Subadar might get information from his spies and get him arrested. Why is the tiger venturing into the lion's den, being fully aware of the danger?

The news of the Subadar's coronation ceremony had reached far and wide. It was difficult to believe that the Bhuyans did not know about it. The peasant was confused. But one thing he was certain of: there would not be much change in the condition of the poor peasants even if the gra-naries of the Choudhury or Dasa got looted by the dacoits. The harvest, whether it was with the miserly landowners or the gang of robbers, would not come into the hands of the peasants who really needed them.

The big man was watching him closely. 'You did not answer my question', he said. 'Will you stop the Bhuyans from looting the Choudhury under these circumstances?'

'How can we stop you, my lord? We are poor people and passing through a terrible time as ordained by our des-tiny. We shall not get drawn into any kind of conflict. If we rob the landowners we shall be sentenced to death, and if we try to prevent the Bhuyans we shall be beaten to death. Either way our lives would be at stake.'

As the two men talked, the sound of rowing was heard from the river. The evil-looking man became alert. He stood up and looked in the direction the sound was coming from. The peasant could guess that the approaching boat belonged to the dacoits and his fear grew intenser. He must get away from this place, he thought. Luckily, just at that time a glow was seen in the north. ' Look, the procession of light!!' He exclaimed in excitement. ' I must leave now', he said and looked at the big man as if seeking his permission. When the dacoit said 'Yes' he left the place. He walked slowly for some time. When he was at a safe distance from the dacoit, the peasant began to run with all the speed he could gather into his body. The big man let out a loud laugh at the panic of the peasant. His raucous laughter made the deserted place appear even more dreadful.

The boat had approached the Patali tree by the time the big man had stopped laughing.

Two of the boatmen jumped into the water and roped the boat to the tree. All the passengers except two boatmen who stayed back to keep guard disembarked from the boat one after another.

***

Chapter-11

Govardhan Dasa

It had been mentioned earlier that there lived quite a few rich and reputed people in the village of Navagram. The readers, by now, have got quite well acquainted with RadhaGovinda Choudhury, the most important among them all. There was another man of almost equal if not the same status in the village; he was Govardhan Dasa. In terms of wealth his worth be ranked just below that of Choudhury. Only a two-feet wide passage between the compound walls of both the houses kept them separated. Govardhan Dasa had passed his childhood in abject poverty. He had lost both his parents prematurely and the poor orphan boy had to go begging in order to survive. He lived in an old, ramshackle hut having two small rooms, and ate only once a day whatever he had got from begging. His mother had left for her heavenly abode when the boy was three. His father, thereafter, had reared him with much care. He was keen to provide his son with some education and had got him enrolled in the village primary school. Govardhan studied in the school till he was seven years old. By this time he had learnt the basics of mathematics like addition and subtraction. Unfortunately, his father too passed away leaving him to face the world alone at a tender age. There was no one to take care of the boy or his education. The village primary school teacher took a couple of tobacco leaves as his fee. But there was no one who could have paid even this to the teacher to make the boy continue his studies. A kindly neighbour, out of pity, agreed to pay the teacher his fees so that the boy could get on with his studies. Slowly, Govardhan began to extract undue favours from the good man. He depended on him for food and all other necessaries. Gradually, he became a burden on the man and his family. Though the man was kind- hearted, he found it difficult to give the boy two full meals a day. Unable to cope with the boy's demands,the man finally drove him out and warned him never to come back. He stopped paying the fees of the teacher and that brought Govardhan's studies to a stop. People who choose to bring up an orphan with sincere love and sympathy are rarely to be found seen in this world. If at all some such people are there, they find it difficult to remain charitable for long for many reasons. A handful of people who help an orphan, do so for selfish reasons. But they treat the poor child abominably.

Dear readers! Life is a complicated business. The ways of the world are neither straight nor easily understood. And for an orphan, life in this world is as tough as penetrating a military formation. Asmall number of such children manage it by sheer good fortune. Otherwise, ninety-nine out of every hundred such orphans, are destroyed by the ruthless warriors that cordon the formation. Only a few receive love and sympathy, that too for only a short time.

It was because Govardhan's luck favoured him, his kindly neighbour helped him for long six months. Govardhan stopped going to school and had to depend on the charity of the people living in the neighbouring villages. It was not that Govardhan did not have any well-to-do relatives who could have stood by him or given him some kind of support. In fact, some of his relatives were rich enough to support tens of orphans like Govardhan. But as it normally happens , none of these callous relatives bothered to cast a sympathetic glance at the boy. If Govardhan ever paid a visit to them, they either abused him or threw him out of their house. But people, who were not in any way related to Govardhan, took pity on him and offered him alms. The life that the ill-fated Govardhan lived, was nothing but a tale of distress. His own suffering and the indifference of the people filled his heart with distrust and distaste for the entire mankind. The world, he came to believe, was an abode of crooked and uncouth people. He looked upon every human being as an embodiment of selfishness. The most important ingredients in the stuff of which make up man, he thought bitterly, were unscrupulousness and treachery. It appeared to him that all the human beings, animals, and birds followed crooked paths of living and turned this world to a dreadful place. He convinced himself that every one in this world was morally warped. Therefore, the cuckoo's song that fills the air in the season of spring, made his soul burn in a fire of envy. Music that has the power to soothe every heart filled him with anger. The beautiful scenes of nature that made the hearts of men overflow with the nectar of peace, filled him with a wild rage; it was as though he was engaged in a personal vendetta against the whole world and everything, animate or inanimate, in it. The concept of beauty had lost its significance for Govardhan, and all the beautiful objects of this world appeared before him as though shrouded in a layer of evil. So intense had become his cynicism that he considered even God Almighty who reigned supreme over the universe as evil and malicious.

The pain and suffering a person has to undergo sometimes turn him totally unscrupulous. No wonder that the scorn and the contempt and the cruelty of people he had endured, had killed all tender emotions in Govardhan and transformed him into a man with a heart of stone. The death of all softer instincts, the shadow of uncertainty that constantly hung over his future, and the cynical outlook he had developed, had turned Govardhan to a ruthless, dangerous creature.

Though Govardhan had taken the selfishness and hypocricy of the world for granted, people still continued to give him alms. A good number of people offered him alms fearing that some mishap would befall their family if they incurred the poor man's ill-will, while others did so out of pity. But these acts of charity did not do much to change Govardhan's temperament. He experienced a savage delight when he extracted something from people by cheating them in various ways.

Nothing remains the same forever. Joy and sorrow visit man's life alternately. Faith in God does not guarantee anyone permanent happiness. In the same way, one that harbours a grudge against God is not subject to unremitting hardship.

Such a statement might dispose the readers to be a little skeptical. It is a controversial topic and cannot be analyzed easily. However, man should always keep himself prepared for change. Govardhan had already spent twenty years full of penury and pain. One day it so happened that he got no alms in the village. He walked two *kosas* from Navagram and reached another village. Unfortunately, he did not receive any handouts even from the people of that village. Exhausted by the long walk Govardhan stepped onto the verandah of a house and stretched himself there in order to rest his limbs a little. The owner of that house was one Chintamani Mohanty who happned to be a building contractor. He obtained contract from the government to construct bridges, roads, and office-buildings. It was his job to engage labourers on a daily-wage basis and supervise the work of construction. He had grown extremely rich through craft and cunning. He was mean and shrewd, and it was said that his cunning combined with his meanness had enabled him grow so rich. He had no qualms about cutting down little amounts from the wages of the labourers who worked under him and get it into his own pocket. Most of the men want to get rich. But all of them cannot perfect the trick of cheating the poor out of their hard-earned money. It requires a particular mindset and a special kind of meanness in one's character to do so. It would not perhaps surprise the readers that these days one comes across many men like Chintamani in this world. To live a life of luxury at the cost of others and to grow wealthy by exploiting the poor have become the order of the day.

Let us not dwell upon these matters any longer. The day Govardhan had fallen asleep on the verandah of Chintamani Mohanty's house he was away from home on some work. Only his wife and his daughter were at home. Mohanty's wife hailed from a decent family; but after her marriage to Chintamani she had relinquished whatever little virtues she had acquired through her decent upbringing. However, she was not inclined to harm others. The disappointment born out of her inability to deliver a male child constantly gnawed at her heart. A daughter, their only child, was born out of her second pregnancy. All other children had died a premature death. The couple had given up all hopes of a son and seriously contemplated adopting a boy. But they had not yet found a suitable boy. The

daughter, Kautuki, was fifteen years old. Her parents wanted their prospective-son-in-law, to live with them at their
house after marriage.

It was mid-Vaisakh and the summer heat was
unbearable.The air smouldered under the wrathful frown
of the sun. All living beings not excluding the plants swel-
tered and suffered in the scorching heat. It was miday and
silenced reigned everywhere. The occasional harsh cawing
of the crows that broke the silence turned the atmosphere
even more dreadful. Very rarely would people brave the
sun during these hours of the day. The rich, however, could
afford the various modern systems for cooling the air and
therefore were able to drive the discomfort away. But the
poor could not afford these. For some of them, the tyranny
of fate was more oppressive than the tyranny of the sun.
They preferred the punishment of the latter to the penury
Fate had inflicted on them. These people were forced to
come out of their houses to earn their bread, even though
they had to face the unpitying sun. When they felt tired,
they sought shelter under the shade of some tree.

Chintamani's wife had eaten her mid-day meal.
Before retiring to her bedroom for a nap she went to the
front room to bolt the door. She opened the door to look out
and her eyes fell on the sleeping Govardhan.

The human heart often behaves strangely. Sometimes the most kindhearted people behave in an extremely cruel manner, while the unkind and hardhearted ones
sometime melt with pity. Sometimes the heart revolts at the
sight of beautiful objects, while it is drawn towards ugly,
unattractive things. Chintamani's wife guessed that the boy
had had nothing to eat. The pity she felt for the boy soft-
ened her heart. The boy's appearance impressed her and

she felt that s if the boy was someone of her very own. A thought crossed her mind: 'I wish he was a boy of the *karana* caste, I would then get Kautuki married to him and ask him to live with us'. She woke the boy up, asked him inside and offered him food and good clothes. Her hopes grew stronger when she came to know who the boy was and learnt the details of his family.

At last Govardhan's agony came to an end. He felt as if the moon had dropped into his hands without any effort on his own part. He stayed with the family of Chintamoni Mohanty for one long month. He also had had a number of opportunities to exchange endearments with Kautuki.

Human life follows a mysterious course. Man strives hard to achieve something, but all his hard labor proves to be an exercise in futility; he sits back disappointed, cursing his fate. And sometimes everything that occurs seems to go in his favour; fortune knocks at his door when he least expects it. Events that are preordained by destiny are bound to occur whether one works to bring them about or not. No logic can explain the inscrutable laws of life. No amount of analysis or reasoning can unravel its mystery. In the end one has to accept that everything that happens in a man's life is decreed by destiny, or are the results of the deeds committed in one's previous life. The idea that had come to the mind of Chintamani's wife probably was approved by destiny, and therefore the incidents that occurred thereafter translated it into reality.

As for Kautuki , Govardhan appeared to her fairly handsome, and she guessed she would be happy to have him as her husband. The relatives and the neighbours also approved of the match. Finally, when Chintamani returned home after a month he also did not hesitate to give his consent to Kautuki marrying Govardhan. The marriage was solemnized a week of his return.

Inscrutable are the ways of providence. It is beyond man's power to comprehend the cosmic order that maintains an eternal harmony in the universe. God willed it that poor Govardhan who lived in a hut and begged for food, would suddenly find himself in a world of wealth and luxury. Not long after his marriage to Kautuki, Govardhan's parents-in-law passed away. Govardhan became the sole heir to Chintamani's huge property. But, like most people, he had a genuine attachment towards his native place. So, he constructed a big house on his own homestead land in village Navagram and came back to settle there. Though he had been immensely rich, the miserliness that was almost abominable, and the greed that prompted him to earn money by unfair means, continued to define his character. No one liked his nature that was evil and ruthless. But Govardhan cared little for people's opinion. In course of time he became the father of three sons. People admired and at the same time envied his good fortune. 'Govardhan is a lucky devil; how could a man like him be blessed with three sons?' They said openly. But Govardhan did not pay any heed to these remarks.

In a village located close to Navagram there lived a man called Sadasiva who was a widower. His wife had died when Sadasiva was sixty. Govardhan was on good terms with this man; it was not unusual since their attitude and temperaments matched. Shortly before his wife's death Sadasiva had adopted the third and youngest son of Govardhan. The boy was still a baby; apprehending that no one would be there to take care of the baby Sadasiva toyed with the idea of taking a wife. But no one was willing to marry his daughter to a sixty year-old man. In the end a very poor fellow, tempted by Sadasiva's property, and and driven by the hope that his daughter would at least get proper food and clothes at her husband's home, agreed to the proposal, and Sadasiva married for the second time. He loved his second wife more than his own life, and she, too, showered her genuine love and affection on the baby boy. A couple of years passed; then death snatched Sadasiva away from the mortal world. The second wife was very young and the son too was a small kid at the time of Sadasiva's death. The maternal uncle of Sadasivafelt that, if the father of Sadasiva's second wife was given the charge of looking after his dead son-in-law's property, the man, being extremely poor might be tempted to appropriate everything in course of time. Therefore, in consultation with Govardhan, this uncle of Sadasiva decided to keep the property under his own control. He took the matter to the court and finally became the legal custodian of the property. He, too, kept the boy in legal custody. Sadasiva's widow, on the other hand, had to go without food for days on end; but the uncle cared little for her.

The villagers roundly condemned this act of selfishness. Pestered by the aspersions cast on him by the people, and their sarcasm and censure, the man decided to give up the custodianship of Sadasiva's property. But in the mean time he had transferred quite a sizable amount into his own pocket. Govardhan intervened in the matter at the proper time and made an appeal at the Subedar's court for making him the boy's custodian.

Like a large fish swallowing a tempting bait dangled by a cunning fisherman Sadasiva's uncle was carried away by the false counseling of Govardhan and gave his consent in the matter. So, Govardhan obtained the custodianship of Sadashiva's property and brought back his son to his own house. The merging of Sadasiva's property with his own filled Govardhan's heart with great joy. He was not bothered at all about Sadasiva's widow who now begged from door to door, and cared not to flick a glance of sympathy at the poor woman, let alone offer her shelter in his home.

Alas! Her poor father, out of greed, had agreed to give his daughter in marriage to a sixty year old man; he had hoped that his daughter would live in comfort. It had never occurred him even in his dreams that destiny had stored such days of misury for his daughter.

Sadashiva's widow, like someone caught in the perilous vortex of life, whose violent, merciless whirl tossed her here and there, wandered aimlessly and prayed to God desperately to put an end to her accursed life. The villagers time and again approached Govardhan on her behalf and requested him to help the poor woman. But Govardhan was not at all moved by their appeal, nor was he affected by the misery of the woman. As it was his abominable miserliness was deeply detested by the villagers; his total callousness towards the sufferings of Sadasiva's widow turned them hostile. They would not have hesitated to tear the man alive but for the fear of the law. A woman who had owned a large property until recently had to beg on the streets and go without food for days together. What an irony of fate!! Govardhan's wife, Kautuki was no less a miser than her husband. She was born and brought up in a family where she had learnt lessons in deceit and selfishness. Living with a man like Govardhan had turned her heart even harder. She had adorned herself with the jewellery which had once belonged to the wife of Sadasiva; but whenever the poor woman begged for mercy Kautuki treated her scornfully, and drove her away. Sadasiva's widow left the place with tear-filled eyes. Deep sighs escaped her as she walked away in great pain and anguish.

Time rolled on. And it so happened that within a few years all the three sons of Govardhan fell victims to death one after another. Astonishingly, such a terrible stroke of fate did not seem to have any noticeable impact on Govardhan's nature. He had perhaps planned to carry all his wealth away with him to the other world. Despite the severe punishment meted out to him by fate, Govardhan's heart did not soften towards Sadasiva's widow.

On the other hand, the forbearance of the woman was pushed to its limit. Hunger had emaciated her; and the hard blows of a ruthless fate had completely shattered her moral strength. The tattered piece of cloth she had covered herself with was no longer able to serve its purpose. Life became so bitter and terrifying for her that she decided to put an end to it. One day people found her dead body hanging in front of Govardhan's house.

It was a sight painful enough to rend the one's heart. Oh God !! What was your intention? What lesson did you want to teach the world through such an incident?

How must the poor woman have felt before she decided to kill herself? She must not have had any choice other than this. This would have appeared to her to be the only way to bring an end to all her sufferings. Was the woman, who received the love of a rich husband, and had cherished in her heart colourful dreams of a happy and comfortable life, destined to quit the world in this manner? Wasn't there a little room for her in this vast world? Readers, I can't find words to express the sorrow that stabs at my heart. O' God!

The Creator of the Universe! Only You can understand the mysterious laws of life, your own Infinite Power.

We, puny, finite human beings, will not be able to make sense of them. Dear readers, have you ever come across reprobates like Govardhan and Kautuki? You might have; God has filled His world with all sorts of characters. These illustrate extreme form of cruelty and inhumanity. The miserable end of Sadasiva's widow had outraged the villagers; but it had brought about no change in the nature of Govardhan and his wife. The one person in their family who was affected by all this was his daughter, his only child whom death had kindly spared. Though born of selfish parents, and raised in a family that was a stranger to human virtues like compassion, and goodwill, she was like a lotus that grew in a patch of mud. God had gifted her with noble qualities. Her body was delicate like the lotus-petal, and her heart was soft as its pollens. Like the fragrance of the lotus, her virtues permeated the air. It was therefore not surprising that the sufferings of Sadasiva's widow had melted her tender heart. The ill-treatment that the poor woman received from her parents had strengthened the girl's feeling of sympathy for her. Several times had the girl helped her without the knowledge of her father and mother. But her help could not have sustained Sadasiva's widow for long. The young girl was utterly disgusted with the behaviour of her parents towards woman and protested it only to receive their scornful reprimands.

The shocking death of the wretched woman had filled her with feelings of revulsion, but it was not within her power to do anything to teach her selfish parents a lesson. She, however, had a strong hope that they would be duly punished one day for their evil deeds. Readers, you have already been introduced to this beautiful and virtuous young woman. She was Rasakala. She was the one who had knocked at Kalavati's door on that full- moon night of the month of Pausha.

***

CHAPTER-12

Bhandeshwara

The readers by now must have guessed that the Dasa the poor farmer and the big man were talking about under that Patali tree near the statue of Lord Mahadeva on that full-moon night of the month of Pausha, was no other than the Govardhan Dasa mentioned in the previous chapter. They too might have correctly guessed that the boat that had arrived there had carried Raghunath Pattnaik and his associates. Sardar Singh, who had come earlier in the evening to inspect the arrangements, had posted the big man under the Patali tree to keep a vigil. It was also a security measure adopted by him. If by any mischance some thing went wrong the man could send some signal to the boat while it would be in the river and alternative measures could be adopted.

Stepping out of the boat, Raghunath Patnaik approached the big man and collected all the necessary information from him. The man gave him an account of the conversation he had had with the poor farmer of the village. The dissatisfaction that seemed to be brewing amongst the poor of the village pleased Raghunath. Thereafter Raghunath addressed his gang of dacoits and gave them necessary instructions. He also warned them to be particular regarding the timing of the raid. Having received orders from their chief the dacoits broke into small groups and proceeded in different directions.

Readers, let us shift our attention to Bhandeswara and have a look at the arrangements being made there for the procession of light. It was not just the auspicious occasion of the full moon night of Pausha for which all those preparations were going on. In fact, such arrangements were never made earlier for this particular occasion. But that day people were busy carrying in flowers, garlands and festoons, and lights of various shapes to the place. The word had already spread that the subedar was to be felicitated that night and a procession of light would be taken out in his honour.

A little below the village of Navagram there was a wharf that went by the name of Pandav Ghat. One could see a number of such Pandav Ghats in different villages. It is believed that when the Pandavs were exiled and lived in forests they boarded ferries or canoes in order to cross the river from these points. It is neither easy nor wise to waste time and energy in verifying the authenticity of these myths. The people in those villages believed it without questioning its authenticity. Anyone who tried to contradict this would only antagonize them. Yet it was comforting to know that in this modern age people still had not forgotten The Mahabharat written by Lord Vyasadeva.

To the south of the Pandav Ghat there stood the temple of Lord Mahadeva who was worshipped by the local people as Bhandeswara. The vast glade to the south of Navagram had acquired its popularity because of the presence of the Lord there. Popular myths are associated with the emergence of different deities in different parts of Orissa. The case of the emergence of Lord Bhandeswara was no exception. The myth goes like this:

Yudhisthira, the eldest of the Pandavas, was a great

devotee of Lord Shiva; he wouldn't drink a drop of water before he took bath and offered worship to the Lord. Once, while they were in exile, the Pandavas walked through the forest near the glade. Yudhisthira, after having taken bath in the Mahanadi, looked for an image of Lord Mahadeva to offer worship to him. But he couldn't find one and therefore did not take either water or food that morning. Having walked some distance with wife Draupadi and his brothers, Yudhisthira got tired from hunger and thirst. His brother Bhima went about in search for an image of Lord Mahadeva. He searched amidst the shrubs and bushes in the vicinity but found none. Finally, he brought a long-stemmed earthen vessel, pitched it upside down in the ground in order to make it look like the image of Lord Shiva. He called his brother Yudhisthira to the spot and showed him the upper half of the vessel that rose from beneath the ground and closely resembled the deity. Yudhisthira, under the impression that it was actually the image of Lord Shiva, offered worship to it and walked on accompanied by his wife and brothers. Bhima stayed back and, when his brothers had moved a short distance, he struck the vessel with his heavy club. The vessel was shattered into pieces. And lo! Out came the image of the lord from inside it. The Lord had emerged from the bowels of the earth, piercing the crust of the earth above and had fixed his abode there since that day. The Lord was popularly known in the region by the name Lord Bhandeswara since He had emerged from a vessel or bhanda. After the image lay exposed to elements for many years, a devotee had built a small temple there. A small pond lay close to the temple. Every year on the occasion of Triveni Amavasya a festival was celebrated there. Many women, in order to seek the Lord's blessings to have a male child came here to offer their worship. They used to take bath in the pond and search inside the water. If they got hold of either a snail or an areca-nut, they swallowed it whole and then went inside the temple to have a 'Darshan' of the Deity. And their wishes were granted. Because of the festival that was celebrated with pomp every year and the great faith the people there had had in the Lord's power, the place still retained its importance.

The light the poor farmer spoke about to the Bhuyan dacoit and had hurried away from his presence, and was now seen from this glade on the southern side of the village, where Lord Bhandeswar's temple stood. The task of arranging the gaslights of various designs, shapes, and colours was almost complete when the fellow got there. Different varieties of gaslights like the flambeaus, fluorescent lights, phosphorescent lights and many others were fixed in ornate holders and sconces and were placed in neat rows. Near each of them stood a man waiting for orders on receipt of which he would carry it and walk. There were also an assortment of fireworks ready to be ignited. Fireworks in the form of trees were fixed on both sides of the road. There were musicians, and the instrument players too were ready to play the orchestra. Everyone was eagerly waiting for the subadar. The ceremony would begin soon after he arrived.

Every thing was ready; but there was no sign of the subedar's palanquin. The delay in his arrival prompted people to let their imagination run riot and invented a number of reasons that could have caused the delay in his arrival. They thought that some untoward incident might have prevented him form reaching the festival-ground in time. There were some who talked about the prowling tigers while others mentioned the bandits. A lean but powerfully built man who appeared to be quite upset and disturbed was seen pacing about the festival-ground. He was feeling annoyed at the way people voiced their apprehensions aloud.

After about an hour the flame of a torch was seen from a distance. The lean man grew immediately alert and turning excitedly gave orders to start the procession. As soon as they received the orders the light-carriers placed the gas-lights on their shoulders, the orchestra began playing and the fireworks were lighted. There rose a loud hubbub as people began talking excitedly to one another. The melody of the music floated around, the resplendence of the lights as well as luminous fireworks dazzled the onlookers, and the sound of the firecrackers reverberated in the air.

The palanquin of the subadar reached the festival-ground. Ten sentries carrying guns and cudgels walked in front of the palanquin.The men carrying the lights walked along with them. The band of musicians and the orchestra players followed suit. The procession moved in the direction of village Navagram.

***

CHAPTER — 13

Two Friends

⁀I am here, apa, open the door.' --- The mellifluous voice of Rasakala that carried the sweetness of the cuckoo's notes reached Kalavati's ears. The words made the strings of her heart vibrate. Its soft, soothing touch subdued the notes of pathos ringing there before Rasakala's arrival. Energy seeped into Kalavati's weary body at the prospect of spending some time in exchanging pleasantries with Rasakala of whom she was extremely fond. She wiped the drops of tears with the end of her saree, got down the bed and opened the door for her. After Rasakala entered she slipped the bolt back into the socket and taking her hand led her to the bed. 'Rasa, let us sleep. There is no sign of the procession as yet. I shall wake you up when it arrives.' Both the young women lay down on the bed resting their heads on one pillow.

Life is strange! The intentions of Lord Almighty are still more so. It is beyond man's power of understanding how and why He brings two human beings from totally different walks of life together. These two young women living in utterly dissimilar circumstances lay together on the carelessly spread out bed sharing one pillow, like two playing-balls set to rolling by some invisible hand had dribbled along the intricate paths of life and come to stop at one particular spot. Their lives were conditioned differently; their aspirations were not alike too. Still they were close friends. Each thought of the other as her very own. The bitter pangs of a long separation tormented them even if they stayed away from each other for just a few moments and when they met the chords of love in both the hearts vibrated in unison. Their hearts sang a note of love just remembering each other even when they were not together. How sweet are the sentiments of friendship!!

The tie of love had pulled two human beings from two completely different spheres of life. It was a marvelous exhibition of the Lord's art of creation. Readers! Can any other form of affection match this divine love? The raging tides of sorrow in Kalavati's heart ebbed at the sound of Rasakala's voice outside and a soothing soft stream of love started rippling across it. Rasakala had gone home at her mother's bidding to have her supper ; but the atmosphere of her home brought back to her the memory of Sadasiva's widow, and, an overwhelming sense of sorrow, like a gust of wind, pulled at the delicate strings of her heart. When she came back and stood in front of Kalavati's door the violent undulations of despair and gloom had calmed down. At that moment of togetherness Rasakala and Kalavati became one, each losing her individual identity in the other. As the doors of their hearts opened to let each other in, so did the door of Kalavati's room. And led by the loving hand of her friend Rasakala got into the bed and lay down; guided by similar emotions Kalavati too lay down by her side. The physical eyes could see two different human beings lying side by side in one bed; but to one who understood the way their souls were fused together, it would appear as if two human forms had merged into each other to become one.

What a marvelous manifestation of love! What an amazing artifice of Destiny! The only witness to it was the lowered flame of the lamp which Kalavati had kept burning while she waited for Rasakala. Rasakala could feel the wetness of the pillow as she rested her head on it. She upraised herself a little and gazed at the face of Kalavati who lay by her side. Her eyes were open. In the dim light of the lamp Rasakala could detect the faint stains of dried -up tear under the eyes of her friend.

"What are you looking at?" Kalavati asked Rasakala when she found the latter looking intently at her face. Like the clear autumn sky overcast with un-seasonal clouds, the mark of freshly wiped tears under Kalavati's eye cast a shadow of gloom over Rasakala's face.

"Apa, have you been crying?" She asked with tear-filled eyes.

Rasakala's words soaked with the nectar of unpretentious love cooled the raging flames of sorrow in Kalavati's heart. Her body trembled a little and her love for Rasakala came rolling down her cheeks in the form of tears. No one, after the death of her husband, spoke to Kalavati so lovingly or revealed such concern except Rasakala. Her care and love reminded Kalavati of her dead husband Raghunath and her kind words soothed her heart and soul. She, because of this reason, longed for Rasakala's company. It was her love for Rasakala that found expression in her tears. She wiped the tears away with the end-border of her sari and said fondly: " It was nothing. You go to sleep." But Rasakala would not give up so easily.

"You have shed so much tears that the pillow has been soaked, and you are asking me to go to sleep as if nothing has happened? Tell me, why were you crying like this?" Kalavati realized that Rasakala would not let the matter drop unless she received a satisfactory answer. But what would she tell her? How could she narrate her tale of woe and burden her innocent heart with her own sorrows? Yet, she had to give some plausible explanation to Rasakala. So Kalavati said: "You had gone home, I was feeling lonely and depressed; what more is there to say?" Kalavati's tears had disturbed Rasakala; her reply made the younger girl even more concerned.

"Apa, I don't come to sleep in your room every night. I came today in order to watch the pageant of light and the ceremony. But on other nights you sleep alone. Do you weep like this every night? From today I shall never let you sleep alone. I shall come every night to sleep in your room. Oh! How much tear you have shed! The whole pillow has been soaked wet."

What could be said in answer to this? How could the volume of tears be measured? Was it so easy to define the exact cause behind one's sorrow with accuracy? Kalavati cast about for an answer but could not find one. She put her fingers fondly under her friend's chin to lift her face and said, " Rasa! How could I explain things to you?------- ------ "

She spoke in a voice wet with emotions, and as she did so tears flowed again washing away the feeble sand-bank of her patience. It was the limit. Rasakala could not contain herself any further and burst into tears. As she tried to wipe away Kalavati's tears with the end-border of her sari she said guiltily: " Apa, have I come here to make you cry like this?"

How innocent, how unpretentious her words were! How divine was the love that filled their hearts! The honesty of the sentiments they revealed had an unworldly quality about it. Readers! Do you think that the taste of the nectar that the gods drink can even be compared with the sweetness contained in those words? The emotional impact they had on Kalavati made her feel faint. The reaction of Rasakala was quite natural since she possessed a tender, guileless heart. God has sent her to earth only to shed tears of grief, Kalavati thought. But she had unwittingly made the person she loved the most and who was an epitome of love, share them. The load of this guilt made Kalavati lose consciousness for a moment, but she came back to reality in the next. Rasakala was not aware of this. She only saw Kalavati close her eyes for some time.

Kalavati decided to keep her emotions under control. With extraordinary patience she composed herself and tried to stop Rasakala from crying. " Please, don't cry", she urged. "I shall not be able to hold back my tears if you do."

Young Rasakala was cofused; she had wanted to know the reason behind Klalavati's sorrow because Kalavati's tears were too much for her tender heart to bear. But it was Kalavati who was asking her to stop crying with a warning that she would start shedding tears again if Rasakala did not listen to her. " I shall weep if you will ----------" , she mumbled. Kalavati settled herself a little more comfortably on the bed, " No, no I shall not weep anymore". She assured Rasakala, " You stop crying".

"All right, now that you have become quiet I shall not cry anymore." She said. And thus both of them stopped crying.

One was shedding tears in the loneliness of her room. The other one came, wanted to know the cause of the former one's grief and began to weep. In the end, their love and concern for each other forced them to keep their emotions under control, and both calmed down. But Rasakala's question remained unanswered. She kept quiet for some-time and then said: "Apa, why don't you eat rice two times a day?"

The question which made Kalavati cry and which she had wanted to avoid was this time framed in a differ-ent manner. But she had promised not to cry; besides, too much of weeping had worn out both of them. She was feel-ing in a way lighter after having shed the tears. She did not want to answer the question but her silence would upset the girl. " It is not good for me to eat rice two times a day", she replied calmly.

" But you used to eat two meals a day earlier; after the death of brother-in-law you are eating just once. Today you have eaten a little something late in the evening. Would such fasting be good for you? Why are you going through this torture?"

"Rasa! It is not torture. Actually I have no appetite. How can I eat when I am not hungry? I have lost my ap-petite after your brother-in-law passed away."

Too much of weeping has made you lose your appe-tite. Tomorrow onwards I shall keep in constant company with you. Then you cannot weep, your appetite will come back and you will have your meals regularly."

"You are talking like a child. Even if I feel hungry I cannot eat more than once in a day."

"Why can't you?" Rasakala exclaimed in surprise.

"You need not know all these details my dear. Let God fill your life with joy. I shall spend the rest of my life in peace if you live a happy life."

"But Apa, tell me the truth." Rasakala insisted. " Why are so many restrictions imposed on a woman after the death of her husband? You were used to adorn yourself with ornaments and expensive clothes. You were used to put lac-dye on your feet and the spot of vermilion on your fore head. You have given up those habits. Does not it mar your good looks?" Rasakala asked in innocent curiosity.

"You are still an immature girl. You are growing up but you still think and talk like a child. How can I explain these things---- All you need to know is that the sashtras forbid adorning oneself.

"Why do the sashtras do so? Why should a woman be doomed to a life-long suffering because her husband has died?"

"Again you talk like a small child. What the sashtras say is right. For a wife, her husband is an incarnation of God. I have explained it to you several times. A widow, whom her God has deserted, should have no interest in worldly pleasure. No other deed could be more virtuous for a wife than accompanying her husband to the other world as a sati, but it is not always possible. As for me I could not be a sati; I have survived. But what is there in my life to enjoy? I have to practise the austerities of widowhood. If I do not perform the duties of widowhood with discipline, it would mean the breach of a sacred vow. My body and my soul were dedicated to someone, and that someone has left for his heavenly abode. But that does not mean that I have got back my body and soul. How happy had I been with him! I devote myself to serving God in the hope of getting united with him in the other world and live happily with him there forever." Kalavati stopped abruptly. Her voice broke.

As she spoke to Rasakala, more than once a sob almost choked her, but her promise not to cry forced her to fight back her tears.

But it was no longer within her power to do so. The image of her husband Raghunath flashed before her eyes. Had that image had a body, Kalavati would have embraced it with all the force of her love. The disappointment resulting from the realization that it was not real accompanied with the memory of her loss overwhelmed her with grief. Her voice choked and tears, ran down her cheeks.

A nervous Rasakala quickly wiped Kalavati's tears with the end-border of her sari; "Apa, didn't you promise not to weep?" She asked haltingly. Kalavati came back to herself and made a strong effort to restrain herself. "No, no Rasa, I shall not weep any more. I just lost control over myself." Without her knowledge Rasakala's eyes had grown moist. She wiped her eyes and asked "What is death? Why do people mourn the dead?"

Kalavati was overcome with the innocence that underlay the apparently simple question. She was unable to find an answer that could satisfy the girl. But would Rasakala let it go so easily? Kalavati did not think so; after a little deliberation she told

"Rasa, your love for me has moved me greatly. But what can I say in answer to your question?" The girl persisted. "Tell me please, Apa, what is death?"

"When a soul is redeemed, it leaves the temporary shelter of the body and returns to its permanent abode; this is what we call death."

"So, brother-in-law is redeemed and has gone back

to his permanent abode. Why then, should you mourn his death?" Rsakala asked as if she understood the whole affair.

They had come back to the same topic once more, despite Kalavati's sincere efforts to change the line of conversation. Young Rasakala was so concerned with Kalavati's sorrow that she was determined to find out its cause and offer a possible remedy. It seemed beyond Kalavati's ability to ignore the eager curiosity of her innocent heart. How could Kalavati get Rasakala's thoughts diverted into a different track? Whatever she told her hoping to change the painful topic, Rasakala kept reverting to the same subject. Shedding tears would have helped Kalavati to assuage her pangs but there was no hope of that. She had given her word to Rasakala not to weep. She had gone back on her promise once. She could not afford to do it again. She knew that Rasakala would join her if she broke down and wept. Finding no other way she tried to explain:

"Rasa, your brother-in-law has returned to his permanent home. But I did not. I am left alone. The strong tie of love that had held us together snapped and it is not easy for me to brace myself against the painful experience. Rasa, how nice would have it been had I accompanied him to the other world. The reminiscence of that strong bond of love is tormenting me and forcing me to shed tears. The undimmed memory of that togetherness has tethered me to this austere vow. I am moving without stop, carrying that severed tie of love, praying to God day and night. May He grant my prayers and let me have a dip in that nectar of love in afterlife."

Kqlavati's explanation seemed to overwhelm Rasakala's tender heart. She lay there quietly, her mind heavy with thought; sleep eluded her eyes. The eagerness to watch the procession of light had long since ebbed away. Kalavatis words, soaked with deep melancholy, had the power to melt the hardest of hearts. Rasakala's curiosity, her eagerness to know the cause of Kalavati's sorrow seemed to have disappeared. What she had just heard from Kalavati filled her with a deep anguish. Suddenly the sound of a firecracker filled the tranquil night-air. It was soon followed by the sound of other firecrackers that began to burst one after another. The loud noise, like the rattle of thunderclaps pierced the walls and doors of Kalavati's room and shattered the silence that had reigned there.

***

Chapter--14

The Procession Of Light

Dear readers! Let us leave Kalavati and Rasakala alone for some time and turn our attention to the procession of light. The procession slowly moved forward in the direction of Navagram. The lights, in various attractive shapes and colours, were fixed inside narrow holders. These were carried by men who walked in two neat rows on both sides of the village-path. Along with them walked others holding artificial banana and other fruit trees. In the midst of this flamboyant resplendence moved a large number of onlookers. It appeared as if a winding river of people that had somehow got cut off from its source, flowed between the banks of light. The crowd that moved outside the procession created an impression of water overflowing river-banks. Doesn't water from other sources rush in to a river during the floods? Here, too, people swarming in from different directions mingled with the main current of the crowd and in no time it became dangerously thick.

As the pageant of light neared Navagram, the sound of fire-crackers and the loud hubbub invaded the silence of the village. There was no getting away from the noise. The loud noise drove sleep away from the eyes of the people. Everyone woke up. The men, caring little for the cold, covered themselves perfunctorily with coarse bedspreads, or shawls, or just with the end-parts of the clothes they wore, and hurried out. The women called out to one another and hastened outdoors. Some young mothers ran to the thresholds of their houses scooping up their sleeping babies in their arms while some others in their enthusiasm to watch the procession forgot their kids. The kids, in a half-asleep and half-awake condition, howling their lungs out, tottered to the place where their mothers stood.

The light-procession was still at some distance. Those young mothers could have woken up their kids and carried them outside but the eagerness to watch the lighting-procession made them forget their babies. Thus every house at Navagram suddenly came to life. The village air was filled with the din and bustle. Indeed, who would not be eager to see the procession of light? Even the poor people, who did not get a square meal a day, did not want to let go of this chance. What to speak of others?

The procession was yet to reach the outskirts of the village. Only bright glow was visible from the distance. But the loud noise produced by the milling crowd combined with the sound of the orchestra made people shout at each other when they wanted to say something. Some villagers had gathered at the outskirts of the village. The moving pageant of light amazed these spectators. Its splendour had dimmed the moon. The moon, as it was, had lost much of its radiance caught in an icy net of mist. This additional splendour seemed to have vanquished its glamour and declare a total triumph over its pride. The ear-splitting boom of the firecrackers, like canon-shots from the enemy-barrack pierced the luminous, cloudless sky and shook the kingdom of the moon. The sound of the crackers bursting lingered in the air for quite some time. The echo rattled through the sky and created an impression that the bullet-shots from the canon had wrought mayhem in the moon's domain. When more than one such bomb burst at the same time, it seemed as if the sky would crash and the moon, wrenched out of its orbit, would drop on the earth.

The procession moved on slowly, haltingly, like a pregnant woman, stopping at places where the tree-shaped fireworks and others that spread colourful lights were ignited. The spell-binding combination of colour and light was a joy to the spectators. The blazing light not only enabled the spectators to have a clear view of the procession, but traveling far into the night-sky it seemed to mock at the pale glimmer of the stars and the moon. Much in the same way the sight of a comparatively more beautiful woman gives complexes to others watching her and makes them turn their faces away with a feeling of belittlement, those heavenly bodies tried to look away from the resplendence of the fireworks.

The three-fold entertainment arising out of the three sources, the light, the colour, and the sound, exhilarated the onlookers. People, floating in that current of exhilaration, moved along the procession and finally reached the village of Navagram.

***

Chapter-15

The Raid

The crowd that had gathered at the outer precincts of the village let out a loud cry of joy when the light-procession approached; the sound of the cry travelled fast to the other end of the village. It had the quality and touch of that loud welcoming cheer with which the subjects greet their king. There is nothing puzzling about it. At that time Orissa was not an independent province; the Maratha subedar ruled over it. The crowd rightly cheered the approach of the *Naib*, (the representative of the Subedar), who was no less than a king for the people of Orissa.

The sound of the loud cheer was also heard in Kalavati's room. Both Rasakala and Kalavati , their hearts heavy with sorrow yet bound to each other with the string of love, were lying on the bed. Their earlier love for each other had attained a new fullness. Kalavati sincerely wanted to lay open her heart before her dearest companion, and Rasakala was eager to listen to her. How could the sounds of the outer world have made any impact upon those anguished hearts that had just experienced the bliss of divine love? It entered their ears, swept past their hearts without creating any impression there. There was no space left for worldly thoughts in the hearts of Kalavati and Rasakala.

Kalavati had stopped speaking, and Rasakala kept gazing intently at her moon-like face that glowed with an intensity of emotion. Rasalala pondered deeply on what the older girl had said earlier about love, about death that severed the ties of love, and so on . The sound of the bursting of firecrackers entered the room but not their minds. That night the affection of Rasakala had reached an absolute totality. And no obstacle coming in its way had the power to hinder its flow. The swelling flood of her love was eager to gather Kalavati's heart and set it afloat there forever. She had made up her mind not to leave Kalavati alone even for a moment.

"Apa, young that I am, it was not easy for me to grasp the meaning of all that you have said; but your sorrow born out of your loneliness has terribly upset me, and I promise that from now on I shall never let you to brood over your loss and shed lonely tears." Rasakala said after keeping quiet for a while.

Readers! Couldn't such words elevate the listener's heart to the utmost height of emotion? Kalavati's heart was overwhelmed with the sincerity of Rasakala's concern and care. The deep love that they felt for each other rendered the whole mundane world and its joys meaningless. The picturesque beauty of our earth that reflect the architectural excellence of God Almighty could have proved worthless before the power of love those words were charged with. The pomp and splendour of the procession of light paled by comparison.

The scalding heat of sorrow was slowly cooled down by the nectar of love Rasakala's words sprinkled on it. Kalavati sat quietly for some time allowing that serene calmness spread over her whole being. Both were wordless. The bustle outside assaulted the silence in the room. But how could it disturb the mood of the unearthly happiness that permeated the hearts of the two friends? Can the small flame of a lamp spread far its light under the blazing sun?

There was a long silence. Kalavati looked at Rasakala's young face. It reflected the severe agitation that went inside her. She realized that the tormenting ecstasy was too much for Rasakala's tender heart to bear. She had read about how Lord Krishna revealed himself before Arjuna in his true majesty. Arjuna was not able to stand the radiance emanating from the Lord for long and entreated him to assume his human form once more. It could be extremely difficult for a girl of Rasakala's age to endure the ecstasy of the revelation any further. As she was older, Kalavati thought, it was her duty to turn Rasakala's mind to lighter things. She tried to find out a way to change the topic of their discussion.

All earthly objects in this transitory world are wrapped in an illusion. But they cannot tempt man unless he desires to be swayed away by them. Though earthly temptations usually keep away from hearts that tend to take a spiritual course, they endeavour relentlessly to delude man. We earthlings may or may not be aware of it but these two antithetical passions endlessly work upon the senses of man trying to exercise their influence on him. The moment Kalavati decided to come out of the depths of her emotional seclusion, the sounds outside caught her attention. The opportunity she was looking for to distract her friend's mind was close at hand!

"Rasa, don't think of those things anymore. It is no use. Didn't you want to watch the procession of light? It is about to reach here; let's go to the front door." Her excited voice reflected the relief she experienced after sharing her sorrow with her friend. The mention of the procession jerked Rasakala out of her thoughts. "Oh yes, there is such an uproar outside. The procession must have entered the village. Come, come." She said eagerly and getting off the bedstead quickly the two of them hastened to the main door. The procession had come half way through the village by that time and was heading in the direction of Choudhury's house. The two friends kept the front door ajar and peered round it.

The procession approached. First came the artificially designed trees. There were a number of them: coconut trees, plantain trees, and many more. Beautiful gaslights shaped like swans, fishes, lotuses came after the trees. Artificial flowers of various colours and shapes followed them. Fluorescent lights having a tapering shape that created an illusion of narrow-stemmed glasses along with several eye-catching artworks were carried with great flourish. In the midst of these, there played the orchestra. The splendid combination of colour, light and music held the spectators under a spell. They vociferously showered praise on the workmanship of those who had arranged the procession. Rasakala and Kalavati stood at the half-open door, looking at the pageant of grandeur with unblinking eyes. Someone set fire to a cracker that the local people knew by the name of the "rising moon". The dazzle of the firework, was for a split second mistaken for daylight. The blinding light baffled the onlookers. Before anyone could guess what happened, there rose a great hue and cry. The commotion that followed shook the entire village.

No one knew what exactly caused the commotion. As Kalavati and Rasakala kept looking at the disturbing sight people began running in all directions. The men carrying artificial trees and gaslights ran as fast as their legs could

take them. The air resonanted with the screams of frightened human beings. Just then, along the sandy stretch of
river Mahanadi to the north of village Navagram, bombs
went of. The ear-splitting sound sent shockwaves across the
village. A louder boom from behind the Choudhury-house
synchronized with them. The compound walls were   hit
with tremendous force from the outside; they came down
with a crash. Kalavati and Rasakala shrieked in fear and
the next moment fell on the floor, unconscious.

***

CHAPTER-16

Sardar Singh

Taking leave of Raghunath, Sardar Singh got into his
boat and the vessel sped away in the opposite direction. Moving unusually fast the boat quickly left the village
of Tarito behind and reached the meeting-point of three rivers. The oarsmen were in no way inferior to those rowing
Raghunath's boat. If both the groups were made to stand
together, it would seem that men possessing equal vigour
and strength were chosen for this job of manning the boats.
As the boatmen of the two boats were equally strong and
equally skillful in handling a boat, both boats moved away
at the same speed, one downstream and the other upstream.

It was a noiseless, chilly night. Silence reigned everywhere. No one was in sight. The moon and a few stars as if
shivering in the ice-cold air, blinked at the earth from the
blue sky. The blue waters of river Mahanadi caught the reflection of the moon and the dimly twinkling stars and made
it appear as if there were two skies, one above and another below. The glow-worms that circled the trees standing
on both sides of the river were like the eyes of those trees
with which they witnessed the twin images. This beautiful moon-blanched landscape one glimpsed through the
icy film of mist brought some sort of relief to the earth that
writhed under the tyranny of winter. But Sardar Singh and

his men had no eyes for this moonlit scene. Their minds were focussed on the mission they were on and the increasing speed of the boat added to their enthusiasm.

From the meeting-point of the three rivers the boat changed direction and entered river Chitrotpala. This holy river, branching out from Mahanadi at the delta region has meandered to the east. Since sages were believed to have fixed their abodes on both sides of it in ancient times the water of this river is considered to be holy and people touched it with reverence. The river unceasingly sang the glory of God in sweet murmurs for having received the redeeming touch of the holy sages. Those wise sages have long since departed but the river has learnt from them a great truth of life and moved along its path of duty never stopping for a while, singing joyfully her gratitude to God. How many people ennoble their lives by following the path of wisdom shown to them by their wise mentors? How many of us have learnt the truth that a sense of dutifulness is the essence of all religion, and how many of us would prefer to dedicate their lives to the practice and preservation of such wisdom? Would anyone try to learn this from river Chitrotpala?

Sardar Singh's boat headed east. The river seemed to giggle gaily as the boat sailed on. The boat and the river seemed to be talking to each other. Why was the river so delighted at the touch of the boat? Was she happy to receive the boat because she thought it was helping to fulfil a noble mission? What could be so noble about the mission of these robbers that the river, instead of feeling morose, expressed its joy? The readers would come to know about it at a later time. All the same, the eager waters of the river quickly carried the boat to its destination.

The boat drifted towards the shore. It was, however, not a usual ferry-ghat or wharf where the boat finally stopped. The dacoits never roped their boats to the wharfs used by the villagers. Instead they chose secluded spots at a little distance for mooring their boats. Only they knew where these were located. Other people did not have any knowledge of that. In such an unfrequented spot, a little away from the wharf called Bateswar where the temple of goddess Bhagavati stood, the dacoits moored their boat. Two other boats of a different make were moored there. They were larger in size than the m*a*l*n*gi boat of Sardar Singh, more like small battle-ships. They were the famous *jaliyas* used exclusively by the dacoits of Kujang. They were specially built cargo-boats for carrying merchandise and were used by the Bhuyan dacoits for trade and commerce. They were also used as the getaway vessels by the Bhuyans to carry the loot after a raid. Several oars were fitted to such boats, their numbers varying from sixteen to thirty. They were manned by hugely built, devilish-looking boatmen. It is easy to guess how fast the boats could move. The motorboats designed by the Englishmen having technical expertise could not move faster than these.

Sardar Singh alighted from the boat. On the river bank, about fifty men waited for him in a grove, ready to set about their mission. The grove resounded with the call "Lord Mahavira" when Sardar Singh appeared. The sound travelled far, tearing open the heart of the slumbering earth. Immediately ten torches were lighted. These men shook the dust off their bodies and wound their clothes tightly around their waists. After offering salutations to Goddess Bhagavati at the wharf of Bateswar they strode towards the house of Mahapatra, evil-looking cudgels in hand. It was past midnight. The house was plunged in silence. Everyone was fast asleep. Mahapatra himself, the sole heir of his uncle's legacy, lay asleep in the ornate bedstead of his uncle and enjoyed happy dreams. His aunt had passed away just a month back. The days preceding her death were extremely painful for the woman; the sighs she heaved revealed the agony she was passing through. But the morbid thoughts of his aunt's suffering and her painful end never crossed the selfish nephew's mind. Mahapatra's father, a poor man, could not afford to give his son an education and left him under the care of his wife's brother. Shortly afterwards, Mahapatra's father departed from this mortal world. His wife, Mahapatra's mother, soon followed her husband. No one took care of the house they lived in and Mahapatra's parental house tottered on its way to dilapidation. His maternal uncle's house became Mahapatra's permanent home after the death of his parents. His uncle and aunt had no children of their own and the couple showered all the love and affection on the orphaned boy. In course of time the idea of adopting a male child crossed their mind. But their love for their nephew had not lessened. Therefore, they decided that if at all they adopted a boy, the property must be equally divided between Mahapatra and their adopted child. To Mahapatra, the idea of a rival appearing on the scene was repugnant. He had long since set his greedy eyes on his uncle's immense wealth. A murderous rage took hold of him and he connived to prevent his uncle from going ahead with his plan of adopting a male heir. Very cunningly he poisoned his uncle and established his ownership over the huge property. He took the title of Mahapatra and became the master of everything. Now that he became all in all, Mahapatra totally neglected his widowed aunt. The poor woman cursed Mahapatra from the depth of her heart. Fortunately for her, she did not live long. She left the world about a month after her husband's death. On that full- moon day of *Pausha* it was exactly one month after her death.

We can recollect how the stonewalls of Chodhury's-house were razed to the ground. Almost exactly at the same time, the noise inside the house jerked Mahapatra out of his pleasant sleep. He, to his utter dismay, noticed that the dacoits had forced the doors and were carrying away everything they could lay their hands on. Outraged at the audacity of the intruders, Mahapatra lunged forward to stop them; instantly Sardar Singh's sword chopped his head off, and the headless body of Mahapatra crashed to the ground. The dacoits carried the loot to their boat. Before leaving the place they fixed the severed head of the ungrateful villain to the point of a bamboo-post following the order Sardar Singh and pitched it in front of the ransacked house. It looked like a flag holding aloft the symbol of sin to teach a lesson to the world.

***

CHAPTER-17

The Mound of Jatia

Towards the far east of the sand-bank where the abode of Lord Mahadeva popularly known as BudhaLinga stood, a large hillock resembling an island in mid-ocean, reared its head above the deep waters of the Mahanadi. Hemmed by a beautiful forest this large mound of earth seemed to welcome the weary merchants traveling to distant places for trading, and beckon the hermits who looked for a sequestered spot for meditation. Lifting its head up the hillock also invited way-worn animals roaming in search of a comfortable shelter. This outcrop of rock in the middle of river Mahanadi was popularly known as the *Jatia* hillock. It has been mentioned in an earlier chapter that the barrages, monuments to English architectural skills, had brought down the water level of the river. Besides a good portion of of the mound had been worn away by the currents lashing it relentlessly, in the way the arrogance of a proud man gets dissolved in the invincible current of Time. Though a sizable part of the hillock had been eroded, the pictorial beauty of the hill never fails to leave an indelible imprint on the memory of whoever visits the place even for once. Indeed the natural beauty of the mound of Jatia excelled the loveliness of all other small and big hills in river Mahanadi. The Creator of the Universe, while painting the picturesque landscape of Orissa seemed to have paused here for a while to give it a few more fine strokes with His celestial brush. The precipitous landmass all round the hill, and the tall trees there thickly entangled with flowering creepers, stood like the huge, ornate walls of a fortress as if to protect the hill from all kinds of outside attacks. The rushing water-currents dashed against the walls and turned back like a vanquished enemy troops producing a gurgling sound like the angry cry of frustration of a retreating army. The creepers bearing multi-coloured wild flowers embracing the trees tightly and gazing happily at their lovely reflections in the water spread there as though to prevent all sorts of trespassing.

Inside these nature-made boundaries are found occasional growths of thick-foliaged trees that further enhanced the beauty of these. Several kinds of flowering shrubs even though untended stood studded with blossoms of captivating colours like a group of devotees with bowed heads felicitating the Creator for his excellent art-work and offering Him gifts of bouquets. There were hundreds and hundreds of them, and amidst those there grew bramble bushes that were loaded with tiny, delicious berries. They seemed to be present everywhere inside the natural boundaries of the fortress holding baskets of Nature's nectar-filled fruits ready to quell the thirst and hunger of the weary wayfarers. Winter is the season of these berries and they are available in plenty in the month of *Pausha*. Hence in this month, many people from nearby villages, mainly kids, came to the mound of *Jatia* during the day to eat the nectar-filled berries. But no one remained on the hill after sunset for fear of Hanuman Das who, it is said roamed about the hill riding a tiger.

The events narrated in this text occurred in that period when the mound of *Jatia* derived most of its fame and popularity on account of being linked with the name of Hanuman Das. But a major part of this famous mound, in course of time, has slowly fallen away. Hanuman Das too has departed from the world. They, like all earthly objects, have fallen victims to Time and returned to dust. They were likely to have been lost in oblivion had not the memory of people been bringing them back to light time and again.

In those days the mound of *jatia* and Hanuman Das had always aroused the curiosity of people. In times of trouble they used to seek the blessings of Hanuman Das at the *Jatia mound* which, they believed would protect them from all kinds of danger. Even the Bhuyan dacoits of Kujanga never failed to pay their respects to Hanuman Das after completing an operation. They believed that it would bring bad luck unless they paid a visit to the great man on their way back.

In the center of the mound there is a large patch of thorny trees that bore small berries. A narrow track cut across the forest and went far into the depth of the forest. The track was flanked on both sides by the thick foliage of these trees. The tendrils of wild creepers that entwined the branches on one side were entangled with similar growths on the other forming a natural canopy that kept out the sun. Moving along this track one would experience the feeling of being inside a tunnel. The spot was utterly desolate; one who walked along the dark, shadowy path would be likely to experience a sense of detachment from the mortal world existing outside. It was impossible to stand upright and one had to crawl along the tunnel to reach its opening. At the end of the tunnelled path, under a large banyan tree there was an anthill decorated with flowers and sandal-paste. A hut that was made with the branches and leaves of trees stood near. In this hut lived Hanuman Das.

The presence of the anthill and Hanuman Das in the mound of Jatia has an interesting legend about them.

Somewhere in the past a cowherd boy used to go to the mound every day with his herd. He played and rested under the tree while the cattle grazed. One day at noon he found one milch cow missing from the herd. Thoroughly upset the boy wandered about the mound looking for the missing cow. He moved through the forest of the prickly berry trees searching desperately for the animal and finally found it standing over an anthill. The boy watched the cow in utter amazement as milk dropped from its udder on the anthill and the rivulets of milk instead of flowing down got soaked into the anthill as if some unseen presence in that anthill was sucking the milk away. Curiosity prompted him to break the anthill and find out what lay inside. But the next instant his religious instincts held him back. Some thing inside him told him that perhaps some noble soul had sojourned in that hill and the cow poured her milk on the anthill to nourish that noble one. This incredible spectacle filled his heart with a serene joy and ecstasy. The entire universe appeared before him as a cow offering her milk to the Divine Creator. A sense of gratitude and reverence for the Great Creator flowed out from the cow as milk and the divine presence immanent in all beings and all objects and each and every particle here sucked that milk of devotion.

What a marvellous interpretation!!

The boy stood transfixed, mesmerized at the sight in front of him. Then he began to dance intoxicated with the newly discovered spiritual joy. He realised that the whole of the universe existed in God. This Supernal Creator extracts the essence from His creations in the form of virtues and devotions, manifesting Himself by His own will and choice in the animate and inanimate objects of the Universe. In other words, the essence of everything returns wherefrom it comes, to its origin, to God Almighty Himself.

What a marvellous pattern of organizing things where one action leads to another till the chain makes a full circle ending at the point where it had begun!

How mysterious is the design of that Supreme Artist!!

Wouldn't one on learning this truth of our existence dance ecstatically?

The cowherd boy forgot who he was; he forgot everything that connected him to the world outside. He lost all attachment to his home and family. Nor was he any longer anxious to come back from the mound before nightfall as he used to do. His parents would no more fondly call his name, 'Nabaghana' because he was no longer Nabaghana, the cowherd boy. As ordained by Fate his days of herding cattle were over. His soul was redeemed. The light of the Truth he discovered had illumined his being and his face and body had acquired a glow of divinity. His near and dear ones who caressed him with love not long before shrank away from that radiance.

What great changes could take place in this world within a brief moment! Indeed, it is beyond man's power to understand that mysterious force that controls all actions and all events. A young boy that grazed cattle in the jungle and played under the thorny berry trees his mind occupied with all sorts of worldly thoughts just a while ago got suddenly inspired by the knowledge of the *Brahma* and stumbled on the truth of creation and existence that even the

great sages had failed to grasp after long years of meditation? It is because God had willed it to happen! Such are the
instances He places before the world to teach man lessons of
truth and morality in order to guide him towards the path
of salvation. For some more time Nabaghana remained in
euphoria of realization that had dawned on him. Then he
stopped dancing. Making a broom of leaves he swept the
place clean and sat there quietly lost in deep thought. Tired
as he was he drifted into sleep a little later. God appeared
in his dream and bade him to make the mound of Jatia his
permanent dwelling place. The next day Nabaghan built a
small hut there using the branches of trees and leaves and
moved into it. he assumed the name Hanuman Das and
stayed there. His parents came and implored him to return
home. Nabagahna refused, saying; "I am no longer your
son Nabaghana". He tried to explain to them, " I am Hanuman Das. I am under a pledge and I ask you not to make
me deviate from my path by your emotional entreaties. Go
back and have faith in God. It will ensure your well being."
His parents came back, broken-hearted. The village people
also went there and tried to dissuade him from following
the path of renunciation. But no one succeeded in bringing
him back.

The fame of Hanuman Das, as God had willed it,
spread far and wide. He could cure incurable maladies.
Patients were relieved of their pain at the touch of the great
hermit. Parents begot sons with his blessings. So strong
was people's sense of gratitude for Hanuman Das that they
bowed their heads in respect at the very mention of his
name. Soon word spread that Hanuman Das roamed about
the hillock riding a tiger every night to see if his devotees
lived comfortably or not. There is no need for us to probe
into the matterany further in order to test the veracity of

the hearsay. But it undoubtedly proved the overwhelming influence Hanuman Das exercised on the minds of people. It was not just a trivial matter that people would believe somebody could roam around in the depth of night riding a tiger! It indicated their firm belief that the monk possessed supernatural powers.

There was only one saint besides Hanuman Das people looked upon with similar reverence. He was Giridhari Das, the saint that lived and meditated in the beautiful arbour in the forest of *Kaijang*.

On that eventful full-moon night of the month of *Pausha* Hanuman Das had invited Giridhari Das to the mound of *Jatia*. Both the hermits in the solitude of the forest spent a long time in meditations and prayer. Late in the night each ate a little of the *prasad* (offerings of fruit and other items made to God during worship) and walked up to the edge of the mound. They sat down quietly there and watched the beauty of the moonlit Mahanadi. At the same time they also talked about different subjects. While they were discussing things, about ten *jaliyas* (large cargo-boats that could move at great speed and were used by the dacoits as getaway boats) approached the mound from the direction of the east. The readers have been well introduced with the *jaliyas* earlier. It was mentioned how indispensable these boats were for the dacoits. Such boats could move with the speed of lightning when manned by the Bhuyans. The speed could be even five to ten *koshas* in an hour and the dacoits, after committing a burglary at one place could sail with the booty to a great distance within a short time. Because of their incredible speed it was almost impossible to chase them and catch up with the dacoits.

The boats slowed down and drifted towards the

mound of *Jatia*. An oarsman from the first boat jumped to the land holding the rope and tied it to the trunk of a tree. He bowed his head respectfully greeting the two monks.

" My dear fellow, the arrangements seem to be too elaborate tonight" , Hanuman Das said.

"My Lord, tonight's adventure will be really exciting." The man answered and stepped down to the lower edge of the mound. Immediately, sixteen men got off the boat and paid respect to the monks bowing their heads. A small crowd now gathered in that lonely place. The oarsmen kept roaming about the mound. All of a sudden the thunderous sound of blasts coming from the sandy stretch of the bank of Mahanadi seemed to shatter the tranquility of the mound. No sooner did they hear it than the boatmen untied the *jaliyas* and rowed away quickly from the mound in the direction the sounds came from.

***

CHAPTER-18

The Booty

The readers might not have forgotten the discussion between Balabantara and Raghunath in the isle of Nandikeswari about some action. Time has come for unravel-
ling the mystery. We know that a loud uproar was raised
when the light procession reached Choudhury's door in
Navagram. It was so terrifying that the grand procession
was scattered in no time. The huge crowd melted away. No
trace of the glamour and pomp remained, nor was a single
unlooker in sight. Just before the procession got scattered
and people ran helter-skelter in utter confusion amidst the
hue and cry, the light of the gigantic cracker had dazzled
the place, turning the night bright as day, like the flame of
a lamp that burns radiantly before going off. The men that
walked carrying the lamps ran away in panic still holding
them. The instrument-players also vanished from the scene.
Within moments the resplendence was lost in the darkness
of the night. The grand celebration came abruptly to a terrible end. People must have noticed with what pomp and
grandeur the thick patches of un-seasonal clouds appear
in the sky before they break into heavy shower but after
sometime the lightning and thunder vanish and the clouds,
all their energy spent, disperse leaving no sign of their presence in the sky. In the same manner, the light ceremony
after a brief show of pomp and splendor, melted away into
darkness. The crowd dissapeared like the rain-clouds dis-

persing. The village streets became lonely once more. No local inhabitant was seen there, let alone the spectators who had come from nearby villages. The palanquin was nowhere seen. Nor did its brave-looking escorts who moved along it carrying guns and metal <u>clubs .</u> Moonlight continued to wash the earth as before. The blinding light of the procession could not make any impact on it. It seemed that the promise the artificial light has made to defeat its celestial counterpart had been ridiculously defeated. It could only manage to make a display of its false glamour just for a very short time The moonlit-earth seemed to laugh at its empty bravado. How long can the beauty of artificial things challenge eternal beauty ? The moon and stars laughed; the light of their laughter danced from one end of the earth to the other. The people who came to watch the ceremony from other villages returned laughing at the vain glory of the show. The only ones who could not laugh were the villagers of Navagram.

The thundering sound with which the stone walls of Choudhury house crashed almost synchronized with the commotion outside, sending tremors of shock and terror through the whole village. The startled villagers immediately guessed that the Bhuyan dacoits had arrived. All the doors and windows were instantly closed and people with their wives and children desperately prayed to God to save them from the marauders. As the noise outside died away the loud thud of the walls falling became more distinct and frightening. As the walls fell one after another the fear of people increased at the sound the crashing walls made. Silence prevailed after all the walls fell to the ground.

The dacoits perhaps faced a little resistance at the Dasa house, but two feeble shrieks were heard. The dacoits raised a cry "Victory to Lord Mahavir" which reverberated in the air. People were more terrified when they heard it. The large cargo-boats had in the meanwhile cruised to the riverbank near Navagram. The robbers who boarded the boat climbed down and rushed to the house of Dasa and from there to Choudhury's house. Every movable thing like the groceries, utensils, clothes, arms and weapons were carried along the village street from both the houses and were loaded onto the boats. The dacoits kept marching about the village like nocturnal animals till the operation was over. The loading over, Raghunath Pattnaik signalled his fellow-men and instantly there rose the loud cry "Victory to Lord Mahavir". The deafening sound shook the village with the force of an earthquake.

The mission was complete. The dacoits strangled Govardhan Das and his wife to death by the orders of their chief. They tied the dead bodies to two separate bamboo posts and planted them on both sides of the front door of the house before leaving the place. The corpses were kept hanging from the bamboo posts like symbols of retribution.

The dacoits returned from the site of burglary. As ordered by Raghunath Pattnaik they carried the unconscious bodies of Kalavati and Rasakala to the boat. The boats loaded with the booty headed for the mound of Jatia.

***

CHAPTER-19

The Meeting With The Hermits

The two hermits were still sitting on one end of the hill. They knew that Raghunath Patnaik would come to meet them. They could not have slept peacefully knowing that they would have to get up and meet Raghunath. They, therefore, preferred to keep awake. Sitting on the mound they watched the pristine beauty of the moon-blanched landscape and sang the glory of the omnipotent Lord. Readers, have you ever guessed how soothing to the heart could be the conversation between two such men who have abstained themselves from all worldly pleasures through a vow of renunciation ? Only those who understand the true essence of their conversation will relish it.Others would consider it tasteless as a sour and saltless dish.

The boats reached the Jatia mound. All the oarsmen stayed back to keep guard. Raghunath's boat too was fastened to a tree. Only Raghnnath alighted from the boat. The two hermits gladly welcomed him. Raghunath touched their feet with reverence and they gave him their blessings wishing him a long life.

"Had the exciting booty been collected without problem"? Hanuman Das inquired.

" When the blessings of a noble soul like you are with us, could there be any problem?" Raghunath replied gratefully. "But how is it that both of you great saints are here together?' he asked.

"Brother Hanuman Das invited me here today. On learning that you have come here, I too have been waiting for you". Giridhari Das said pleasantly.

Hanuman Das said again, "We were savouring the beauty of nature. The moon is caught in the icy net of mist and is experiencing the biting chill of the winter, but still it illumines the world. See how pleasant the earth looks bathed in its radiance. We were just wondering who would have filled the earth with such soft soothing light had the moon not been around? It would perhaps have been engulfed in darkness and shedding tears of dew."

'Patnaik', Hanuman Das resumed in a serious voice, ' In these troubled times, you have appeared like the moon. May God bless you to carry forward your mission without any obstruction."

The kind words of the hermit filled Raghunath's heart with humility and respect. He folded his hands and said humbly, "Maharaj, relieving people's distress has become the avowed mission of this humble servant of yours. The consequences of my endeavour in this regard depend on your blessings. But I do not deserve even the one hundredth part of the praises you have showered on me.'

Hanuman Das was about to say something but Giridhar Das cut in, ' You deserve all of it. No one else but you have ventured to perform this difficult task. You have brought glory to your parents. May the Subadar suffer from a hellish agony in his own palace and may God make you the King of Orissa.'

'Please do not say such things.' Raghunath protested

in humility, ' I do not have any such ambition. I shall be happy if I can successfully fulfill the vow I have taken.'

Hanuman Das glanced at his friend and said , 'Did you see how polite and how intelligent Raghunath is!! In my opinion he should not be the king of such a province where the subjects have lost their self-respect. They have been reduced to the level of mere animals. They are unfit to enjoy independence. Servility has seeped into their blood. Unless a sense of duty to their native land is aroused in each of them and revives their spirit, they would continue to be tyrannized by rulers of different kingdomss. However, they are fortunate that a god-send has appeared in such hard times to render them help.' He turned to Raghunath and asked, 'Have the booty from other places reached here?' It was obvious that Raghunath had earlier consulted the hermit about that night's expedition. He had met Hanuman Das the night before and had given him a detailed account of his plan. So Hanauman Das had prior knowledge of the places that were to be looted that full-moon night by the dacoits. He had also extended his silent support to Raghunath .

Raghunath had remained standing as he had not been asked to sit down. He was also not interested to sit for long because he was anxiously waiting for the other cargo boats which were due to arrive there any moment. Just then he could see the faint outline of the boats in the distant river. 'See, the boats are coming', he exclaimed in excitement.

The two hermits rose to their feet. They could see the boats speeding towards the hillock. Hundreds of oars struck the moonlit waters that glittered like liquid silver. The foamy water rose and fell on both sides of the boats like silver flames, burning and going off at regular intervals. Giridhari Das watched the beauty of the scene in amazement. 'How many boats are there?' he asked.

'There are thirty boats. Many of them are coming from Devidwar and Vaideswar. The booty collected from the house of Radhagovinda Choudhury only is loaded in twenty five of them.'

Hanuman Das observed that the boats slowed down, which meant that they would soon arrive at the foot of the hillock. Time must not be wasted, he thought and asked Raghunath not to delay.

'No I shall not delay; we shall leave with your blessings.' Raghhunath said and knelt down to touch their feet again. The hermits uttered their blessings. Raghunath climbed down the hill to make arrangements for the return journey. The hermits also walked back to the leaf-hut enjoying the landscape of the mound which seemd to have been painted silver by the moonlight filtering through the trees.

Raghunath reached down and asked the boatmen to unfasten the boats. He also ordered the boatmen of the thirty cargo- boats not to come close to the mound. The sight of the cargo boats , all fully loaded with the booty, filled Raghunath with joy. He stepped on to his boat and signalled his associates to move.

'Victory to Lord Mahavir' all the dacoits called out at the top of their voice. The echo rose from the river and travelled miles. The boats shot away across the river.

***

CHAPTER-20

The Villa Of Lalbagh

The boats loaded with the plundered goods crossed the canal of Taldanda soon and entering a narrow strait that emerged out of the Mahanadi and was flanked on both sides by dense growth of forests disappeared out of sight. We need not follow them any further.

Readers, let us meet the Subadar at the villa of Lalbagh in Cuttack.

The eventful full-moon night of *Pausa* finally came to an end. It was morning. The sun had risen only an hour or so before. River Kathjori glided along just below the villa. The night before, the river, shrouded in fog, looked like an endless ocean. The mist had dissolved in the light of the morning-sun, and river Kathjori, like someone released from a long confinement, flowed away giggling happily. Close to the river-bank, just above the water level, stood the enormous villa of Lalbag. There was a large stone-floored courtyard adjacent to the villa.

The old villa of Lalbagh where the Subadar lived during those days has long since been renovated. In its place now stands a bungalow that flaunts the British architectural expertise. It is used as the residence of the British Commissioner, the representative of the Queen of England. Earlier there used to be a large two-storied building near the entrance where the watchmen and security guards lodged themselves. Though the villa was renovated, this outhouse, dilapidated beyond repair, had remained standing there for quite some time. Snakes and reptiles made the ramshackle house their hunting ground. At a later time, since the old building seemed to mar the looks of the main bungalow , it was completely demolished. The ladies residing in the villa of the Subadar used to pass time in recreation and merry-making on the large stone-floored patio. But now no one sets foot there.

Readers, most of you must have seen the Lalbag mansion at Cuttack. But the time during which the events narrated in the novel had taken place, the villa wore a majestic look. The present bungalow does not retain even a fraction of that majesty. The grandeur of the original bungalow constructed by the Marathas has evaporated with the end of the Maratha hegemony. When the king belonging to a particular clan or dynasty loses his control over his domain, a king of another dynasty seizes the scepter of power. The new king always looks down upon the edifices and architecture of the preceding era. Slowly, those sculptures and edifices that retained the touch of the artistry and craftsmanship of the previous era disappear from view. There must be very strong reasons behind some such structures of the earlier age remaining untouched. But the villa of Lalbag was one that fell victim to the new order and had to shed its old glamour. The two-storied building that served as the guard house too has recently been pulled down. It is tempting to imagine how ornate and luxurious the own living quarters of those who held the office of power must have been, if the house built for the use of guards could be so large and elegantly designed. The Marathas had always been in favour of pomp and luxury. It would not be an exaggeration, therefore, to say that the beauty of Lalbag palace was incredible.

Before the barrage at Naraj shackled the free -flowing Kathajori, the river had stored a large volume of water just below the stone steps that descended from the villa as if paying her tribute to the architectural excellence of the Maratha builders. But long ago, when the events of this novel had transpired, the volume of water reserved under those stone steps of the villa as well as the depth of the river there were comparatively greater. Perhaps the river paid her humble respects to the villa in this manner those days. The river looked more gay and beautiful perhaps because the Maratha ladies who enjoyed royal privileges bathed themselves in its water. The touch of the royal persons gratifies all and precious is the joy that emanates from the sense of that gratification. River Kathjori, therefore, enjoyed eternal happiness being at the service of members of the royal families. But her earlier luster has dimmed after she was shackled by the barrage built by the mighty British government, which has always been partial to its own vested interests. Besides, the ladies of British royal families did not prefer to take bath in the river. Still, the Kathajori paid her tribute to the villa and its residents and perhaps because of that she still rippled away happily.

The view of the Kathjori from the upper parts of the villa is even more charming. The dense growth of trees on the far side of the river was like a natural wall that fixed the limits of the river. Its green tenderness seemed to mock at the massive walls of stone of the villa on this side. But the stone walls, unruffled by the mockery, stood as proudly as ever.

In the distant horizon, like a backdrop to the treewall, the mountain range raising its head high, unfolded a panorama of beauty. Viewed from the far side the conterminous man-made column of trees behind the stone wall that displayed the creativity of God's most intelligent child, presented a similar picture as if it challenged Nature's artistry.

Just like the white sand-bed of river Kuakhai on the far side of the river Kathjori, glimmered through the occasional opening amidst the cluster of trees the whiteness of the grand villa of Lalbagh flashed before the eyes penetrating the thick column of trees planted in its foreground. If one looked west from the roof of the villa he could see the white temple of Lord *Dhabaleshwar* on the blue-topped mountain standing like a light-house and sending signals to the sailors, guiding them towards the path of virtue. A look at the other direction would bring before the eyes the picture of a faraway woodland that looked like encroaching into the river as if determined to hold its progress in check. Thus the view of the Kathjori, thus, from the top of the villa was exceedingly beautiful. River Kathjori, that rose from the holy Mahanadi like the noble-hearted daughter of a spiritually inclined mother. Its noble descent and its sweet water had increased its beauty many times over. Could there be any doubt about the saying that a woman's beauty is enhanced by her virtues?

Readers, let us turn our attention to Subadar Sambhu-ji Rao Ganesh, the royal representative of the Maratha empire in the province of Orissa. You have been told already that this Maratha ruler was a tyrant. He had levied several kinds of taxes on the people of Orissa soon after being appointed as the subedar here. He had also imposed tax on the lands that were earlier rent-free. People of Orissa had to endure the same kind of misery as the subjects of any other state would under the reign of an oppressor as this one. There was no one to do anything about the problems and difficulties they faced. The Subedar had no ears for anything except an account of the regular increase in the taxes. The clerks and the accounts manager, too, knowing their master well, did not bring any other matter to his notice. Hence the misery and the suffering of his subjects crossed all limits. Calamities both man-made and natural, added to their troubles. It has already been mentioned that the full moon night of the month of Pausha had passed. It was early morning and the sun had just begun to peep from behind the thinning curtain of mist. In the spacious outer hall of the villa of Lalbagh, Sambhuji Ganesh, the Subedar was busy with his his office work. He had settled himself comfortably on a fluffy mattress. A few pillow-cushions were neatly arranged around him. A round spot of sandal-paste that shone on the subedar's forehead seemed to brighten his face. But though white and round-shaped like the moon, the mark of sandal-paste did not bring any joy to the supplicants waiting at the hall the way the moon does with its cool beams. It scared them instead. "This spot has appeared as a symbol of the forest fire; it will not stop till it burns Orissa to ashes," people used to say. Close to the mattress where the Subedar sat his legs crossed under him, a coarse carpet was spread. Here was seated Choudhury (accounts-manager) sat. The clerks and other employees seated themselves on the two flax-mats rolled out on either sides of where the Subedar and the Choudhury were seated. There were four cushioned arm-chairs set along the wall on which small, cylindrical pillows were placed neatly. The Subedar used to recline on the arm-chair when he found the time to relax. At the back of the Subedar's seat, long benches were placed against the wall. Behind the benches stood a large wooden shelf where several bundles of palm-leaf documents lay in a pile. The furnishing of the Subedar's court lacked the elaborate neatness of that of the British governor. The quality of the judicial procedures here was also proportionately poor in comparison to that of its British counterpart. One thing that was found in excess here was a selfish interest in exploiting the poor subjects.

On that day, people from various parts of the state had arrived in large numbers at the villa to put forth their grievances before their ruler. They had gathered in front of the courtroom of the villa daring the biting cold. The system of obtaining application forms for stating complaints by paying court fees was not then in practice. The supplicants were cruelly driven away even after they bribed all categories of employees from the top to the bottom. It was by sheer chance that a few of them came to the Subedar's kind notice and received small remedies to their problems. Those few returned home thanking their stars. It was not that the Subedar himself was an epitome of honesty. The shenanigans of employees of lower rank were secret affairs. It was not so in the Subedar's case. He took the lion's share of the bribe and he accepted it openly, calling it a gift. No one could question the actions of men in power.

Today, the Subedar's court was in session. Everyone appeared to be busy. Choudhury Radha Govinda sat on the coarse carpet and was intently studying some papers. The record-keepers were writing non-stop on palm-leaves with styluses. While the court work was going on inside, a crowd of supplicants stood waiting outside. But none of them had been called in. Whenever they talked a little loudly the guards struck at them with their canes. The brokers acting on behalf of the Choudhury and the clerks were busy collecting their own shares of bribe.

The Subedar turned to look at the Chudhury, " I had asked you to prepare some documents. Have they been ready?" He inquired.

"Yes your Lordship, the papers are ready" came the prompt reply. The Subadar asked him to read out the papers, and Choudhury unrolled a sheaf. The bottom edge of one piece of paper was joined to the top of another and the total length of the document, when unrolled, must have been five feet or so. It contained a detailed account of lands that were either donated to the Brahmins as or lands given away to people as service-tenures. It also mentioned from which of these lands tax was being collected and which others could be suitable for levying tax. Towards the last part of the document, a few lines were written about the famine and the present condition of the state. Radha Govinda read out the matters relating to the collection of the revenue and was about to go through those last few sentences when a sentry entered the court-hall. He announced that a poor farmer was getting impatient to meet the Subedar. The Subedar ordered the guard to bring the man in. The fellow stood at the door of the courtroom and kept peeping inside. He approached the Subedar as soon as the guard signalled him to enter. The Subedar gestured him to wait until the Choudhury finished reading the report. The Choudhury went on: " This year Lord Indra has been kind to our state as he is to most parts of the earth. There has been plenty of rain and people do not have any problems. The farmlands have yielded good harvest and the harvest has been gathered comparatively earlier this year. This clearly proves that the farmers are no longer lethargic; they have been working hard and therefore more resourceful. What could be a better news than this?"

The Subedar was extremely pleased when he heard this. He ordered the Choudhury to prepare a list within a period of fifteen days of the rent-free lands that could be taxed. " The government of Maharasthra has been able to strengthen its grip on Orissa because of your sincere endeavour and efficiency," the Subedar said addressing the Choudhury. "The Bhonsla of Nagpur has praised me because the collection of revenue here has increased four-fold in the recent years. But the credit goes to you. I shall double your salary if you can manage things in such a way that taxes could be levied on fifty percent of the rent-free land and seventy-five percent of the lands given away as service-tenure. The Choudhury was delighted to notice the signs of satisfaction on the Subedar's face. "No problem my lord", he said with enthusiasm. "I shall leave here tomorrow to make a tour of different places and do as you say."

The farmer stood waiting. He was filled with a rage when he heard what the Choudhury said. He knew Orissa was ravaged by a famine. He himself was a victim of the calamity. Heavy rains had washed away the paddy seeds sowed in the fields and later excessive heat scorched the seedlings that had somehow sprouted. As the harvesting of the pre-autumnal paddy was severely affected by the heavy rains and the burning sun the farmers had desperately pinned their hope on the winter-paddy. But Lord Indra ,the god of rain, showed no mercy. The early rains had destroyed the seeds sown in the lands and the unkind autumnal sun did the rest of the damage. There was no crop left for harvesting. Even a sheaf of straw was hard to come by. The armers shed tears of despair. Withered by the heat of a furious sun the shrunken paddy stalks looked like strands of flax. So pathetic was the sight that it made farmers faint out of despair. They collected some of those dried-up stalks of paddy and kept it in their barns with a hope to show them to the officials who would come to collect the taxes and get some relief. Could anyone that knew what a bad time the state was passing through have been able to keep calm on hearing the outrageous lies told in the Choudhury's report?

Readers, perhaps the lies mouthed by the employees like Choudhury does not surprise you. It is quite natural. Our country is at present under the British rule. The Englishmen are supposed to be the most civilized in the world. But the local people that worked under the British officers did never hesitate to present such false reports for their own vested interests and for incurring the favour of the officials holding high posts. These selfish employees hide the truth from their superiors without the slightest compunction. When all through the country people suffered in the hands of the native officials even though the nation was governed by civilized rulers like the British, why should one be surprised at the falsehood of selfish flatterers like the Choudhury who uttered blatant lies just to be in the good books of the Subedar who represented a faulty system of administration put in place by the Marathas? The readers may not therefore find it strange or absurd. But such an atrocious distortion of truth was bound to rouse resentment and hatred if not surprise. And so the poor farmer seethed in anger when he heard the report being read out. He knew the Choudhury well enough; he was also aware what a wicked man the Subedar was. He too had kept track of the manner in which the Choudhury and other local clerks projected a completely different picture of the state before the Subadar. Unable to control himself any longer, he blurted out : "My Lord, this servant of yours has a submission to make. I shall bring it to Your Majesty's kind notice if permission is granted."

The Subedar during his discussions with the Choudhury had glanced at the man and noticed the anger in his eyes. He was curious to find out why he was so angry. "Tell me, what is your grievance", the Subedar said. The man took the large bundle he carried on his back down, and began to open it. The Subedar, the greedy man he was, thought that the bundle must have contained a large gift and was delighted. The temptation of a gift always thrills habitual bribe-takers. But the Subedar cloaked his excitement under a false modesty and said, " Don't worry about the gift; first tell me what is your problem." The man stopped untying the knots of the bundle. He joined his palms together in a gesture of respect and answered in a humble voice. " My lord! What gift can a wretched creature like me offer—

Your Majesty?" He pointed at himself and continued, " My Lord, just have a look at me. Once upon a time I used to be the famous Das Khadanga, a man of strong muscular build. People used to treat me with respect. But hunger has reduced me to a skeleton. I have lost my health. That is not all. I have sold away all the valuables and jewellery to provide food to my family. I have come this far using whatever little strength my body still retains to seek your mercy. My future is now in your hands. I shall present before you whatever little I could manage to bring to you as gift for you." Saying so the man bent down and resumed the earlier act of untying the bundle.

Anyone could have easily guessed that the man had been starving. So thin and transparent was his skin that one could easily count the ribs under it. The tangled network of the blue-black veins about his belly looked like black lines of Fate that disfigured and destroyed his life. The upper-half of his chest under the shrivelled skin looked as grotesque as the bare patches on a mountain after the sun had peeld off its coating of snow. The hollows just above the collarbones formed by the loss of flesh under the shoulders resembled the dark caverns of that mountain and the pointed shoulder blades that stood out like the scraggy peaks of the mountain accentuated the ugliness of those caverns. The concavity of the neckline was gone. The neck had become taut and straight, and like a decrepit, crumbling bridge struggled to connect the pinched face to the shrunken body without any show of shame. His face looked haggard and wary. The man had large eyes that were stretched up to his ears. Earlier they must have looked beautiful on a full, healthy face. But now those large eyes had receded deep into their sockets and looked frightening. In short, the man was a sorry spectacle of hunger and destitution. The Subadar observed all this; he was pleased with the man who, he thought, did not forget to bring a gift for the Subadar even if he himself had gone without food for days together. To curtail some of the extra expenses in order to get a gift for somebody is one thing, but to go without food for the purpose is another. The difference between the two acts is something that requires no elaborate explanation.

Giving a gift to somebody without feeling burdened brings pleasure and satisfaction to the giver as well as the receiver. But under Maratha rule it had become customary to present something to the officials occupying high positions whenever a subject came to meet them. People were compelled to bring a gift whether they could afford it or not. The officers expected it and were pleased to receive it.

What could be more unfortunate than this? If a man cannot have any pity for another man in pain what traces humanity are left in him? How strange had become the order of the day!!

The greed of the Subadar was like a fathomless ocean ready to devour everything that was dropped into it. The size of the bundle was tempting and the Subadar eyed it greedily imagining the large gift that would soon make its appearance. Eventually the man opened the bundle and to the astonishment and disgust of those that were watching curiously took out a few sheaves of blighted paddy-stalks from it. " My Lord, this once healthy and strong man called Khadanga has fallen a victim to the dreadful famine. These blighted paddy-stalks will tell you the tale of my misery." Khadanga said in a choked voice. The dreaming Subadar was jolted back to reality. He cast a crushing glance at the man who looked like a skeleton. 'The man did not bother to bring him even a bunch of greens', the Subadar thought tohimself angrily. He tried to figure out why this man who called himself Khadanga had brought these ridiculous objects to his court. The Choudhury's report stated that the subjects of Odissa were living in peace and comfort. Nowhere in the report was it mentioned that the farmers were in distress due to unfavourable weather conditions. 'And this man has the nerve to present himself before the indomitable Subadar and produce these worthless things as evidence to disprove the facts supplied by one of his most trusted employees!!' the Subadar fumed and glared at Khadanga with bloodshot eyes.

"How dare you!" he shouted. 'You have brought these hay-stalks to my court and produced them here to disprove the facts presented by my trusted subordinates as soon as you have heard the Choudhury's repor. Everything is fine with the province. What an audacity to tell me that people are passing through a hard time ! You wil be duly punished if what you have said is proved to be untrue" , the Subadar said angrily.

The Subadar's reaction made Khadanga hopeful; if not his commiseration, at least the Subadar's anger and doubt might lead him to order an inquiry. But it had never occurred to the unfortunate man that the Subadar had no such intention. He already knew that famine had struck Odissa. If some landowners died there would be fresh settlement of the estates. Men would die, but the land would remain.

Selfish and greedy men like the Choudhury had given the Subadar the tempting impression that the government could claim its right over the lands of deceased owners, which, when tilled properly would yield enough crop, and that would mean an increase in the revenue. The ill-fated farmer had no knowledge of all this. He was inspired by a false hope that probably the local employees would be assigned the duty of an inquiry. With folded hands he pleaded, " My lord, your kind self might take a little pain to pay a visit to our village and see for yourself the condition of your subjects. You could ask your employees to make a tour of the village to verify the truth of whatIhave said. If I am proved wrong I shall readily step on to the gallows." He paused here. He noticed that the Subadar still glared at him and guessed that whatever he had said had aroused the Subadar's anger rather than his sympathy. Anyway, he thought, like many others he too was going to die of starvation. What is the harm if he lost his life in the Subadar's hands doing some good for the people of his land? He continued, "My Lord, the embodiment of justice ! You sit relax here trusting the report of men like the Choudhury. But the reality is very different. Fate has turned against our village. Our farmlands yielded a very poor harvest this year. Famine has broken out, and to make matters worse, the Bhuyan dacoits have made a comeback. Your Gracious Self may findout from the Choudhury what has happened to his own house." The Choudhury's mouth turned dry out of fear when he heard this. The glow of satisfaction that had spread over his face after reading out the report vanished immediately. He was a man of niggardly nature. The very apprehension that his carefully hoarded riches could be looted by the dacoits drained the blood out of him. His eyes became glazed, and an insane fear cast a dark shadow over his face. "What has happened to my house?" His voice grew hoarse in a frenzy of despair.

What an irony of Fate!! Did the readers get an idea of its unseen but mysterious powers? Did they realize that it is God Almighty who holds the Universe under His supreme control,and   pronounce the final verdict?

Different people react differently to bad news of this kind. Some refuse to believe it; some others believe it but their brains instantly start to devise plans for redress, either by recovering the lost goods or by getting the culprits captured and punished at any cost. But there are some like the Choudhury who believe it and get overwhelmed with grief. The enormity of the shock renders them temporarily lifeless.

Nevertheless, there could not be two opinions on the subject that such utterly inhuman people like the Choudhury deserve the severest of punishments. The Choudhury had gone on amassing wealth as long as fortune favoured him and had derived unlimited happiness out of it. Fate might have granted him this favour for reasons unknown. Perhaps it had other plans in store. When the reservoir of the Choudhury's sin filled to its brim Fate found the opportunity it was waiting for and struck. The heard-hearted man was bound to accept his hard luck. Everything in this world is ordained by Destiny. No one can deny that the unseen hand of Destiny directs man's every action.

The man from Navagram looked at the woebegone Choudhury: "I don't know exactly but when the compound walls of your house fell with a loud noise all ran back to the safety of their own houses. I stood on a narrow foot-track and saw the dacoits carrying away things from your house to their boats. They also looted the house of Govardhan Dasa.

The Choudhury felt as though he was struck by a thunderbolt. The shock, with the speed of lightening, travelled from his brain to other parts of his body. His vision was blurred, he felt as if he had lost his power of hearing. His whole body became numb. He was going to fall backwards when the Subadar caught hold of his hand and pulled him forward. The numbness passed and rivulets of tear streamed from his eyes as soon when he came back to his senses. The Subadar was silent for some time.

"You don't worry", he said soothingly. " I shall leave no stone unturned to track down the criminals. A thorough search will be carried out and each and every place will be turned upside down and I shall not rest until the culprits are caught." The Subadar glanced suspiciously at the man from Navagram and said, " I think this man is at the root of all these—why else had he come all the way here to break the news?" Saying so the Subadar called one of the guards and ordered him to get him handcuffed.

The poor farmer's head began to spin when he heard this. But the next moment he decided to leave everything in the hands of God and stood patiently. He was sure that one day or the other he would have fallen a victim to the wrath of the famine. To bring the grievance of the people to the attention of a Subadar who was so unwilling to pay heed to it was a suicidal act, he thought. What was there to worry then if he was falsely implicated as a confidante of the dacoits and was sent to the scaffold? The man stood still, clutching desperately at his patience. His only worry was his family. The news of this death would shatter his family members. But that could not be helped. He prayed to God to look after his family and tried to keep calm.

The great Subadar, the so called embodiment of justice' took a piece of paper and began to record the statement of Das Khadanga.

The Subadar: Your name?

Das Khadanga :   Dasarathi Das alias Das Khadanga.

Subadar :   Where are you from?

Das Khadanga: Gopalpur.

Subadar :   At what time did the dacoits break into the Choudhury's house?

Das Khadanga: About an hour or so after midnight.

Subadar: Why were you at Navagram at such late hours of night?

Das Khadanga: I came to know that the felicitation ceremony of the *Naib* (the Deputy of the Subadar) would be celebrated at Navagram. I had gone there to place my grievances before him.

The Subadar was surprised. He had no knowledge of any such ceremony or procession. When asked, the Choudhury too expressed his ignorance about the ceremony. This strengthened the suspicion of the Subadar. He was sure that the man was lying and was somehow connected with the crime.

"What ceremonial procession?" The Subadar asked. "I have not given anyone the permission to take out any such procession."

Das Khadanga: "My Lord, I know nothing about that. I had only heard that the *Naib* was taking out a procession of light and gone there to meet him and bring my problems to his kind notice."

The Subadar: You are a liar! I am sure that you are involved in the crime. Well, how did you know that it was the Bhuyan gang that committed the burglary?

Das Khadanga: I met a Bhuyan dacoit near the statue of *Budhalinga* on the river bank.

"You are now trapped!" the Subadar said excitedly. "Why did you talk to him knowing him to be a dacoit?" He demanded.

Das Khadanga: As I was passing by his eyes fell on me and he called me. Why else should I talk to him?

The Subadar trembled in rage when he heard this. It is often seen that persons occupying high offices apply their incredible wit when judging things for themselves and deliberately disbelieve the truth. The Subadar gritted his teeth in anger.

"You are a dastardly liar. Give out the names of the other dacoits, or else you will be sent to the gallows at this very instant", he said menacingly. How could the innocent man know the names of the dacoits? He kept quiet and the outcome of his silence was obvious. At the orders of the malevolent Subadar the guards lashed his shriveled body and black and blue weals were left on his paper-thin skin. The poor man yelled in pain and shed tears of agony. If God had wished that a hunger-worn, shrunken body would have to bear the additional pain of being cruelly lashed at could it have been prevented? The unfortunate man had no alternative other than cursing his fate.

By now, the readers must have guessed that this was the man they had met near the statue of *Budhalinga* on the riverbank. Poor man!! His bad luck kept goading him and continued to punish him in several ways. In the end, after being thoroughly thrashed by the guards he was sent back to Navagram to face a local enquiry. Radha govinda Choudhury, his energy and vigour diminished, also left for Navagram with a heavy heart carrying the office-order from the Subadar instructing Duman Sardar to act as the investigating officer.

***

CHAPTER –21

The Day After

The full-moon night of the month of *Pausha* finally gave way to morning. The people of Navagram opened the doors of their houses and came out. The night before when the dacoits had broken into the houses of the Choudhury and Dasa the villagers were as though turned to lifeless images in an excess of panic. The loud noise of the collapsing walls and the ear-splitting cry of the dacoits after the operation was over had left them shaken and frozen the blood in their veins. No one ventured to come out and look even after the dacoits had left. They knew well that once gone the dacoits would not come back. Still they were too frightened to open their doors as though a tiger sat outside ready to pounce upon them the moment they showed themselves. Even the sound of a mouse scurrying about in the house would startle them. When such was the terror where was the question of coming out to see what had happened? Finally some of them, exhausted with fear and worry, drifted into sleep. Others passed a sleepless night and prayed to God to end the terrible night. A dreadful silence hung over the air of the village.

Eventually, the fateful night came to an end. The cawing of crows outside heralded the approach of the morning. Slowly, one by one, the doors opened and people began to emerge. The gentle morning breeze indicated that the storm that had raged in the night had passed. But the fog still obstructed the morning light. Perhaps it reminded the villagers of the mishap that had taken place the night before. They heaved sighs of relief and thanked God for bringing an end to the dreadful night. Then they walked slowly to the ransacked houses of the Choudhury and Govardhan Dasa. The dacoits had broken through the boundary walls and taken away everything. Nothing was left behind except the dead bodies of Dasa and his wife hanging from bamboo-posts on either side of the front door. The gruesome sight jolted them. At first look they seemed to be alive, but the tongues that protruded out of their mouths were proof enough that they were no more. "Serves them right", the villagers said with some kind of a savage satisfaction.

People made several remarks as they wandered about the site of burglary inspecting the wreckage. "What a great amount of grain and money this man had stored! But he could not enjoy anything in his life," one said. Another came forward and added, " Oh! He was a villain!" "You cannot find a miser like him in the whole world", another commented.

" Do you think the procession of light was just a humbug and was taken out to distract people's attention from the burglary?" Someone wondered.

" Where did the *Naib* run away?"---- one asked in curiosity.

Another replied knowingly, " He was not the *Naib*, he was the chief of the dacoits' gang."

Still another put in, "The dacoits have killed the *Naib*." He tried to be more convincing as he noticed that others refused to believe it and said, " I have seen them do so with my own eyes."

"This man is a fibber. Wouldn't there be any sound had they killed him?" one of them asked.

Suddenly someone remembered the two young women. "Hey, what happened to the daughters of the Choudhury and Dasa?"

"The dacoits have killed them, I have heard their screams", came the prompt reply from another.

"No, no, in that case they would have left the dead bodies like those of Dasa and his wife."

"Perhaps they were asleep and were buried under the collapsing walls."

"But I have seen them standing at the door when the procession of light passed by."

"Do you think that the villains have left them behind and they are still here?" Others asked unbelievingly.

A kindhearted and sympathetic man commented: "Alas! How well-mannered and virtuous both the girls were! How the dacoits must be harassing them! Had the cruel fate stored so much of suffering for these innocent creatures!" Everyone present there was filled with genuine sympathy for the two girls. In this way the spectators formed different groups and voiced different opinions. The debates, discussions, speculations and surmises all blended to make the scene of the dacoity as noisy as a marketplace.

Slowly people from nearby villages thronged in. The quantity of grains stored in the granaries of both the Choudhury and Govardhan Dasa could have easily sustained the famine-stricken people of nearly seven villages for four months or so. But neither of them did bother to spare a little of it for the hungry masses. The dacoits did the right thing by taking everything away. This was the subject around which the debates and discussions revolved. No one felt an iota of sympathy for the loss that both the families incurred. They felt sorry for only Kalavati and Rasakala.

As people kept gossiping, ten sentries, guns in hand, arrived there at the orders of Duman Sardar. The sentries warned the villagers that they would be arrested unless they left the spot immediately. Everyone ran away from the place. The sentries broke into small units and kept guard over the ravaged houses of the Choudhury and Dasa.

***

CHAPTER-22

Two Hermits

The spectators were driven away but the gossip continued. People gathered at different parts of the village
and began to talked about the burglary. Palatable episodes
were concocted with the help of an imaginations running
wild. There are many who can plead quite earnestly in favour of their lies to give them the appearance of truth. They
can   unhesitatingly swear by their lives or by their eyes in
order to prove themselves right. They seem to derive a lot
of pleasure from this. So, the actual incidents now vividly
coloured by the fertile imagination of such people spread
around quickly.

The people of Navagram did not feel sad about what
occurred in the houses of the Choudhury and Dasa. But
they felt apprehensive. The Bhuyan dacoits had made a
comeback. Could there be any guarantee that they would
not strike some other villager in the coming days? They
considered several possible measures to prevent such attacks. It was suggested by some that the villagers would
form groups, and armed with staves and spears keep vigil
taking turns at night. But many others were against theidea.
In their opinion it would be a risky venture since the Bhuyan gang as an adversary was far more powerful than the
untrained and physically weak villagers. The proposal was
dropped. Soon after, another group of villagers came up
with a new suggestion: the villagers should approach the

Subadar and pray to him to appoint a few security guards to keep a watch and protect the village against the attack of the Bhuyan dacoits. But there too was a catch here. The selfish and cruel Subadar might not agree to spare his men for the purpose. Moreover, the robbers armed with lethal weapons might always prove stronger than the sentries. The debate went on ceaselessly till someone came out with the idea of seeking the advice of hermit Hanuman Dasa of the Jatia mound. The idea of meeting Hanuman Dasa and take his advice appealed to everyone and was unanimously accepted. It was decided that they would sail to the mound of Jatia on that very morning.

The two hermits woke up in the early hours of dawn. Having finished the routine chores of washing and bathing they praised the name of God and offered Him their gratitude for creating this beautiful earth. Thereafter they meditated and chanted His name. It was an amazing sight--- the hermits sitting motionless, rapt in meditation, their senses conquered by their spiritualism and willpower. Their eyes were half open, as though they were seeing God in person and communicating with Him in the language of the heart. Where else could their faces have received that divine glow from?

It is not within the power of ordinary human beings like us to fathom that mystery. We who call ourselves modern and westernized and take pride in it tend to ridicule and look down upon such saintly characters. Our fascination for western culture

has tempted us to think of them as thieves, lechers, or fugitive criminals. Have we ever tried to probe the mystery of that meditation which these noble men so passionately engaged themselves in? Their spiritual wisdom is beyond our comprehension, so too their actions. We have neither the spiritual bent of mind nor the knowledge to assess its worth. Hence we present them as negative characters just like the jackal had declared that the grapes were sour. If we had that wisdom, nothing could have prevented us from admitting that the spiritual powers of these saints could absolve the sins of many like us. The hermits sat in meditation for two long hours and their souls experienced the serene joy of being transported to an elevated state of bliss while still confined in their mortal frames. The joy of that experience lent an unworldly radiance to their faces. Their meditation over, the two hermits came out and pointed out to each other how the fog had started to lift in the light of the morning sun. That is the way all evil and negative thoughts leave man's mind when it is illumined with the light of spiritual wisdom. As they watched the scene the two hermits once more began to sing the glory of God. Readers, the behaviour of these two hermits may appear abnormal to some of us but isn't such abnormality hundred times more desirable than the insane pursuit of material prosperity? Blind indulgence in acts that have no spiritual worth is nothing but madness.

Slowly, the blanket of fog lifted and the sunlight shone on the water, the land around and the lush green vegetation. The boats carrying the villagers moved off the river bank in the direction of the mound of Jatia. In a short time they reached the mound and the men alighted one after another and walked in a file up to the place where the two hermits stood. The villagers prostrated themselves at their feet and offered their salutations to the noble souls. The hermits blessed them and asked them to sit down. They sat down in rows, thanking their good fortune that had brought them the opportunity to come face to face with the two great tiger-riding hermits in one place.

" Is anything the matter? Why have so many of you come here?" Hanuman Dasa asked.

A man called Sanatan Mohanty, who was articulate and vocal, was chosen by the villagers of Navagram to voice their grievances. He sat in the front row, facing the hermits. " My Lord, is there anything which passes without your knowledge? It appears as if the end has arrived. We shall drown ourselves in the river unless you assure us that you would protect us. We have come here to tell you of what we are going through" Sanatan said.

"As far as I know no harm has been caused to you people." Hanuman Dasa said calmly. "Why then are you so alarmed?"

" How can we not feel miserable if your noble self speaks like this? Have you no knowledge of the incident that occurred last night?" Sanatan asked. His voice was a blend of anxiety and despair.

Hanuman Dasa:	Yes I have. But that has happened in the houses of the Choudhury and of Govardhan Dasa. Your homes have not been plundered.
Sanatan :	My Lord, what valuables are there in our houses to be looted? You know we are passing through a hard time. If it continues for a while longer we are going to perish very soon. Perhaps that would be better. Are you not aware of our misery My Lord?
Hanuman Dasa:	Why do you panic when no harm is caused to you?

Sanatan:	My Lord, when the houses close by are set afire isn't that something to feel worried about even though our own houses have escaped the danger?
Hanuman Dasa:	But the fire has died away. What is there to feel so disturbed about?
Sanatan:	True, the fire has died out. But once the fear of fire has been aroused in the mind, we have to remain alert, and ready with water-filled pitchers to put out the fire.
Hanuman Dasa:	All right, do that. All of you keep your water-pitchers ready and use them when a fire breaks out.
Sanatan:	But My Lord, wherefrom shall we get the pitchers of water to put out such fierce fire?
Hanuman Dasa:	How can I tell you? You have to look for them out if you need them.
Sanatan:	That is why we have come here, to look for pitchers of water that will put out the fire.

The way in which Sanatan Mohanty spoke, and his witty replies amused Hanuman Dasa. Giridhari Dasa also silently admired the man's presence of mind. One or two villagers had tried to interrupt the conversation but held back when others asked them to keep out of it. All listened intently, curious to know where the conversation would lead. An amused smile flickered on Hanuman Dasa's face as he said,

"Sanatan, are you out of your mind? You come to

look for the paddy-pounder in a hermit's hut? Go. Make an appeal to your Subadar. He will protect you."

Sanatan could no longer restrain himself. He fell at the feet of Hanuman Dasa and pleaded: "My Lord, please do not deceive us. You are sending us to the Subadar whose nature you know full well. Please tell us whether the currents of the troubled time would sweep us to our doom or we shall be steered to the safety of the shore."

"Sanatan, who can save you if God does not will so? All of you pray to God and have faith in Him." Hanuman Dasa advised.

Sanatan joined his palms together and prayed, " My Lord, what you say is true. The flames of famine have spread to every corner of our land. The attack of the Bhuyan dacoits is adding fuel to the raging flames. There is no other alternative left than praying to God. But we are ignorant men. We do not know the proper manner of offering up prayers to Him. That is why we have come here."

The innocence underlying in the words of Sanatan could have moved anyone. Giridhari Dasa patted his back, " Well said my son" , he said. Hanuman Dasa embraced Sanatan affectionately. " Sanatan, your words have proved how pure your heart is. But do I have the ability to make God listento my prayers?"

"Maharaj, only you can act as our benefactor. None but you can invoke His blessings for us." Sanatan begged. Others joined him : "Yes Maharaj, only you can pray to Him on our behalf and obtain His blessings for us." This gesture of faith and devotion moved Hanuman Dasa. Faith and devotion are the essence of spiritualism. The heart that harbours these two qualities will never be defeated. He praised the faith of these innocent villagers in his heart. Then, like one drunk with divine love, he rose to his feet and raised his hand. " The God you seek blessings from is full of kindness. Nothing in the world can frighten you if you have true faith in Him. He punishes men like the Choudhury and Govardhan Dasa who defy Him in their blind pursuit of material wealth. He does this for the well-being of the world. All of you should place your trust in Him and offer Him your sincere devotion. He will certainly listen to you and prove that He *is* really The Saviour of His Devotees."

A loud cry of " *Haribol*" rose from the crowd. The name of the Lord that hundreds of men cried out in unison made the waters of the river ripple in reverence. The name of Lord *Hari* came echoing back from both its banks and travelled far into the air carrying the news of Nature's joy at the utterance of the Lord's name. Before the echo died out, Hanuman Dasa asked them to take the Lord's name for the second time and again the people cried out '*Haribol*', this time in a doubly loud voice. The echo of this second cry stirred the air around the mound of Jatia. When hundreds of voices cried *Haribol* in a chorus at the bidding of Hanuman Dasa its sound resonated in the distant horizon.

The villagers, now relieved of their worries having received the assurance of the great hermit, offered them the rice and vegetables they had brought along with them. After consulting each other the hermits asked the villagers to start making arrangements for cooking for a grand feast. Immediately after receiving the order the men began digging large fireplaces and making other arrangements for the feast.

***

CHAPTER-23

Paradeep

To the east of Taladanda, a narrow strait that branched off river Mahanadi, flowed in the direction of the sea. It merged with a small river called Kujanga on its way and assumed a frightening breadth where it fell into the Bay of Bengal. It was a natural reservoir that supplied water to a vast area. Local people had named it as *Patakunda* (the silk-tank) perhaps because they were able to gather in a richer harvest using its water that made them affluent enough to buy silk garments. To the north of this huge natural reservoir the main stream of river Mahanadi flowed murmuring sweetly, to hold the hands of the Bay of Bengal that gathered her in an eternal embrace. The vast landmass between the reservoir of *Patakunda* and river Mahanadi looked like an island. This island was called Paradeep. In the middle of the island there stood the invincible, massive palace-fort of the mighty rulers of the Sandha Dynasty.

Readers! Those of you that have seen the fort of Paradeep in its present condition cannot deny that the remnants bear testimony to the aura of majesty which had once surrounded it in the past. But every worldly thing is bound to get caught in the ever-spinning wheel of time, and perish. The wheel of time had brought about the fall of the powerful kings and the fort of Paradeep that was once the symbol of ethereal beauty has disappeared from the scene. There was a time when its grandeur used to send tremors of fear to distant lands; the splendour of the palaces of the gods in Heaven appeared dull when compared to its incredible beauty; its proud banner had held aloft the glory of the Gajapati kings of Odisha. The name itself was enough to make the most vicious adversaries cower. But the gigantic structure that had once spelt indomitable power and iridescent glory has crumbled. The progeny of the Sandha Dynasty, now shorn of their vigour and valiance wander about the place like ordinary men. The trenches and moats that surrounded the fort-palace still exist but tears of nostalgic memories in place of water now flow in them. The forests are there too but the trees there no longer bear luscious fruits to satiate the hunger of the passersby; instead, their pale withered looks bring tears to those that set their eyes on them. The successors of the mighty Sandha Dynasty still live here but they do not have the gallantry and gusto in their character that their invincible predecessors had. The qualities have been sadly replaced by a kind of lethargy and languor that have stolen the radiance of power from their faces.

What brought about this shocking change? Change, however, is the law of life. The world is constantly on the move. The fall of the Sandha Dynasty is a small matter compared with the decline of the great Gajapati dynasty that had contributed a lot to the rise of Kujanga. When the Gajapati rulers could not survive the ravages of time, how could the kings of the Sandha Dynasty evade their downfall? But the real reason behind the decline of the Sandha kings would break one's heart. Indian kings always prefer a lavish life-style. Their love for luxury and their vainity had forced them a number of times to admit defeat before foreign invaders. Even now India is not able to summon up enough strength to rise against the British. This same love of luxury had led Kujanga to its doom and hurled the honour and pride of its mighty kings at the ocean.

The predecessors of King Janardan Sandha had collected large sums as revenue from their estates. It was not that they did not love luxury but these kings had managed to fill the royal treasury with millions of rupees. But King Janardan seemed to have been born and enthroned as the king of Kujanga under an evil star. His extravagance emptied the royal treasury. Financial constraints compelled him to borrow from several creditors. The interest on the amount he had borrowed, like the wide-open mouth of demon *Rahu*, gobbled up everything. The estate owed a huge sum of money to the creditors even after millions were paid towards the interest amount. The creditors, now aware that the royal treasury has become emptiy, went to law courts in full confidence, obtained a court-order that directed the king of Kujanga to place the estate under auction and pay the creditors from the amount received from the sale. King Janardan had passed away in the mean time and was succeeded by his son, Vidyadhar. The young man, whose role was that of a king only in name, soon realized that the debts of his forefathers had put the kingdom in chains. The estate was going to be ruined unless it was freed from the bondage of debt. But he had neither the means nor the power to release the estate from the hungry clutches of its merciless creditors. The conditions were beyond help, the estate stood on the brink of disaster. In the end, some kindhearted officers of the British Government held a meeting to discuss the matters relating to the crisis Kujanga was passing through. Moved by compassion for the once glorious kingdom that was heading fast towards a catastrophe, they decided to include the estate of Kujanga as a special *tahasil* in a larger district and pay the creditors back on behalf of the king of Kujanga. But they had to obtain the king's consent for executing the proposal. Accordingly, they sent a message to King Vidyadhar. King Vidyadhar came up to the bank of river Mahanadi but he did not cross the river to meet the officers on the other side. His so -called trusted advisors and well-wishers who had enjoyed great comfort and luxury during the heyday of the kingdom betrayed him at the moment of crisis. " Do not go to meet the English officers", they warned Vidyadhar, "They will place you under arrest." The innocent king, failing to comprehend the real intention of his unscrupulous courtiers, returned to Kujanga. Eventually the 355 square miles of rich, fecund land was auctioned off just at 550 thousand rupees for re-paying the loans and the glory of the Sandha Dynasty vanished forever.

The bidding had taken place on the 18th of May in 1868. Driven by a vain hope to retrieve the lost honour a case was filed in the court and the rest of the money that was left after the recovery of the loans was spent n meeting the expenses. Nothing remained in the end and the successors of the mighty Sandha Kings were reduced to ordinary, poor people that roam the streets.

Such incidents come to pass almost regularly. In times of need people usually approach moneylenders and seek financial help from them. But these helpful creditors turn dangerous if the borrowers fail to repay the loan on time. Earlier there was a saying, " Where there is wit there is strength", but in the present time it could be presented with a slight modification: "Where there is money, there is strength". It is the business of the creditors to loan out money and recover the debt on time. This is what they had to do. They could not be blamed for not being kind to their borrowers. If people do not act wisely and if they do not return the money they borrow on time the creditors would obviously make them dance like puppets. Several families in the rural Odisha fall victim to these rapacious money-lenders and face disastrous consequences. Though they saw this happen time and again people of Odisha seem not to have learnt any lesson from their experience. May be, they are helpless; the crooked course that Time has taken is leading the poor people of this land to their ruin.

Let us not dwell on the topic any longer. We have digressed far from the principal storyline. The turn events took in the present story had necessitated bringing in the history of the great fort of Paradeep and that of the the kings of Kujanga. While describing the fort in its present condition, one's mind got automatically transported to the distant past and was forced to indulge in nostalgia. It was during those days the fort of Paradeep was a paragon of beauty. It held its majestic head high and flicked smiling glances at the ocean. Trade and commerce flourished; people voyaged to distant places in ships loaded with precious merchandise. There was a constant flow of money to the royal treasury. Since irrigation was facilitated by natural canals the farmlands yielded a rich harvest and a lot of money sluiced into the treasury in the form of land-revenue. (To express it figuratively, the man-made moats around the fort brought in, as it were, immense riches defeating the god-made canals.) Indeed, the the moats encircling the palace were impassable, and matchless in beauty. It is not possible to imagine its real beauty without seeing it. It was so wide that four of the large cargo boats could be easily rowed across it at one time. The moat was as deep as it was dangerous, infested with snakes and crocodiles. The fort had only one entrance and it was under the constant surveillance of sentries possessed of enormous physical prowess. A giant -sized clock fixed at the top of the magnificent portals of the huge entrance announced the time of the day. Inside the fort there stood the massive, ornate palace. The enthralling beauty of the palace put the viewers in the mind of the palaces in heaven inhabited by gods.

It is quite obvious that that the palace of a king who reigned supreme over a vast, fertile land and to whom the ocean, that is believed to be the treasure-house of gems, had given the gift of natural reservoirs like lagoons and inlets as means for collecting immense wealth, would be as magnificent as that of *Varuna* ,the ocean-god. The king of the Sandha Dynasty lived in the palace with his family. His family was as large as his estate, as if keeping in proportion. In the ladies'-wing of the palace there were hundreds of stunningly beautiful ladies on whom the Sandha king had generously bestowed his royal love.

The aura of majesty that surrounded the temples inside the fort is difficult to describe in words. In the not-too-large area inside the Paradeep-fort there stood the temples of as many deities as there are in the holy land of Puri. A number of festivals were celebrated in those temples with pomp and splendour throughout the year. The heart of Paradeep throbbed with the excitement and the enthusiasm of the large crowd that thronged there to observe the festivals.

The fruit orchards and the flower gardens yielded a large variety of fruits and flowers and offered the king basketfuls of them as a token of their gratitude. As was mentioned earlier the fort of Paradeep was surrounded by natural moats like the inlets and lagoons. The constant supply of water to the land kept the vegetations lush and green round the year. The quality of fruits that grew there was so rich that they seemed fit to be enjoyed by gods, not men. The evergreen-meadows could have been aptly described as the roaming ground of the nymphs of heaven. tired and wornout people preferred to spend some of their time in that salubrious surrounding enjoying the pure air that helped them shed their fatigue. During leisure hours they came here to picnic and danced and made merry. Such was their exhilaration that it seemed to intoxicate the sylvan goddess. The king had no worries, nor did his subjects have any problems. People earned a lot doing little labour; the apprehension of an attack from any outside enemy never crossed their minds. It was obvious that Beauty would choose such a peaceful land as her permanent abode. Indeed, Paradeep was a land of beauty and splendour. One who saw it during its heyday must have been forced to recall the kingdom of Lord Krishna at Dwarika described by the great poet, Magha. If someone charmed with the beauty of the place described it as the image of Heaven reflected in the ocean-water, such a comparison could not be dismissed as ridiculous or far-fetched. But this image of Heaven could not retain its glory for long. Towards the second half of the nineteenth century, the prosperity of Paradeep began to deteriorate. Wealth earned easily, and the love of power diverted the Sandha kings away from administrative matters and made them utterly indifferent to the problems of their subjects.

The court-room of King Janardan Sandha was located in the front section of the palace. Every day, the court was held for three hours. During the two sessions, one in the morning and the other in the afternoon, the king and the court officials remained present in the courtroom and the grievances of the subjects were placed before them. The rest of the day and the entire night were devoted to merry making.

The condition of the kingdom and its subjects is bound to suffer if the rulers can't spare the time to address their problems. The welfare of the state will certainly be in jeopardy when people at the helm of the affairs do not care to devote adequate time for ensuring its progress and betterment. There will undoubtedly be trouble, and taking advantage of the prevailing anarchy, any foreign ruler would try to occupy the kingdom. The kings who indulge in luxury have no moral scruples and honour and glory cannot be sustained without such scruples. Nevertheless, the kings of the Sandha Dynasty deserve thanks because they spared at least three hours of a day for their subjects. There are several states where the kings did not spare even that much time to look into the problems of their states. They enjoyed themselves and left the affairs of the state in the hands of unreliable deputies who lead the state to disaster.

It has been mentioned that the court was kept open in the first and the second half of the day. The supervisors and the *dewans* attended both the sessions. All the courtiers, starting from the Rayagurus to the Bhattabrhmas, sprang into action the moment it was announced that the king would be making his appearance in the court-room. Most of the courtiers held such titles of honour. Like in other states, in Paradeep too, it was not difficult to receive titles of honour from the king. One had either to present a sum of five rupees as a token of respect, or address a few flattering expressions the king when the latter was in a good mood. The king would unhesitatingly confer a title upon the person and he would walk out of the courtroom thrusting forward his chest in pride. The British government, too, conferred such titles or distinctions upon its officers; such titles usually indicated the importance of the title-holder's office. But here the case was not so. In the court of the Sandha king there was no dearth of distinctions and titles. Sometimes, the titles of honour the courtiers held were difficult to pronounce correctly. There were titles like the Jhatpat Singh, the RanaHandol, the Bhattabramha, the Rayaguru. In addition to these there were also titles such as Dian Bagha, Himmat Singh, Ranachhanchana, Mardaraj Shardula and many others. The people of Paradeep craved these titles and affixed them to their names as symbols of authority. The foreign-returned persons these days are put off when they are not addressed as Mister something. The court officials of the Sandha Kings were far more serious about their distinction. They considered it a deliberate insult on the part of somebody who did not address them without using their titles of honour and reported the matter immediately to the king. The king took the matter even more seriously and considered it a grave offence to ignore the title conferred upon the courtiers by his royal self. He imposed a fine on the wrong-doer.

This was the manner in which the dignity and the honour of the titles were preserved. Only God knows what benefits and joy people derived from it. But, to decent people a title appeared like the tail of a monkey dangling from one's posterior.

It was the day after the full-moon night of the month of *Pausha*. The king had occupied his throne in the spacious court-room and was discussing various administrative matters with his ministers and counsellors at about the same time when poor Dasa Khadanga, in the custody of guards was sent to Duman Sardar for interrogation. Ba-

habalindra entered the court-room. He offered his salutations to the king and stood waiting. 'Why, Bahabalindra,
when did you return? Did everything go well?" The king
asked with a smile. "Your Majesty, we have just reached
here. Pattnaik is waiting outside. He will appear before you
with your permission." Bahabalindra replied. The king was
pleased to learn that the operation had been successful and
the boats, loaded with the booty, had arrived. He sent a
guard to usher Patnaik in.

The courtiers withdrew. The clerks immediately tied
the papers and documents into neat bundles and put then
on the shelves. They were glad that the court was adjourned
earlier than usual that day and that meant there would be
time for a leisurely bath and a well-cooked meal. The king
never involved his courtiers and ministers in matters related to the dacoities. It was an altogether different sphere of
activity and there were people with specialized knowledge
of the matter to be cosulted.

After the courtiers and the clerks left the courtroom,
Raghunath entered with his associates. He greeted the king
courteously and seated himself. Then he gave a detailed account of the operation to the king. He did not forget to add
that it had yielded highly profitable results. The king was at
once pleased and amazed when he heard of the wondrous
adventure and thanked Raghunath Pattanaik effusively for
masterminding the operation with skill and efficiency. He
glanced at Mayadhara and asked amusedly, " Uncle, what
special role did you play in this operation?"

Mayadhara was overjoyed when the king addressed
him so affectionately and replied, " Your Majesty, Pattanaik
sat in the palanquin in the guise of the *Naib*. I was asked to
bring up the rear. So I walked behind holding the gun and

tried to lift the spirits of our men." The king could guess the meaning that lay hidden in the words and laughed aloud: "Pattanaik, next time, you ask uncle to sit in the palanquin as the king." Raghunath Pattanaik and other dacoits roared with laughter at the joke. The dacoits gave the king a list of things looted. The king set apart goods that were to be given away to the needy people, and chose the articles that were to be kept in the palace.

At the orders of their chief the dacoits left the court-room. When he was alone with the king Raghunath told him that the dacoits had abducted a beautiful woman from the village Navagram. He prayed to the king to give her shelter in the palace. The king agreed.

Having obtained the king's permission, Raghunatha immediately made arrangements for Rasakala to be trans-ferred to the palace. He entrusted Mayadhara, Bahabalin-dra, and Baliyar Singh with the task of distribution of the looted goods. After this he boarded a smaller boat and tak-ing Kalavati with him sailed swiftly away from the water-trench of the fort of Paradeep.

***

CHAPTER-24

The Grand Feast on the Mound of Jatia

About the same time as Raghunath left the fort of Paradeep with Kalavati, cooking for the grand feast at the mound of Jatia was almost complete. Large containers filled with rice, pulses, curry and other food-items were placed in rows close to the fireholes.. The hermits asked all the villagers to assemble at one place. In the morning there were fewer people. But when the firewood started to burn in the fireholes the smoke rose up and went swirling past the tall trees and reached the sky. People in the village saw it. Lured by the thought of good food men, women and children in large numbers boarding small boats and rafts headed for the mound of Jatia. By the time the cooking was completed the size of the crowd at the mound had nearly doubled. The hermits asked them to stand in rows. Then the hermits took some water in their hands, chanted *mantras* and sprinkled the water around the food-containers. After he paid worship to the gods in this manner the hermit Hanuman Dasa addressed the crowd:

"Brothers", he said, " Today is an auspicious day. We could not have assembled here at this holy mound unless God had willed so. We would not have been so fortunate to enjoy an occasion such as this without God's grace. Let us take the name of that merciful God with absolute sincerity and devotion. All of you say in unison *"Haribol"*. The villagers called out *Haribol* in unison at the top of their voice. They called out three times. Every time they cried out the loud sound went cleaving the surface of the river to the distant horizon and its echo came bouncing back to fill in the gaps between the calls. This way the cry of *Haribol* lingered in the air around the mound of Jatia for a long time and reverberated in the sky above. The two hermits kept their eyes closed as long as the name of Hari resonated in the air. The loud utterance of the Lord's name had not only set the sky astir, it also had sent their blood pulsating with reverence and gratitude for the Supreme Being. As the sound trailed off and the air became calm again, Hanuman Dasa went on: " Brothers, did you see how fortunate we are? To get united at one place at one time and take the Lord's name together is no small matter. It is beyond our powers to understand how the Lord of the Universe makes His children spread His glory all over the world. He is great; great is His power and Supreme is His sovereignty. Brothers, I entreat you, never ever forget this. You know that the famine, its enormous jaws open, is threatening to take our state in its deadly grip. In these troubled times you have all gathered here and organized the ceremonial feast. You will all eat together sitting at one place. The spirit of brotherhood you have displayed in this manner is quite impressive. You must preserve and maintain this spirit in future and share your joys and sorrows. Always remember that God is great. It is at His will that our lands yield good crops and it is at His will too we suffer from calamities like the famine. We need neither question nor analyse His mysterious intentions lying behind all these. We have to bear our sorrow with patience, but that will not be possible if we are not inspired by a spirit of brotherhood. The spirit that has led you to come here to take part in this ceremonial feast must fill you with strength to overcome the sufferings the famine has brought in--- Om Shanti! Shanti! Shanti!"

Hanuman Dasa closed his eyes after he spoke and sat down to meditate. Giridhari Dasa too did the same. The noble words of the hermits as well as their unshakable Faith in God overwhelmed the listeners. A deep reverence and love for that Great Lord brought tears to their eyes. The two hermits rose and asked the men to say *Haribol* in a loud and cheerful voice. They did so *Haribol* three times as they had done earlier. The devotion and faith with which they took the Lord's name might have shaken His throne in Heaven.

God is always fond of His devotees. He loves to remain in their hearts bound by their faith and love. The cry of *Haribol* that rose straight from the hearts of the simple-hearted villagers spread in all directions and filled the earth with a kind of pristine joy. The hill of Jatia bathed in the showers of that joy acquired a divine freshness.

Following the instructions of the hermits they sat down in rows. Another group of villagers served them. Different dishes were served on leaf-plates. The feast began. It was a wonderful sight. People belonging to different castes and creeds sat in one place, eating from the leaf-plates, taking no notice of the differences of ideas and opinions. It echoed the extraordinary sentiments of humanity of the people of Odisha that rose above all sorts of narrow-mindedness resulting from differences of caste or religion. It is here in Odisha Lord Vishnu has fixed his residence in the form of Lord Jagannath. The huge tree that was felled to supply wood for the making of the deity was believed to symbolize the strong caste system that prevailed in Odisha at that time and the felling of the tree proved the Lord's rejection of the evil system. The tree was felled so too was the system.

It would be ridiculous to question the wide-spread influence of 'Vaishnavism' on Odisah after witnessing how people of all castes beginning from the brahmins to untouchables eat the m*ahaprasad* from each other's hands inside the temple. It was the influence of Vaishnavism that inspired the people of Navagram to partake of the ceremonial feast that day and eat together forgetting their social differences. Readers, I must admit that the caste system prevailed in Odisha in those days as it did in many other states. And it was rather more rigid here compared to that prevailing in other states. But, while eating the *Prasad*, people completely ignored it. The merits of such a gesture, in my opinion, need not be elaborated on. Alas!! Had every Indian been initiated to the doctrines of Vaishnavism in this manner, a new life-force would have been generated in our country. Would a time ever come when we would see the entire nation pulsating with such a spirit of brotherhood?

The feast came to an end. People praised the two hermits, cried *Haribol* and got up. They climbed down the mound, washed their hands and drank water from the river. They came up to the hill once more to bid farewell to the hermits and stood around them, waiting.

Hanuman Dasa realized that it was the proper time to explain things more clearly to them. Raising his voice, he said, " I doubt if you have ever before eaten with as much satisfaction as you have today."

" My Lord, we have never eaten food with such relish." The villagers replied in a chorus. His face lit up with a blissful joy Hanuman Dasa explained: " Look, the feeling of contentment is the most important indication that God gives to man. When you felt that you have eaten with real contentment, you must understand that God has been kind to you and had desires you to be satisfied. God, who trules over the world is "Absolute Vaishnava". This world is His most cherished creation. He infuses objects here. Each and every particle of this earth reflects His divine presence. You yourselves are Vaishnavas and are true devotees of God. Remember that what I have said now is the essence of the religion you follow. You should never think of anyone as not being one of your own kinsmen. Try to realize that Death has stepped into our state in the guise of famine. No one can assess how many lives it will claim. I advise you not to lose patience in these hours of crisis. You know that man has no power to question the commands of God. Admit and accept it as the will of God. Do your duty with patience and honesty as long as you live. When a starving man arrives at your threshold think of him as your own brother and render him whatever help you can. Give him food if you can afford to do that. Now promise me you will do so-------- !!"

The villagers had stood listening to the enchanting words of the great hermit. " Yes we will" ---- came the reply in a chorus when Hanuman Dasa finished. " I am extremely glad to hear this," he said. "God helps those who care for others. Bear this in mind, and perbform the noble duty of helping the poor and the needy. God will steer you safely through these turbulent times. Never fear. What is there to fear once you have surrendered yourself to God? We know that God Almighty has opened up several avenues for your well-being. It is up to you to choose the path you should follow. This transitory world belongs neither to you nor to me. We are just going on a journey like everybody else. We are born here to carry out the wish of that Supreme One. Relieve your mind of all worries and fear and go back home. Trust and adore God, and take his name. Learn the truth that He is behind everything that you do, and everything that comes to pass in this world. Leave yourself in His hands and live in peace."

Hanumana Dasa spoke with fervour.

The sun had completed almost half of his journey towards the west by that time.

The nectar-sweet words of Hanuman Dasa enthralled the listeners. When he stopped, the people cried out *Haribol* three times even before they were asked to do so.

It was as though an overflowing fountain of love and devotion had swept over them. Alas! We modern men have so little time to enjoy such bliss!!

Would we ever be fortunate to have a little spare time to take a dip in that fountain of faith when the powerful currents of western civilization keeps us permanently adrift, thrusting us constantly after worldly gains till we are drowned in the ocean of stress and strain?"

The monks blessed the villagers. Crying out *Haribol* as loudly as possible, the villagers, their spirits fully revived after listening to the noble words of the hermits climbed down the hill. They boarded the boats and set off for the village.

***

CHAPTER-25

The Judgement

After attending the ceremonial feast the men came back to the village. The utterances of the name of God and the religious sermons had sprinkled the divine potion of bliss over their hearts and a new energy had filled them. As it is the days are short in the months of winter. Moreover, the visit to the mound of Jatia and the feast had taken up a lot of time. By the time they reached the village day-light was beginning to fade and a thin film of mist had spread over the horizon like a translucent screen of smoke. The smoky haze of the winter twilight had triumphed over sunlight. The undaunted sun-god, who held unlimited power, failed to pierce the blanket of fog the winter evening had wrapped around the earth at Time's command with his invincible spear of light. Ashamed of his defeat the indomitable sun-god, his face pale and drawn, beat a shameful retreat and hid himself behind the western horizon.

It is by the supreme command of inexorable Time that days and nights and different seasons visit the earth taking turns. What could it be called other than the charismatic power of God? Isn't this one instance enough to shatter the arrogance of a proud man? And what can one be called who fails to learn his lesson from instances such as this except a fool?

Before they reached home the villagers driven by curiosity went to the place of the burglary. By that time the number of security guards had been doubled there. Duman Sardar himself was present at the spot and saw to it that peace and normalcy were maintained in the village. A large number of people had flocked to the place because an officer of a high rank had come to cerry out inspection. Small-time tradesmen, vendors and wayfarers returning from the marketplace had stopped by to see what was happening. These outsiders and the villagers together formed a large crowd. There was quite a hubbub but it was not as uproarious as it was in the morning. Most of the onlookers observed intently what steps the officer was taking to preserve normalcy and maintain peace in the village. At the same time a lot of debates, discussions and criticism went along in a subdued tone. Men from other distant villages brought several such incidents into their purview of discussion. Some stood a little closer to Duman Sardar. They offered him suggestions so that the job could be carried out in a disciplined manner. There were a lot of noise but as it has been said earlier it was less than the morning. It was getting dark; the curtain of mist was was growing thicker. Animals and birds producing a lot of noise like a troop of soldiers returning from the battlefield made their way back to their homes. Duman Sardar, too, thought it was time to return. He called the security guards and once again explained to each of them their duties. As he was about to ask the crowd to vacate the place Dasa Khadanga was seen coming there escorted by security guards. The Choudhury of Navagram walked behind him. You might have seen how people in Calcutta walk behind the coolies who carried their luggage. Radhagovinda Choudhury followed Dasa Khadanga and the guards in the same manner in which one walks behind baggage-carriers. The fear that his carefully hoarded valuables might have been robbed had continued to haunt him all the way. That was now replaced by the fear of the culprit escaping from the clutches of the guards. The miser that he was, he did not like to spare even a little of his money. And, similarly, his miserly eyes did not cast even a passing glance at any other object. His gaze was steadily fixed on the man that walked ahead of him. He suffered from a death agony as his imagination continued to form dreadful pictures of his house being burgled by the dacoits. The waste of a single paisa causes unbearable pain to a miser like Choudhury. And this man was coming home oppressed by the terrible knowledge that the savings of his entire life had been stolen away. It was but natural that a shocking news as this one would make his heart stop beating. His one-track mind was focussedon one thought: "My money", " My money" — His mind went on reiterating this silently as if he had nothing or no one else to think of except this. Such a heartless creature was he that the thought of poor Kalaati did not cross his mind even for once. When learnt of his loss of property he never bothered to ask anyone what has happened to Kalavati. He had loved her like a daughter once upun a time and had entrusted her with the responsibility of the entire household, and remained away from home for days together busy earning money. The poor girl had looked after him with the genuine love of a blood-daughter and never neglected her duty even after being thrown into a malestorm of woe by cruel fate. The thought of such loving daughter did never cross Choudhury's mind nor did he feel even a grain of sympathy for the poor girl. Did the loss of money wipe out the memory of Kalavati completely from his heart? It is quite astonishing that such outlandish creatures live on this beautiful earth. Perhaps Lord Almighty has accomodated such villains in

His beautiful world with a purpose----- to teach lessons in moral responsibility to human beings.

The shock of the loss was so overpowering that it paralysed Radha Govinda. He walked on looking vacantly, feeling an emptiness around himself and a void within. Much notice had not been taken of him as long as he was outside the village but the moment he entered the village the whole place became abuzz with loud whispers.

"The villain will die of shock when he sees the condition of his house." Someone remarked. " You had never cared to spare a quarter-seer of paddy for someone in dire need----now see how all your carefully hoarded grains have been taken away ---- ", another sniggered. " The miser went hungry and amassed wealth, ---- serves him right!" Yet another added. The sarcastic comments did not seem to stop. Nobody uttered a word of sympathy. The village urchins stood a little away, clapped and sang;

The miser doubles his wealth

But it slips away through dacoity or stealth

Radha Govinda did not pay heed to these taunts. His mind drew a total blank and nothing entered it. Yet, at the slightest nod of his head the brats giggled mischeviously and ran away from him. The news of Choudhury's arrival had spread through the village with the speed of the lightning. As soon as they heard it people hurried out of their homes to see Choudhury. The crowd that had gathered near that wreck of a house that was once the invincible mansion of the Choudhury rushed towards the outer limit of the village to watch him arriving. Soon a large number of people gathered near him and an endless stream of debates and discussions seemed to flow out. The acquaintances of

Dasa Khadanga were stricken with grief and sympathy for the man when they saw his plight. No one would believe easily that Dasa Khadanga could have been involved in the crime in any manner even if he was seen with the dacoits. People had to admire the sharp intellect of the Subadar that enabled him to make such an accurate analysis and connect the poor man with the burglary!!

The frail, emaciated figure of Khadanga was proof enough of his innocence. Those that did not know him personally found it difficult to believe that such a hunger-worn, pale-looking man could ever have any link with the dacoits. The very idea of Dasa Khadanga being involved in such a large-scale burglary was absolutely ridiculous, to say the least. But the great Subadar had believed it and people had no alternative but to commend his credulity. The sad plight of Dasa Khadanga triggered off a debate. As the Choudhury walked on people followed him, and the debates and arguments continued. The women folk of the village also came out of their houses and watched the Choudhury and the crowd that moved along with him as eagerly as they would watch a marriage procession. But the Choudhury did not cast a glance at anyone; his vacant mind did not register anything.

Is it true that the mind of a miser is too narrow to make his perceptions so strictly limited? The circumference of his thought is so stringently shrunken that it admits entry to only some specific things and the countless spectra of this broad, beautiful world are never allowed admission there? May be it is so. The world appears before one just the way he perceives it. To a generous, goodnatured man the world appears as a beautiful place, but a narrow-minded man can never have a broad view of things. The only world a miser's mind recognizes is his wealth. Once the wealth is lost everything is lost for him. The world becomes a black void. He cannot see anything there. So great was the sorrow of losing his material possessions that the thought of his daughter had completely escaped his mind; how could it be expected of him to take note of the comments of the outsiders those surrounded him? He was, in a way, not himself any more. The world was lost to him. Nothing interested him; everything appeared as repulsive as poison. The satisfaction he had derived from earning money through unfair means had vanished. He did not have even the least possible hope that his lost wealth could be recovered from the dacoits. The tides of emotion began to swell higher and higher as he neared the village. As he entered it the sky above him seemed to crash and scatter about him. His body shuddered in a frenzy of sorrow. He was bathed in perspiration. For a berief second he lost conscousness and regained it in the next moment and walked heavily towards the house. The closer he got to his house the faster his heart began to beat. The rushing waves of sorrow seemed to wrench his pounding heart off his chest. It became no more possible for him to keep control over the paroxysms of madness. He found it difficult to breathe. Death, he thought, must be a hundred times better an experience than this. Alas!! Was it for this he had saved the money? Why had he dedicated his entire life to the mad pursuit of amassing wealth? Of what use was it? He had throughout remained under the illusion that money could buy happiness in this world.

But how could money bring happiness to one if he does not have the right to spend it?

An excess of sorrow numbed Choudhury's mind; his body felt weak as if all life had been drained out of it. He dragged himself as though urged on by some mechanical force. He was slowly losing all powers of reasoning. His head whirled so fast that he felt like being thrown down by its force. It whirled even faster when he realized that he had almost reached his house. He could at that moment of truth re-live the painful experience of hoarding money. Only one thought, "my money", "my money", with the speed of a water-current seemed to rush through his veins along with blood. His behaviour at that moment displayed the absolute form of egocentricity. The enormity of despair emanating from a sense of permanent loss rendered him as lifeless as a puppet. Men with even a little common sense could guess that the Choudhury was on the verge of losing his sanity.

Finally, the ruined house that had once been his dear home came into view. The terrible picture he had thought would be awaiting his eyes since he had heard the news of the burglary rose vividly before him. The sight of the wreckege filled him with an emptiness that paralysed his senses for a few moments. As soon as his mind could register the immense impact of reality his last breath was emptied out of his body. The next moment his lifeless body fell on the ground.

***

CHAPTER—26

Salvation

Could the soul of a miser be redeemed? Could the soul of one who has never tried to realize God through devotion, has ignored morality, and has never performed noble acts like charity or helping a fellow man in distress or never engaged in meditation, ever attain salvation?

Attaining salvation is not easy or else people would not have bothered to abide by any moral principles. There is no tangible evidence to prove that a man's soul has attained salvation. It is beilieved that nothing accompanies the soul to the other world except the virtues derived from the noble deeds of the dead man because he reaps the result of his deeds, noble or ignoble, during his life-time. The respectful recollection of those virtues by posterity may be the only acceptable proof of a soul's attainment of salvation.

Radha Govinda knew that the world belonged to God. He accepted God as great only because he believed Him to be the absolute owner of the great wealth of the world. His interest in God, therefore, was born out of the malicious intention to steal God's wealth and make it his own. Otherwise he had neither fear nor reverence for God. But sinners can never enjoy true happiness. Had it not been so, he would have been respected and praised by people in his lifetime and remembered as a good human being even after death. But men like the Choudhury are never favoured by fortune. In this case, too, the obvious happened. The shock of losing his life-time's savings proved fatal for Radha Govinda. One look at the wrecked house killed him instantly. When his lifeless body fell on the ground with a thud people rushed in to see what happened. There was a loud uproar. 'O, the sight of his ransacked house has killed the villain", hundreds of voices exclaimed. " He has carried his money to the other world on his head", some others jeered. The air rang with the made by the crowd that had thronged the spot. Duman Sardar and the security guards made their way through the milling crowd and reached the place where Radha Govinda's dead body lay.

As he was familiar with Radha Govinda's nature, Duman Sardar had been expecting that the man would not be able to stand the shock. His death, therefore, came as no surprise. " The unfortunate man probably deserved such a death", he thought to himself. People were still busy talking about the Choudhury. " The dacoits have looted his house; no one remained to continue his lineage or light a clay lamp in his name. But none of the villagers felt even a tinge of sympathy for the dead man. Their remarks and observations reflected their anger and hatred for the Choudhury. Readers, try to think and analyse for yourselves. How could a man that was thoroughly disliked by people, could receive their love and sympathy after death?

Duman Sardar, along with some men of experience examined the Choudhury's body to find if there was any sign of life. There was none. Then he searched his clothes. But it was useless. Nothing except the official letter addressed to Duman Sardar was recovered from his clothes. The letter had been kept carefully, in the waist-fold of his cloth that was wound seven times to ascertain absolute safety. Duman

Sardar decided it would be better to make arrangements for the removal of the body before reading the letter. Curiosity prompted him to cast a passing glance at the letter. Then he folded it and handed the letter to a sentry standing by. Thereafter he consulted the people who were present there for making arrangements for the cremation.

Radha Govinda had no kinsmen. Everybody who was even slightly acquinted with him and his nature had felt nothing but a bitter dislike for him. "That villain was as reprehensible as an untouchable", they said to Duman Sardar; " Let the low-caste untouchables carry his body away to the cremation ground."

Dear Readers, Radha Govinda had earned nothing except people's ill will

during his lifetime. His immense wealth could not buy him anything except their hatred. Duman Sardar knew how the villagers despised Radha Govinda; he had expected that they would react in this manner if they were asked to carry the dead body of Choudhury. Yet he decided to give it another try and requested them again to manage things somehow. But they did not change their decision. Finding no other alternative Duman Sardar ordered a sentry to send for some untouchables. Now the question as to who would perform the funeral rites arose. It led to a lot of debate and discussion.

"Throw his body in the cremation ground. The scavenging birds and beasts will devour it," someone suggested. "Are you out of your mind?", another cut in. "Even jackals and dogs won't touch him. He had tortured us enough while alive, now the stench from his rotten body will pollute the village air. He will continue to torture us even after his death."

Others laughed aloud when they heard this.

"He is right", said Duman Sardar. "It is often noticed that even the carrion-eaters are averse to touching the dead body of a sinner." The discussions went on but no solution emerged. In the end, Duman Sardar suggested that the most convenient way to get rid of the body was to throw it into the river. The men from the untouchable casts were asked to drag the body to the river and then fling it into the water.

Alas, Radha Govinda!! Was this what you had aspired for? Was this what you wanted to gain from your insane pursuit of wealth? Let alone carrying along yuor savings them selves, you were not destined to carry even the satisfaction of having saved enormous wealth to the other world. Your death would not perhaps been so pathetic had you realized that wealth never belonged to any one. Alas, RadhaGovinda!! What a lesson in morality your sad end has taught this world!! God must have sent you to this earth with a purpose. But your ignoble deeds had belied that purpose.

You have proved your unworthiness through your selfish deeds. Why should anyone spend any money for you when you in your entire life time had never spared a single pie for the poor and the needy? All your carefully hoarded wealth was snatched away. You witnessed your ruin with your own eyes. What more was there to be seen? Your dead body did not deserve even a pyre made of bamboo sticks. You have never felt a grain of sympathy for the hunger-worn, dying human beings of your own village. You had earned money from the Subadar by giving false information in your report. Why should anybody speak a few kind words in your favour? You refused to recognize basic human values; the world therefore rejected you as useless. Because you had indulged in stealing other people's money you became a subject of their abhorrence. The way of life a man follows determines the nature of his death. How can any one hope for salvation if he had never pursued the path of truth during his life time? How could the soul of a man whose dead body was dragged away by the low-caste *chandals* ever be redeemed?

A group of untouchables arrived and, ordered by Duman Sardar, pulled the dead body away and flung it into the waters of river Mahanadi. People watched the body floating away and continued casting aspersions on the Choudhury.

The rotten body might have got stuck at some unknown place by the river and filled the air with its stench. People who lived there must have cursed it for polluting the air.

It was dark by the time the Choudhury-episode came to an end. The bystanders returned home still discussing the subject. Duman Sardar, too, headed for his place of posting. Dasa Khadanga, in the custody of the security guards, went with him.

***

CHAPTER-27

Duman Sardar

Two rivers, Paika and Chitrotpala, had branched out of the holy, vast and bottomless river Mahanadi in two opposite directions at this spot. The Mahanadi has narrowd here and looked like the concaves belly-line of a woman who lay in a relaxing posture, taking a deep breath stretching up her arms. The dense forest of Kaijanga appeared more fearsome when viewed from this spot. On one side beyond the forest was village Barada flocked with green patches of thick-foliaged trees that gave it the appearance of a woodland, and Kisan Nagar on the other looked as colourful and lovely as a flower-garden. The enchanting landscape sprinkled a potion of bliss on the heart and infused a new life into men living under the permanent threat of a merciless Time that rules the world by the Law of Impermanence.

There, on the river bank, was a dense growth of varieties of fruit-bearing trees like coconut mango and the jackfruit. The trees that bore tasty, luscious fruit not only enhanced the beauty of the river bank, they also constantly lured the work-worn boatmen to stop their boats and rest for a while to shed their fatigue. The water-level was not deep here and sandy patches stood out at different places in the river bed. The sight of water-fowls and sheldrake couples sporting delightfully in these shallow pools of crystal-clear water drove away the fear of crocodiles or any other dangerous reptiles there and compelled the viewers to believe that earth is an abode of beauty. The river-bank witnessing the enchanting sights smiled. She decked herself happily with wild flowers that filled the air with exotic fragrance.

Readers! This was the lovely spot where the village Tarito, mentioned in an earlier chapter, was located. DumanSardar, the deputy of the Subadar, lived here in his huge, ornate mansion which was more or less like a fortress. It might not have been as imposing as the Subadar's villa at Lalbagh; nevertheless it was a sort of a replica of the later. The castle was a stone-sructure, and therefore was strong. Deep and wide moats were dug around the castle and were filled with water as a protective measure against the attack of any outside foe. Those water-filled trenches were flanked on both sides by thick jungles of bamboo. But they did not mar the beauty of the trenches in the least. Just as way the moat was an ideal place of sport for the swans and the other aquatic fowls the bamboo bushes were fit stage for the dancing and singing of birds like peacocks. Readers, so dense and impenetrable were the bamboo-bushes on the outer side of the moat that someone standing beyond it could not imagine that the huge, fort-like residence of the Maratha official stood inside.When the wind passed through the hollow reeds of bamboo an eerie, uncanny sound issued from them which could have been easily mistaken for the wild screeches of a witch or some such unearthly creature. The scary environment was sure to give the creeps to any outsider that happened to pass by but to local people such sounds meant nature's music that enraptured the listeners and held them in a bondage of love.

Returning from Navagram, Duman Sardar crossed

the trench and entered the castle-gate. Dasa Khadanga, in the custody of the security guards, walked after him. Duman Sardar was a man of great physical strength and that was one of the reasons why the Bhuyan dacoits of Kujanga admired him. Men of such physical build were rarely found among the Marathas. He was not only strong but was handsome, too. The muscular arms that reached down to his thighs, broad torso, rock-hard thighs, strong and shapely shoulders, his thick curved eyebrows and the long eyes that seemed to have stretched up to his ears were enough to frighten an enemy as strong as a monster. Yet, his face exuded such a calmness that people who knew him personally instinctively loved him; and strangers could not but stop a while to gaze at his face. He was a man of efficiency and skill as well and not a malicious character like the Subadar. He was good at taking care of the day-to-day problems; at the same time, he was capable of dealing deftly wth the administrative affairs of the state. He had kept track of the activities of the criminals in the area under his jurisdiction. It was not difficult for him to track down the culprits if a crime occurred there. Readers, is there any doubt that such an able man will always draw everyone's attention and be in the good books of his superiors? He never had to face any resistance from his subordinates since they liked and respected him. Duman Sardar sincerely worked for the well-being of the people and had genuine sympathy for the poor and the needy. Sometimes he tactfully went against the instructions of his superiors in order to help such people. He was endowed with many noble qualities and the village of Tarito was proud to have him.

This noble character was not a stranger to the Bhuyan dacoits.Duman Sardar had apprehended that the vagaries of weather in Odisha would bring about a devastating famine that would destroy many innocent lives. He had apprised the Subedar of the problem and prayed to him to take appropriate precautionary measures. But in stead of receiving any sympathetic or positive response from th cruel,selfish and inhuman Subadar Duman Sardar was subjected to severe admonitions for the offence of bringing such matters to his notice.

The reproach of the superior as well as his indifference to the suffering of the poor had badly bruised the tender heart of Duman Sardar that remained hidden under a hard and sturdy exterior. Like streams of clear water flowing from rocky mountains, tears of regret had streamed down the cheeks of the man who appeared so tough outside. Duman Sardar felt it was his moral duty to help the people and he was determined to do it even if it cost him his life. Leaving everything in the hands of Fate he took a trip to Kujanga and discussed the matter with the Sandha king. After a long discussion it was finally decided that to get the crop and the cash and other valuables that the selfish land-owners like the Choudhury and Govardhan Dasa had hoarded in their houses robbed by the Bhuyan dacoits could be the most appropriate solution. Raghunath Patnaik readily agreed to extend his help to carry out the plan. Duman Sardar returned from Kujang after having entrusted Raghunath Patnaik with the leadership of the entire operation. By the king's orders he was introduced to the gang of robbers as Sardar Singh and they addressed him by that name. Readers! This 'Sardar Singh' we have met earlier in this narrative.

He was none other than Duman Sardar. There is no need to explain that the dacoits, having received the cooperation and support of Duman Sardar, were able to fulfill their mission without any difficulty.

By this time the readers might have also guessed that Duman Sardar *alias* Sardar Singh knew every detail about the burglary that had occurred at Navagram. He, therefore, knew it for sure that Dasa Khadanga was not involved in the act of robbery. At the same time he was aware that the Choudhury was one of the most trusted subordinates of the Subadar and the Subadar himself suspected Dasa Khadanga. In his letter the Subadar had elaborately explained the points that made him suspect the man. In the letter the Subadar had ordered Duman Sardar to make a proper investigation of the matter and send back Dasa Khadanga alongwith the details of the findings of the investigation. Duman Sardar had, therefore, no power to release Dasa Khadanga although he was convinced the man was absolutely innocent. Hence, there had to be a sham investigation for the benefit of the public; Duman Sardar considered different aspects of the problem. He kept Dasa Khadanga confined in a room; because of the kind-hearted Duman Sardar, the poor man had something to eat at night. After taking food the man lay down on the floor.But sleep eluded his eyes. He felt restless and was sick with worry. So agitated was his mind that he could not feel the stinging cold. The guards sleeping by the door snored loudly. In that dreadful silence the noise of their snoring sounded more frightening to Khadanga. In the course of that single night the news of the arrest of Dasa Khadanga had travelled far and wide. People came to know of his arrival at the village of Tarito. On learning about the Subadar's orders for conducting an enquiry into Dasa Khadanga's possible involvement in the dacoity quite a large number of men, women and children had reached the village of Tarito on the next morning to witness the investigation. Amongst them were the young wife of Dasa Khadanga, his old mother, and his son and daughter. His mother was in her eighties and was a bag of bones. She had somehow managed to drag her frail, skeletal body along that far with the aid of a walking stick. Tears ran down her hollow eyes. She had given birth to four sons, but the other three had departed from the world. By sheer luck, death had spared Dasa Khadanga, and hence he was priceless to his mother. Like the stick to a blind man, Dasa Khadanga was an indispensable support to his old mother. His wife was just twenty-four; she walked on holding her three year old son by his hand, and cradling a suckling baby-girl in her arm. She was a beautiful woman. She was also a devoted wife and a woman of noble virtue. Her beautiful face, wet with tears, was as pale as the dying moon in the dawn. Time and again the little boy asked, " Mother, where is my father?"

"In the Sardar's house. Come on, we shall meet him there." The grief-stricken mother spoke these tear-soaked words of consolation with great effort. Readers can well imagine the mental agony of Dasa Khadanga who had to suffer imprisonment for no reason, leaving his family in utter distress. Words fail to express the anguish the man went therough. His family was so poor that it was difficult for them to get a full meal even under normal conditions. Imagine the misery this family had to go through when its only earning member, its only support, was in prison. And to add to their misery the deadly famine waited to devour everybody. Khadanga's heart was rent with sorrow when he thought of his old mother, and his wife and his two small children.

Duman Sardar started collecting information and evidence from people of Navagrama and some other villages in the vicinity. This exercise started at about 8 in the morning and continued for nearly four hours. It has been made clear to the readers earlier that the whole process of investigation as far as Sardar Singh was concerned, was only meant to impress the public. Not much information could be obtained from the people regarding Dasa Khadanga's connection with the robbery. Besides, no one said he had seen Dasa Khadanga on the scene of the crime. Nevertheless, Duman Sardar could not declare the man innocent and acquit him since he did't have the authority to do so. He called the old mother of Dasa Khadanga and his wife and children inside and consoled them saying that there wasn't any evidence that could even remotely connect Dasa Khadanga with the crime. He was deeply moved at the pitiable plight of the starving family and ordered an attendant to get some food from his own house for them. But how could food go down their throat when the flames of sorrow corroded their being? Their hearts were filled with premonitions; God knew what was that heartless, malicious Subadar was going to do to their dear one!! The deep agony of the old mother who wept inconsolably seeing her darling son was beyond words. All who heard the wailing of the poor creature could not hold back their tears. The distress and the torment his wife passed through was idescribable. She cast a pathetic glance at her husband and sat there her head lowered while silent tears ran down her cheeks. But she tried to console her mother-in-law and wiped her tears. At the same time, she held her own little son in check, who made several eager attempts to run towards his father. As for Khadanga himself---- he had resigned himself to fate and left his family to the mercy of God and prepaed himself to face whatever fate had in store for him. Still, despite his best efforts, the pain he experienced witnessing the sufferings of his family brought tears to his eyes. This was but natural. He was a human being of flesh and blood after all !

With much difficulty Sardar Singh (Duman Sardar) managed to make the old woman, her daughter-in-law and the two kids eat a little food. He made arrangements for accomodating them in a place close to his house. He also made arrangements for Khadanga to come and meet his family.

Duman Sardar did not complete the enquiry that day even though he did not have much information to collect. The readers are well aware that he knew everything relating to the Navagram robbery. But the Subadar would have been suspicious had Duman Sardar finished the investigation so early. So he let the enquiry go on for eight days and prepared a report, where he mentioned the findings of the enquiry. The report said that Dasa Khadanga was innocent and no evidence could be found to establish his complicity in the burglary. It was also mentioned that the dacoits had left no clue which could have been used to track them. He sent Dasa Khadanga along with the report in the custody of the guards to the Subadar. He explained to Khadanga's mother and his wife that there was a fair chance of his acquittal. Dasa Khadanga's wife and mother followed him to Cuttack.

***

CHAPTER-28

The Sick-Bed

The beautiful river Chitrotpala branching out of the holy Mahanadi flowed smoothly some distance towards the east. It has been said earlier that along both the banks of this daughter of the Mahanadi there dwelt noble sages. Graced by the blessings of those noble souls river Chitrotpala had given birth to a daughter, a small river called Luna, and ecstatic in the joy of motherhood, rocked her in the cradle of earth. River Luna, hence, could thus be called the grand-daughter of river Mahanadi. Because of her narroeness the current was strong and rushed on with great force at places where the river took sharp turns. The trees that stood on its banks, were like friends of hers who watched the grand daughter of Mahanadi engaging in adventures. As she giggled away happily, her joy was transmitted to her tree-friends and made them look fresh and cheerful. The river that had the Chitrotpala for her mother and the Mahanadi for her grand mother would doubtlessly be merry and playful in nature. It looked as if waves not of water but laughter flowed in her and therefore everything around her looked gay and cheerful. The Luna flowing amidst the delightful sylvan surroundings filled the air with laughter, and never failed to endear herself to the animals and birds and all other children of nature bringing them the sweet and clear water that her grandmother had bequeathed to her. Travellers that approached her bank in order to cross to the other side were received with delight and their boats were manoeuvred along speedily to their destinations. The pleasure they experienced when the frolicsome ripples danced around their boats lengthened their life-span, as it were.

Ever eager and ready to add to the satisfaction of everyone and everything around her, the river glided on singing the glory of God and everyone that heard it was enraptured. Why wouldn't they be? The bond of togetherness born out of the gratitude they felt for her because she was a joyful sight, quenched their thirst and entertained them during their journey, doubtlessly made them derive unlimited bliss from the song that was dedicated to God and eulogiged His infinite glory. This was perhaps the reason why several shrines and temples and monasteries had been built on both the banks of river Luna. Noble-hearted saints who dwelt in them followed the example the river had set before them and glorified their lives offering obeisance to God. There was a particular bathing-ghat on one bank of this river called the Sandhya Ghat. Legend has it that, when the Pandavas were in exile, they once walked by this river. It was evening when they reached this place. They took bath here and after performing the evening worship they crossed the river. The ghat where they had crossed the river was later named the Sandhya Ghat. This place was located at about a distance of six kosas to the east of another wharf known as Bateswara-Bhagavati (mentioned earlier in chap-16) Long before the events narrated in this novel took place there was a stone-house near this ghat encircled by a beautiful garden. This house still stands there.

Readers, let's turn our attention to this house and see

what was going on in one particular room of this old stone-house.

A week had passed after that terrible full-moon night of the month of Pausha. It was the eigth day of the dark fort-night following that. A lean moon had risen a short while ago and shone feebly in the eastern sky. It made an effort to bring a little relief to poor earth which was drowned in darkness The cold night was enveloped in a soundless darkness which seemed to throb with a kind of creepy elo-quence. The occasional howls of the wolves and the jackals and the eerie hooting of the owls pierced the thick silence. The sounds were horrible enough to drain the life out of those that heard them.

There was a young man in one of the rooms in the stone house. The room was dimly lit by the feeble flame of a candle. Completely oblivious to the cold and scary night, he sat by the bedstead on which lay a sick young woman. His chin was moist from the tears he had shed; his face looked pale and wan as the moon at day-break. He gazed fixedly at the patient lying on the bed. His mind was com-pletely preoccupied with worries and consternation, while his anxious heart prayed to God unceasingly to cure her. His face hung low and looked like a lotus drooping from its stem in the absence of the sun-light which instilled it with life-force into it. The lotus would raise its face when the sun would rise again; so would he when the young woman would recover from her illness. There was no other choice either for the lotus or the young man.

Besides these two young people there was a third per-son in the house: his mother who was seventy seven years old. Age had completely withered her and the young man had to take care of her, too. Despite the protests of the old woman, her son helped her in most of the domestic chores, fed her with his own hands and personally saw to it that she lived in comfort.

Dear readers, 'wife-worship' has become the order of the day. As long as a son is not married he takes care of his mother. Soon after marriage he turns into a doting husband and starts neglecting the mother who gave birth to him and reared him with immense love and care. He takes no notice of the poor old mother even if she goes without food for days, let alone looking after her. Alas! What a terrible time we live in! Instead of taking care of their old mothers, the sons these days try to push them out of their minds completely. Does his wife love him more than his mother does?

Let's bring this subject to a stop now and return to the young man in that dimly lit room. Unlike most young men of the present times he was a devoted son and believed that life would attain fulfillment if he could take proper care of his old mother. The old woman, moved beyond words by the way her son looked after her, always prayed to God to bless him with a long life full of happiness. The son, by God's grace, did not suffer from any material deprivations. He spent quite a good sum of money on observing religious rites and donated a considerable amount towards charity and could still afford to live a life of comfort. The only sorrow that oppressed him was the death of his young wife; she had left for her heavenly abode about five years ago leaving him alone in this mortal world. She was a noble and virtuous woman. The love and affection she received from her mother-in-law being the wife of her only son had never made her haughty or arrogant. Instead, she always looked for opportunities to return the love and affection she received by taking good care of her. So eager was she to make her mother-in-law comfortable that the old woman felt awkward about asking even for a glass of water. Her daughter-in-law was ever ready to fulfill her every wish even before she expressed it. If she chanced to commit any ittle mistake---and it was quite natural that some problems would crop up while managing the household affairs, she would fall at her mother-in-law's feet and beg forgiveness. Dear Readers, you might dislike my telling all this but the truth is that that daughters-in-law of the present generation wouldn't even dream of touching the feet of their mothers-in-law. They would not hesitate to make their old mothers-in-law fall at their own feet. With a strong belief in the time-less law that man and wife are equally responsible for the smooth running of the world these modern daughters-in-law assume themselves to be all-in-all in the family. They suppose that God has kept these old creatures alive with one single purpose: to serve and be at the beck and call of their daughters-in-law. But the daughter-in-law we men-tioned a little while ago was very different. Her untimely death, therefore, had left her mother-in-law in a state of utter distress and had shattered her husband. From the after the wedding this virtuous woman had dedicated herself to the service of her husband and her mother-in-law. She thought a world of them and believed that no one else in this world mattered to her except those two. She believed that her soul would find a place in heaven only if she could please them with her words and deeds. She attended to the needs of her husband more dutifully than a slave; but the ways of Providence are beyond man's comprehension. It had nev-er occurred either to the son or the mother that this noble woman would leave this world so soon, that she would desert them forever. The two of them had always tried to return her love by keeping her happy in various ways. But events do not always occur according to the wishes of human beings. Death arrived all on a sudden in the form of a fever and snatched her away from her loved ones. Everyone was powerless before death. Her mother-in-law wailed loudly. Her husband wept bitterly but nothing could bring her back. Death is invincible and inevitable. It never listens to anybody's appeal, nor can it be bribed in any manner to make it delay its arrival. The reason why an evil force like death is engaged by God to rob the precious gems from the earth is best known to Him. Maybe Death is exceptionally dutiful and never makes a moment's delay in carrying out the orders of his Master or maybe the pressure of work does not permit him to pay heed to the appeals of human beings. How the old woman and her son had wished that their loved one would live longer! But hard-hearted Death turned down their prayer. The absolute sincerity of the wish to obey the Master's command perhaps had turned it as ruthless as thunderbolt. It was as though the light went out of the family with the death of the daughter-in-law. The mishap affected the old woman's body and mind rather badly; her son, although he went through the terrible pangs of the irreparable damage Fate had caused to his own mind and heart, tried his best to console his mother. But her tears did not stop; they streamed down her old, hollowed cheeks like showers in the rainy season. All the consolations of the world could not assuage her pain. Her daughter-in-law was a strong moral and physical support to her. She was as priceless to her as the pupil of her eye. The loss of someone so precious could never be a small matter. Her death made the mother-in-law blind with grief. Her daughter-in-law was her life; without her the old woman could not bring herself to stand straight. She was like the stick that gave support to her. It was as if the death of her daughter-in-law had sucked out all the energy from her. She was unable to raise herself from the bed. No one, unless he himself had passed through similar conditions, could have been able to realize how devastating her sorrow was. She had given up all hope that she could ever raise herself from bed.

Of what use were all the pains and tears of the ones that were left behind?

Could they bring back the dead?

At the pitiable wailing of the old woman leaves might have fallen off the trees; but Death had no ears for it. That old age had rendered the old woman immobile and helpless would not affect Death in the least. Such things it regularly comes across while fulfilling its duty but the most piteous appeals do not arouse mercy in its cruel heart. Death would never return the one it takes away even if the loving survivors die of grief. There is nothing strange about it. Such things happen all the time in this world. But a human being made up of flesh and blood and capable of feeling emotions cannot accept death so easily. The young man knew this eternal truth. Still he was not able to mitigate his sorrow through his logical reasoning. The tragedy of his life was that he could never express his sorrow openly. He had to conceal his woes in some secret corner of his heart and console his bereaved mother. Time, however, has the power to heal most of the wounds and his mother could manage somehow to compromise with the loss in course of time. But she had become too weak physically and was unable to get up from her bed without assistance. She experienced weakness and a painful stiffness in her back whenever she got up from bed and did a little household work. For this reason she had to remain confined to her bed most of the time. She was everything to her son and the youngman did not neglect her even for a moment. He had chosen to spend his entire life nursing his mother. How noble a son was he!! The mouths of the thousand-headed snake-king *Vasuki* would not be enough to sing a proper accolade to such a dutiful son!!

Despite his concern for his mother the young man disagreed with her on one issue. He was not in favour of marrying again though his mother constantly persuaded him to do so. He wanted to spend the rest of his life nursing his sick and old mother. Often arguments would break out on this point between the son and the mother, the mother insisting on remarriage and the son politely rejecting the idea. He tried to explain to her that it would spell trouble for him in case the second wife turned out to be quarrel-some and disrespectful. The mother knew that her son was right but she also wanted him to raise a family. She had not given up her efforts of persuading her son during all these years—Time had moved on and after five years suddenly her son had brought home this beautiful young woman, who now lay sick in the bed.

The son was thirty years old. The woman he brought home was young. Bringing a young woman home without marrying her was neither proper nor decent. The mother guessed that her son had married the daughter of some poor man, who did not have the resources to perform the wedding ceremony, and had brought her home. But she had no problems with this. The marriage of her son was her sole concern. When her curiosity got the better of her she asked her son to tell her the truth. He explained that the young woman was not his wife; when he had found her she was pretty sick and was lying unattended. He had brought her home since there was no other convenient place where he could have kept her, and he wanted her to get well receiving proper treatment and care. The mother now inquired about the caste of the woman and her son's reply brought the old woman a great relief since she came to know that the woman belonged to a caste not inferior to their own. Sickness had made her look pale; still she looked quite attractive. The old woman was pleased and secretly decided to get her son married to the young woman after she recovered from her illness. The prospect raised her spirits a little. The young man, now relieved that his mother did not object to his bringing the young woman home,, called in a physician to treat the patient and sat by her bedside, attending her. Her condition was critical a couple of days ago and the chances of her survival were almost nil. She seemed to be sinking. The young man prayed to God desperately but her condition had remained unchanged. But her condition seemed to change for the better the next morning and, by evening, signs of some improvement were seen. The young man experienced a little relief, but he did not leave her bedside. The patient opened her eyes once or twice after evening. That was a clear indication of improvement because she had remained unconscious for the last seven days and had not opened her eyes even for once. During those seven days the young man had sat by her bed forgetting the rest of the world, caring little for food and sleep, and had never left her alone even for a moment. He was overjoyed as though the moon had dropped into his hand when he saw her open her eyes. He thanked God from the depths of his heart. A new energy seemed to seep into his body and mind; he nursed her with greater enthusiasm.

It was past midnight. Though the patient did not open her eyes anymore after she had done once or twice in the evening, she was obviously conscious. The young man was sure that the patient was enjoying a sound sleep. Still he kept gazing intently at her to find if there were signs of further improvement.

After what seemed to be hours the patient sighed and opened her eyes; the young man's gaze was fixed on her and their eyes met automatically. The young man thanked God from a heart that now overflowed with happiness. In that brief moment their eyes met her eyes had captured the image of the young man sitting by her bed and stored it in her mind even though she had tried to push it out of her sight by closing her eyes immediately. She felt shy in the presence of a stranger and cringed a little.

There was no further need to try and look for the symptoms that could prove she had regained conscious-ness. The young man offered his heartfelt gratitude to the Lord. His heart danced and his whole body shivered with joy. The happiness surging inside him drove sleep away from his eyes, and he continued to gaze at the face of the young woman.

After a few moments she opened her eyes again, and once more the picture of the young man presented itself to them. She closed her eyes at once and made a feeble at-tempt to put her clothes in order. This instinctive reaction proved that she was in her senses and was feeling shy in the presence of a stranger.

'Who are you?', she asked in a feeble voice. The young man had given up all hopes of her survival. But her reflexes seemed normal and he guessed that her life was no longer in danger. His spirits revived when he heard her speak. Who could say what divine potion was contained in that soft voice that instilled a new vigour into him? He had heard those words from the mouths of several people earlier. But the very same words seemed to pour sweet nectar into his ears when she spoke them. No other voice had made him experience such ecstasy. He knew that he would never forget that experience.

Afraid that she might feel tense and restless if he did not answer her question, the young man said, "You must rest. Don't worry at all and don't burden your mind with meaning-less apprehensions. Think of this house as your own and feel at home. I am Raghunath Pattnaik." He said soothingly.

The reply sent a shiver of excitement through her body. but she felt too weak to respond. She closed her eyes and remained quiet. Raghunath did not say anything more; he continued to sit by the bed and watch her intently. ===

**

CHAPTER-29

The Inner Wing of
Kujanga Palace

We have not met Rasakala after she was sent to the palace of the Sandha king of Kujanga. The dacoits had carried her unconscious body in the boat and she was still unconscious when she was transported to the massive palace of the Sandha king. In the inner wing of that huge palace there lived quite a few lovely-looking ladies. A look at them was likely to make one assume that the king of the Sandha dynasty had brought them together with a mind to treasure all the beautiful women created by God at one place. It is however not possible for one man to enjoy the companionship of all the beautiful women of the world as it is not possible for one man to enjoy all the wealth of the world. The inner wing of the palace was more or less an ex-hibition-ground of beauty and glamour, and this is where the amorous desires of the kings were fulfilled..

The dazzling display of beauty and glamour tends to hurt the eyes sometimes. The ladies that dwelt in this inner section of the royal palace were extraordinarily beautiful. The chief queen was known as the *Pata Mahadevi or Pata Mahadei* while the others were entitled only *Mahadevis or Mahadeis*. There were many young and attractive queens who had married the king just by exchanging garlands; they were like fresh blossoms in the garden of beauty that filled the air with exotic fragrance. Some others bloomed with the joy of having received the royal touch of the kings of Kujanga.

Each one of such queens was attended by at least ten maids. The chief-queen had nearly forty of them at her beck and call. Each of the *Mahadevis* enjoyed the services of thirty or so maids. Elderly queens and the *Rajmatas* too had their maids to wait upon them and run errands for them. In this way, the number of women that lived in the inner wing of the palace could have been almost similar to the number of people living in seven or so villages.

Most of the inmates of the inner-wing were engaged by turn in the services of the king. When a particular queen's turn came , she would adorn herself with expensive costumes and jewellery and present herself before the king. But it was customary that the queens must attire themselves in beautiful clothes and jewellrey in the evening.

Hence, in the evening hours they roamed about the palace that looked almost ethereal in the soft, cool moonlight flaunting their beauty through enticing gestures. The palace, at that time, appeared to have transformed to a celestial garden, where nymphs dwelt. Such was the dazzle of their beauty that it seemed to give complexes to the moon and forced it to hide its beauty under the black scar on its face. If the scarred moon can enthral our hearts, wouldn't the unblemished beauty of those ladies of the palace of Kujanga charm everyone that had the opportunity to cast a glance on them? The jingle of their anklets as they moved about was sure to compel a man of the most unromantic temperament to turn and steal a second glimpse. The tinkle of their waist-bands could have lured saints who had renounced the world.

Readers, the resplendence of the beauty of the royal ladies, the music of their ornaments,

their graceful movement, and their melodious voice that was as sweet as the cuckoo's song, seemed to turn the inner wing of the palace to an abode of the heavenly nymphs. It would not be surprising that just a glimpse of the extensive show of beauty would be enough to captivate the heart of the viewer.

To this place Rasakala was brought.

She had remained unconscious for two days. The chief queen, as fate had decreed felt drawn towards the girl the moment her eyes fell on her. A wave of affection surged in her heart at the sight of Rasakala, and she took care of her and nursed her as though she were her own daughter. Rasakala regained consciousness after a couple of days. She recovered completely after a few more days and was able to move about the palace within a week. Gradually, she made friends with others in the palace. Rasakala addressed the chief queen as 'mother' since she had taken special care of her during her illness. The chief queen was overjoyed when Rasakala called her 'mother'. With a heart overflowing with love and a body trembling with happiness, she kissed Rasakala's forehead and said, " Now I am sure that you were my daughter in some previous life. God has therefore has placed you again in my lap." Those words of affection melted Rasakala's innocent heart. It was but natural. Since her childhood she had never received such love from her own mother. The warmth of the unalloyed affection emanating from the heart of someone who was not related to her in any way would doubtlessely have caused an iceberg to thaw, and Rasakala's heart was as soft as a drop of dew. From the relationship that was formed between the chief queen and Rasakala there stemmed a number of others. So Rasakala found in the inner wing of the palace quite a number of aunts, sisters, grandmothers and so on--- . Rasakala, who came from a family that derided love and affection, was thrown as it were into an ocean where there surged high tides of tender love.

The chief queen stood apart from all the other women in the palace. She was like the most precious among the collection of gems. God endowed her with a loving and sympathetic heart that perfectly matched her beauty. A woman who despite her royal status could be so full of affection and love for everybody is rarely found on this earth. She treated even birds and animals like her own children, and Rasakala was after all a human being. It was but natural that she inspired a special kind of feeling in the heart of the chief queen and received special attention from her. Nevertheless, Rasakala's heart pined for Kalavati. She was no doubt happy in the company of the chief queen and other ladies, but at the back of her mind there lurked a dismal shadow of loss. Hence the chief queen tried to engage Rasakala in various light and pleasant activities to keep her mind occupied and did not allow her much time to miss Kalavati. The ladies in the palace stayed close to Rasakala most of the time and tried to cheer her up. They did that not because the chief queen desired so, but because they, too, genuinely liked her and felt drawn by her innocence and good-natured behaviour. Thus, Rasakala lived like a princess in the palace of Kujanga. The chief queen loved to deck this beautiful young woman with expensive clothes and jewellery. Rasakala, who was constantly haunted by thoughts of Kalavati and was worried about what sort of troubles she might be passing through, was disinclined to adorn herself with ornaments but she could not bring herself to refuse the chief queen when the latter so fondly pressed her to do so. And when Rasakala, looking divinely beautiful in gem-studded jewellery and rich costume roamed about the palace, she created the impression that some goddess had made her appearance in that abode of heavenly beings.

The king himself had grown fond of Rasakala. She was unconscious when she was brought to the palace and was in need of medical attention. The king, following the advice of the royal physician procured the expensive medicines and massage oil for her from different parts of the land. We have to keep in mind that, during those days, the knowledge of a royal physician and his expertise depended largely on the interest shown by his patron. It was with the king's encouragement and support he sought to prove his mettle. Since the king had taken a personal interest in Rasakala's health, there was no impendiment to the physician's prescribing expensive medicines.

We are now under British rule and the popularity of ayurvedic or herbal medicines has diminished. It is difficult these days to find either a good physician or an effective medicine. But in the past such medicines were quite popular and easily available, too. Those medicines, if used with expertise could work miracles. So the royal physician made every effort to get hold of medicines of the best quality for the treatment of Rasakala. The king himself accompanied the physician to the ladies' wing of the palace to have a look at the patient. He had taken an immediate liking to her and had made all arrangements for her to have the best treatment and diet. There was little hope of her survival. The king had asked the physician to take meticulous care of the patient. Besides, he regularly visited her and supervised the treatment. In short, the king grew fond of Rasakala as though she was his own daughter and planned secretly to give her in marriage to Raghunath after she came round. When Rasakala's condition improved noticeably, he disclosed his intention to the chief queen. Delighted beyond measure at the king's suggestion, the chief queen readily agreed to it.

Rasakala, after she recovered from illness, lived in the palace of the Sandha king like his beloved daughter. Rasakala had never met Raghunath. She had never heard of him, nor did she have any knowledge of the truth that the ceremonial procession that had been taken out on that fateful night was actually a cover for the burglary. She could only remember the frightful noise of the walls of the Choudhury house crashing as the procession passed their house. The moment it occurred to her that the dacoits had broken into the house she had lost consciousness. She did not know what happened after that. When she was asked about the incident Rasakala could tell just this to the ladies to satisfy their curiosity. But this little episode, tinged with the colours of their imagination evolved into an interesting story and spread around the palace. Hence, no one in the palace knew the real identity of Rasakala and how she was brought to the palace. Since she was treated by the king as his daughter Rasakala had once taken the liberty of asking him under what circumstances she was brought here and by whom. She had learnt that, after the dacoits left Choudhury's house the king's men had found her lying unconscious there. They had rescued her and brought her to the palace. How could Rasakala have persuaded the king to part with more details? She had to be satisfied with whatever little the king told her. Her parents did not love her and she knew it. But any human being living in this mortal world is bound to get caught in the snare of love and attachment; no one, however hard-hearted he or she may be, cannot afford to be callous to his or her parents. Rasakala, therefore, very humbly tried to inquire about what had happened to her parents. The king, full of sympathy as he was for the young girl, tried to prepare her to accept the bitter truth before breaking the sad news of the death of her parents in the dacoits' hands. He tried to explain to her how cruel, selfish and inhuman her parents were in nature. Rasakala knew this very well; despite it she loved them from the core of her heart. She broke into tears on learning about their death. The king and queen tried to console her in various ways; and Rasakala's soft, innocent heart that was afloat on an ocean of her newly acquired royal parents' love, could not nurse the grief resulting from her loss for much longer.

But she was not able to forget Kalavati. She was constantly haunted by her fond memory. She often asked the queen and sometimes even the king about Kalavati. The only consolation she received from them was that Kalavati was all right and Rasakala would soon meet her. Her heart pined for her dear friend, who was more than a sister. But Fate had kept her locked in a wonderful cell, the walls and floors of which were soaked with soft showers of love. She had no other choice than wait for that propitious hour ordained by Destiny when she would meet Kalavati again. With reasoning of this sort Rasakala tried to soothe her heart that yearned for Kalavati.

Time moved on. Rasakala regained her health and became her original beautiful self. The divine glow of her beauty radiated in the palace and enlivened its atmosphere. The king and the queen, relieved and glad at the same time at the complete recovery of Rasakala decided to send for Raghunath because they had to know what was in his mind before they could broach the topic to him.

CHAPTER-30

Mayadhar

Our readers might not have forgotten Mayadhar the so-called uncle of the Sandha King. He was not somebody one could easily forget. There are two kinds of individuals who are not easily forgotton--- an exceptionally good man who lives in the minds of posterity through his noble deeds, and an exceptionally vicious person who is remembered with distaste even after his death. In the strange world we live in are the two extreme points between which human character is kept confined. Mayadhar had chosen one of those two points for himself and held on to it. The wheel of Time continued to spin ceaselessly; Mayadhar too kept pace with time, and his evil mind unstoppably planned one mischief after another. He was like Duryodhan's conniving uncle, Shakuni in the great epic, the Mahabharat, who had crafted strategies to ruin the Kaurav Dynasty through the battle of Kurukshetra. Uncle Mayadhar had similar evil elements in his character though to a comparatively lesser degree. Like Uncle Shakuni uncle Mayadhar might be remembered afterwards with contempt for his evil deeds. It would be not be surprising if that happened. Mayadhar craved for fame though he had no idea in what way such things would benefit his selfish interests.

Readers, let us pay a visit to Uncle Mayadhar and see what conspiracies his evil mind was hatching. He had set his eyes on Rasakala and Kalavathi when their unconscious bodies were carried to the boat. The unearthly beauty of the two young women had aroused lustful desire in him. But he could not have his way as he was not the chief of the gang. He had to obey the orders of Raghunath whether he liked them or not. He could never have the maidens for himself without the knowledge of Raghunath. He doubted if Raghunath would allow him to enjoy them even if he lay claim to the maidens. It would be futile to hope, Mayadhar thought, that Raghunath would let such beautiful maidens go out of his clutches. But Mayadhar would not rest till he attained the object of his desire by hook or by crook. His scheming mind, tried to discover a way to fulfill his wish.

He had been keeping a close watch on the activities of Raghunath ever since the time the boats loaded with the cargo of plundered goods reached Paradweep. After embarking upon the shore Raghunath and his associates had gone to meet the king. Soon after the meeting with the king was over, Raghunath had sent one of the two young women to the palace and left Paradweep taking the other one with him. Mayadhar, Bahabalindra and Baliyarsingh were entrusted with the task of distributing the plundered goods. This work kept him thoroughly busy and Mayadhar found no opportunity to do anything. The dacoits, after committing the big robbery, were granted a rest period of a fortnight. Hence Mayadhar, like all other dacoits, went to meet his family in the village.But his mind was elsewhere. A lustful mind cannot find pleasure even in the company of his wife and children. Under the pretext that the king had sent for him, Mayadhar left for Kujanga in a haste.

He had decided to meet Raghunath on his way to the palace and have a man to man talk with him. If Raghunath agreed to spare one of the women, Mayadhar thought, it was well and good. But in case Raghunath refused to do so, Mayadhar was determined to have his own way even if it meant a breach of loyalty to Raghunath. Preoccupied with unholy thoughts such as these, Mayadhar set out on his journey and reached Raghunath's place at noon.

Raghunath was still sitting by the patient's bedside, his eyes fixed on her face. He had taken neither bath nor food since morning. How many people in this world would nurse the sick with such loving care? There would be no dearth of friends as long as one lived in comfort and luxury; but only the one that stands by his friend's side when the latter is in trouble could be called a true friend. Selfish friends are like the sun that appears in the sky of one's life during the day-time of prosperity; they disappear leaving no trace of their presence when evening sets in. But a true friend is like the little star that keeps sending its feeble light from the distant galaxy to relieve his friend's distress. Because Raghunath was a benevolent man he sincerely looked after the sick woman. Were he like Mayadhar, the patient might not have lived this long. Madhara had no knowledge of all this. Not that he would have taken any genuine interest in Kalavati's illness or in the unselfish sacrifice of Raghunath had he been aware of these developments. As has been said earlier, Mayadhar reached Raghunath's house by midday. He saw that the front door was closed. So he sat down on the outer verandah to take a little rest. A few minutes later, the doors opened and Raghunath came out. He was going to have a bath in the river and therefore had rubbed his body with oil. He was surprised and at the same time glad seeing Mayadhar sitting outside, and asked anxiously if Mayadhar had had his bath and taken his midday meal. Mayadhar asked Raghunath not to worry about that since he had bathed and taken food before he started from home.

But Raghunath forced him to have some refreshments as it was quite late for the mid-day meal. We know that Mayadhar did not come to have refreshments. His interests lay elsewhere. He said he was in a hurry to leave for Kujanga as the king had sent for him urgently but he would not object to a few sweetmeats as Raghunath was insisting on his having some. He thereafter revealed the true purpose of coming. "We had brought two beautiful young women from Choudhury's house", he said brazenly, " You may keep one of them but you must let me have the other one."

Raghunath instantly guessed in what direction Mayadhar's evil mind worked.

"You know that one of them is in the king's palace, the other one is with me. You can have the latter", he said agreeably.

"You are the chief—you have a claim over the elder one. I want the one you have sent to the palace. I had my eyes on her from the very beginning. But before I could speak to you you sent her to the palace. You can write a letter to the king requesting him to hand the girl over to me."

Raghunath disliked the unabashed manner in which Mayadhar stated his intention. He could understand that the fellow lusted for the younger girl. So strong was Mayadhar's desire for the girl that he was not able to put her out of his mind during his stay at his village, Raghunath thought. He did not hesitate to stop at Raghunath's house to discuss the subject with him even though the king had urgenty sent for him. But he did not show any sign of displeasure that welled within him and said, " I cannot do that. You see, I have left her in the charge of the king. It wouldn't be decent on my part to ask the king to hand her over to you. You can make a request to the king yourself."

Such an answer disappointed Mayadhar. Soon his disappointment turned into anger. "Why can't you ask the king yourself?" He demanded indignantly. "You haven't informed the king about the other maiden and brought her here. Did you seek our consent at that time? You have taken advantage of your position as the chief of the gang and acted on your own. Well, what has happened has happened. But if you don't write a letter to the king I shall bring the truth to his notice" , Mayadhar said threateningly.

One often acts the way one thinks. There is often a harmony between the thoughts and actions of an individual. Mayadhar had lied to Raghunath that the king had sent for him. He had anticipated that that Raghunath would not agree to his proposal and ask the king to let him have the girl. He had hoped that in the worst case such a threat could force Raghunath to write the letter. But Raghunath was not one who would yield to unjust demands. Nor was he a man who would get easily scared. He had his own reasons for not revealing to the king the fact that Kalavati was with him and he was fully prepared to explain everything to the king in case he was called upon to give an explanation. Madhara's threat did not frighten him in the least. "You can do so if you like", he said firmly and strode away in the direction of the river. A frustrated and furious Mayadhar hurried towards Kujanga intending to expose Raghunath before the king.

***

CHAPTER-31

The Invitation

Mayadhar's hard words had surprised and hurt Raghunath. He knew the fellow's ways and tried to remain watchful and alert lest he should bring harm to somebody through his sinister designs. Still he had never expected that Mayadhar could go to this extent to fulfill his perverted intentions. 'Only malicious ones like Mayadhar rush in to swallow fire', Raghunath thought to himself. 'Was it not ridiculous that a rogue like Mayadhar would hope to own the gem of a maiden like Rasakala?'

Raghunath had spent a long week nursing Kalavati and sitting by her bed. Though his worries were not over yet, he felt a little relieved since Kalavati had regained consciousness last night. He was in a comparatively relaxed mood and wanted to take a bath in the river. He was glad to see Mayadhar waiting at the door and expected that the few exchange of a few pleasantries with him might calm his agitated mind. But his hope was cruelly belied. Raghunath did not fear in the least that a man like Mayadhar would be able to bring any harm to him. But he felt a little disturbed thinking that the foolish fellow might get caught in the very trap he has set for his rival. Raghunath could not hold back his laughter as he stood reflecting upon the mischevious yet stupid way Mayadhar's mind worked, and watched him stride away in the direction of Kujanga.

For the last six or seven days it was difficult to make Kalavathi swallow even a spoonful of medicine let alone any diet or liquid food. She had survived on only a few spoonfuls of water and milk. She had begun to recover since last night. By noon the next day indications of recovery could be noticed in the patient. She was given a liquid diet of rice-paste and milk. She drifted into sound sleep after she was given the food. All these kindled the hope of her fast recovery in Raghunath's heart. After that long, stressful week, for the first time that day Raghunath ate with relish. The rice and curry that had tasted so unsavory during the whole of the last week, now seemed to have acquired a divine taste. He felt that he had never eaten such delicious food in his entire life. Who could say what magic flavour Destiny had added to the ordinary dishes that day that they tasted incredibly delicious? Raghunath's mother was glad to see him eat with contentment after so many days. She was afraid that her son had lost his appetite and cared little for food. She could guess that the patient's condition had improved. "Raghu, how is the patient?" She inquired.

" It appears that the fever has come down to some extent", Raghunath replied politely. The answer satisfied the old woman. She joined her palms in reverence and prayed to God for the well-being of her son. She also prayed to Him to rid her of her own painful, burdensome life soon.

The world is a difficult place to live in. Death is the only certainity in this world where everything else seems uncertain. But sometimes to some people death comes as a blessing. How every mother wishes to be outlived by her children! How earnestly does she pray to God to take away her own life first! For a mother her son is priceless and she begs God to transfer all the happiness she is entitled to and even the remaing part of her own life own life-span to her son's lot. Sometimes it is seen that Death ruthlessely snatches this 'more precious than life' son from his mother. Such a blow tears the mother's heart apart. Unable to bear the sorrow she begs for death as the separation from her most dear son renders her life totally meaningless. But we all know that no amount of grieving and tears can deter Death. Nor would it stop in response to our entreatment or appeal.

Only Time can heal the wound inflicted by the loss. When a mother that suffers from the loss of her 'more precious than life' son wails loudly beating her heart in a frenzy of grief

and pitifully begs life to leave her body, no solace would calm her down. It is only Time that has the power to harden her heart into rock. The heart that sometimes fails to bear even the slightest grief gets as strong as steel and can brace hundreds of such cruel assaults of Fate. There are instances of people succumbing to minor or slight ailments. But the mother that so earnestly desires to quit this grim, cheerless world is not able to kill herself despite her efforts to shatter her heart with such forceful beatings. Merciless Fate leaves her alone to go through the pain, to experience the bitter pangs of her irreparable loss. Time, too, does not spare her; it compels her to perform her worldly duties. This is the way of the world. One is not spared his or her share of work just because one is forced to go on living. The world grows sterner in its demands.

Readers, won't you agree now that the world is really a difficult place to live in?

Raghunath's mother had experienced the bitter sorrow of losing her beloved daughter-in-law; but she had lived on. Life had not taken pity on her miserable plight. Life treats everyone equally while exacting its dues. It might be possible to pay what one owes to the king by selling one's material possessions, but it is not easy to settle the accounts of life even after giving our last breath to it. Raghunath's mother had never been miserly in offering her sincere prayers to God asking Him to take away her life, Death would not release her from the coils of mortal life until the time came. She, however, had not failed to realize that it was more than she could ask for to have her son with her in the last phase of her life and she offered her heartfelt gratitude to Lord Almighty for having been so kind to her. Her son was her most valuable possession; she wanted nothing for herself. All she wanted was that her son should live a happy and long life. She was happy because her son had eaten with relish after so many days and because his labours had finally brought in positive results. She ate a frugal meal herself after making offerings of food to Lord Vishnu, and went inside to lie down and rest. Raghunath sat by his mother as she ate and spread out the bed for her. The satisfaction she derived from the way her son took care of her made her bless him from the bottom of her heart. There was no doubt that such blessings would not only increase his life-span many more times but would fill it with real happiness.

Who could nurse his mother with such dedication? Who could endeavour to pay back a debt which actually is unrepayable? Who could see the image of invisible God in his mother and glorify his life by worshipping her? The pages of our sacred texts are filled with innumerable instances of dedicated mother-worship. But we are now living in difficult times. In these days no son cares to turn the pages of such texts; if someone cares to cast a look at them, the changing times wipe them soon out of his memory. The present time is full of instances of old and ailing mothers being beaten by their sons, of mothers living an uncared-for life in the houses of their sons. There are sons who let their mothers starve. Some ungrateful sons abandon their mothers to their fate whereupon the poor mothers suffer from indescribable misery. Sons who bring glory to their families as well as set an example for the world through dedicated service to their parents are rarely found in modern times. Dear readers, won't you agree with me?

It is foolish to hope that people will try to preserve the age-old moral virtues and bring glory to their families as well as to the society through the noble act of mother-worship in an age which tends to steer us away from the path of morality and spiritualism. Fortunate is the son that holds the name of his family high and sets an example for posterity through the noble act of serving his parents even in this modern age that encourages perversity.

When he was satisfied that his mother was enjoying a sound, peaceful sleep, Raghunath went back to Kalavati's room. She had been fast asleep for more than three hours and it was a good sign. Raghunath, his heart relieved of worries, spread out a mattress on the floor and stretched his tired body on it. As his mind kept flitting from one thought to another, Raghunath drifted into a light sleep. But he could not sleep for long since worries about Kalavati's health loomed constantly oppressed his mind. He woke up abruptly and found Kalavathi awake. He felt guilty for having fallen asleep leaving the patient unattended for some time. A man of Raghunath's nature was likely to feel that way although there was nothing wrong in taking a short nap. It could have been an exhaustive exercise for anyone to spend seven sleepless days and nights at a stretch and people might have thought of him as someone abnormal had he not felt the need for some sleep. But since Raghunath was an uncomplicated and simple-minded person, he felt ashamed of this and hurriedly went out of the room in order to fetch a little milk for the patient. He came back carrying a small bowl of milk; he sat by Kalavati and tried to make her drink it.

Since the time she had taken a look at Raghunath last night, Kalavathi's mind was caught in a turmoil. She had never known of any incident of a dead husband returning to life. She had ,however ,heard about Savitri whose chastity could bring back her husband from the clutches of death. But such characters existed somewhere in the distant past. It was a dream-like experience for her to come across a man who nursed her with the loving care with which a husband usually looks after his sick wife. His name was Raghunath; it was the name of her dead husband. Compelled by a curiosity to discover a semlance of her dead husband's appearance in him, Kalavati stole frequent glances at him. She could feel his closeness as Raghunath sat by her bed attending to her needs, and the desire to keep looking at his face seemed almost irrepressible. She began to visualize her own husband Raghunath in him and her mind as though it was under the influence of some spell began to conjure up one fanciful picture after another. She felt she was drawn closer and closer towards this good-natured, caring, handsome stranger as if some supernatural force pulled at her. She was utterly powerless to offer the slightest resistance to whatever Raghunath did.

Raghunath sat by her, half-raised her from the bed holding her hand gently. He placed her head on his left shoulder and fed her milk. Overwhelmed with a sense of gratitude that had rendered her powerless to protest Kalavati drank the milk as if she lay under a spell. The sincerity with which her heart uttered silent prayers for the well-being of this kind-hearted stranger must have been heart-felt. After she drank the milk, Raghunath gently laid her down on the bed. In no time Kalavati fell fast asleep. As Raghunath kept gazing at her face and at the same time offering his thanks to God Almighty, someone knocked on the front door. Raghunath went quickly to the front room and opened the door. Outside the door stood a messenger from the king of Kujanga. Raghunath let him in and closed the door. The messenger handed him a letter which he said had come from the king himself. Raghunath opened the letter and went through its contents. The letter said that the king had not met Raghunath for a long time and that made him unhappy. The letter also carried an invitation from the king asking Raghunath to have a mid-day meal with him. Raghunath was a hospitable man and he gave the messenger some refreshments to eat. He also wrote a humble reply to the king's letter. In that letter he apologised for not having presented himself before the king during all those days because he had to attend a patient at home. The patient was recovering fast and he would present himself in the royal palace within a few days. He sent back the man to the palace with the letter and returned to Kalavathi's room.

**

CHAPTER-32

Khadanga

Duman Sardar completed the investigation and sent a report to the Subadar. Khadanga too was sent back in the custody of the security guards to be presented in the court of the Subadar. Khadanga knew in his heart that he was totally innocent. He had an inkling that the report of Duman Sardar had said the same thing. All this had aroused a hope in him that he would be acquitted of the charges that were brought against him. This hope had emboldened him considerably. The presence of his family members who had accompanied him to Cuttack also relieved him from anxiety to some extent. Nevertheless, the human mind has a tendency to analyse things from a negative angle. Hence, time and again, Khadanga anxiously wondered what would happen to his old mother and his wife and children in case the Subadar pronounced him guilty. He felt dizzy when he thought of it; but the next moment he tried to calm his agitated heart by offering up prayers to God and completely surrendering to His will.

But his wife and his mother could not do that. Nothing could console them or allay their fears. Their faces were streaked with tears from constant weeping. They thought that one would need the accumulated piety and righteousness of seven earlier lives to be free from the vicious grip of the Subadar, who was as cruel as a serpent. Though they knew that the report of Duman Sardar declared Khadanga innocent they had no hope of aquittal until such time the Subadar declared him so.

The Subadar was seething in anger eversince he had heard of the disaster that befell Choudhury. In a frenzy of rage he had sworn to destroy everyone whom he believed to be responsible for it. People who were closely associated with him were aware of the Subadar's wrath, but the outsiders had no no exact knowledge of the magnitude and the intensity of the Subadar's anger. A ruler must be impartial and judicious. It was difficult to believe that a man that holds the scepter could abuse his power to such an extent in order to satisfy his selfish whims. The Subadar was as belligerent as a ferocious beast whose prey was snatched away from under its nose. Such a man could go to any length to carry out a personal vendetta. The people of the land he ruled over had been instrumental in blocking the source of a lavish income by eliminating the Choudhury. Would the rapacious, vengeful Subadar spare them? In fact he had no intention of extending any help to the famine-stricken masses. His cruel callousness had pushed them to the brink of a 'death-in-life' like existence. What could have been a worse punishment than that? The only befitting punishment would probably have been to massacre the people and douse the rising flames of the rebellion. That perhaps would have been preferable to the corroding hunger and the abject poverty they suffered from.

Dasa Khadanga was brought before the red-eyed, wrathful Subadar like a sacrificial animal. The blood flowing in his veins seemed to have been sucked out by the terror he experienced at that moment. But the Subadar's blood that was boiling brought a hard glitter to his red-rimmed eyes. Khadanga's mother and wife waited under a tree that stood nearby. They watched helplessely the terrified, miserable-looking Khadanga. Dreadful anticipations about what was going to happen to their dear one had rendered them life-less. When Khadanga was brought to the court a large number of curious bystanders assembled there to hear what verdict the Subadar pronounced. Almost everyone knew that the burglary in the village Navagram was committed by the Bhuyan dacoits of Kujang. People around were convinced of Khadanga's innocence and it an undercurrent of sympathy flowed through every heart.

None of these things touched the hard-hearted Subadar. He had always kept himself aloof from his subjects, nor did he have any interest in listening to their views or opinions. Only he knew how he discharged the duties of a ruler.

May be excessive greed had drained the sap of humanity from his heart. He shook in fury the moment his eyes fell on Khadanga. "This man is responsible for the death of Choudhury", he thundered. Everyone was shocked out of his wits. The guard could not summon up enough courage to give the report of Duman Sardar to the Subadar. The Subadar kept quiet for some time and then spoke again, " Had Duman Sardar sent a report?", he asked grimly. The guard handed him the report without uttering a word.

The Subadar went through the contents of the report several times. But it did not cool the heat of his anger. Instead it grew more terrifying by the minute as the wrath of a serpent does at the sight of its captive. " Duman Sardar--- a most incompetent person!", he shouted. So frantic was he in anger that he was not able to articulate his accusations clearly nor could he recollect their exact terms. He called out for the guard in a loud voice; the guard appeared almost immediately. " Send this man to the scaffold", he commanded.

Disaster!! The crowd was stunned. The cruel command struck Khadanga like a bolt of lightning. His body stiffened and became hard like a log of wood. He fell down and lost consciousness. His wife and mother who stood watching let out a loud scream and threw themselves on the ground. The two kids were stupefied with fear. Then they began screaming at the top of their voices. Their loud screams turned the atmosphere even more horrifying. All the people who had gathered at the spot were filled with sympathy for poor Khadanga and his family. "Make them get up", "Make them get up", the Subadar shouted to the guards. The guards hurried to raise the fallen bodies and found that there was no life in any one of them. The guards reported the deaths of Khadanga, his mother, and his wife to the Subadar. " Throw the bodies in the river", he gave said and dismissed the court. Then he went inside the villa.

Outside, there was a commotion. The Subadar, had he remained there longer, probably would have got physically assaulted by the angry crowd. But before people could reach a unanimous decision on how to avenge the death of poor Khadanga, the Subadar bolted and locked the front door of the villa. The loud noise outside finally died down and people left the place one by one. The guards threw the three bodies in the waters of river Kathjori. The unfairness of the justice meted out to them would never be alleviated by the clear, cool waters of the river. The currents swept away the bodies farther and farther and finally they were lost to view. But wherever they were seen by people they sparked off a flame of vengeance which, as Fate had decreed it, led the Subadar to his doom.

And what of the two little children?--- Those twin pictures of innocence? What happened to them? They were unable to grasp what had happened and looked blankly at the scene that unfolded before their tear-filled eyes. When the enormity of the loss registered itself in their simple minds they began to wail loudly. Tears of anguish poured down from their eyes.

Oh cruel Fate!! How could you allocate such a great sorrow to these guileless children's lot? Who could give an answer? Was it the retribution for some vile act committed in their previous life? Is this how Destiny makes human beings pay for their evil deeds of earlier lives? No explanation other than this could have been plausible to justify the mishap that befell these two at such a tender age. God Almighty! It is believed that every incident, auspicious or inauspicious, that occurs on this earth eventually brings in some good consequences for mankind. Perhaps the Lord intends something good which lay hidden behind this painful incident and which we, ignorant mortals are unable to see.

Readers, words would fail to describe the sorrows and sufferings of those two little children. there was a guard in the villa who was mourning the loss of his only son who had died a few days back. He took pity on the two orphans and brought them to his own house. He thought that perhaps this would make him forget the loss of his own child, and the pangs his bereaved wife suffered might get assuaged a little when she would see them.

***

CHAPTER-33

A Happy Coincidence

Readers, I can guess that you don't want to spend any more time with the cruel, heartless devil of Lalbagh. Let us come back to the holy and tranquil house of Raghunath located on the banks of the sacred river, Luna. It is true that everything, good or bad, comes to,pass in this world in accordance with the will of God. Yet it is not easy for human beings to witness tragedies like one that took place in the previous chapter. Only a person with a heart made up of stone might bring himself to watch such scenes of abject cruelty. We have no words to describe one who commits such heinous acts.

Kalavati fully recovered from her illness within a couple of days since we had last seen her. Only the physical weakness remained, and it was expected that she would take some more time to overcome it. But the care and nursing of Raghunath and the treatment she received instilled a lot of energy in her and in another few days she was able to get up and move about without assistance. The medicine and diet she had been given must have acted on her illness with exceptional effectiveness. But it was the care and attention she received that really worked the miracle. Good medicines would not suffice unless accompanied by proper diet and careful nursing. Good medicines and diet sometimes fail to cure a patient. But, combined with love and care, they can fight the severest of diseases.

Kalavti became aware of the presence of a third person in the house. From the way Raghunath talked and took care of the older woman, it was not difficult for her to guess that she was his mother. When she could move about on her own she went to the old lady and paid her respects to her, as women usually do, by taking the dust off her feet and rubbing it on her own forehead. She addressed the old lady 'mother' and prayed to her to consider her (Kalavati) as her daughter. She began to look after the old lady with as much care as her strength would permit. Kalavati saw Raghunath every day as long as her sickness kept her confined to the bed. But soon after she got well she spent most of her time with the old lady. There were now few opportuniesnot for meeting him alone. Raghunath was pleased with Kalavati's guileless and pleasant manners. One evening as he was taking his meal, Raghunath told his mother and Kalavati of the invitation from the king. He set off for Kujanga very early the next morning.

The king's messenger had carried back Raghunath's reply to Kujang. Raghunath in his letter had mentioned that he would be coming to the palace in four days' time. The king went to the inner wing to inform his chief queen about it. The royal couple, thereafter, set about making arrangements for a fabulous treat for their guest.

Rasakala, of course did not have an inkling of all these developments. She roamed about in the ladies' wing of the palace radiating the glow of her ethereal beauty. Rasakala exchanged pleasant words with everyone and therefore there was not a single resident in the inner-wing of the palace who was not fond of her. Her good demeanour and winning manners had charmed everyone. There were instances of the king's instructions being ignored, but Rasakala's wishes never went unfulfilled.

Four days passed swiftly in making hectic arrangements. The fifth day arrived. The Sandha king was expecting Raghunath any moment. Though it was not particularly necessary the king had given strict instructions to the sentries posted at the palace-gate to inform him as soon as Raghunath arrived. The chief queen kept on moving in and out of her royal apartment to inquire if Raghunath had arrived. A short while after ten o'clock Raghunath approached the massive Lion's Gate of the palace. The atmosphere of the the entire palace starting from its main entrance to the other side of the ladies' wing grew astir with excitement. The ladies of the palace had no knowledge of the guest's identity. The arrangements that went on in the inner wing under the personal supervision and care of the chief queen, however, had made them guess that the invited guest must be a close friend of the king, that all the preparations were made to honour him. They understood that the king and his guest would eat together in the chief-queen's apartment. When they noticed the joy of the chief queen on hearing the news of the guest's arrival they got extremely curious and hurried out of their chambers to have a look at the guest much in the same way as women rush out of their houses to see the bridegroom in a marriage procession. It was too much of an effort to repress their eager excitement and wait to see him dine with the king. Raghunath approached the king and greeted him courteously. The king stepped down from his throne and took him in his arms as if he had received some priceless treasure. He sat Raghunath by his own side and made enquiries about his well-being. Raghunath was moved and felt gratified at the extraordinary manner in which he was received; the show of such great love and affection touched him deeply. He wanted to know the reason for which the king had invited him. The king replied that it was the sincere wish of not only the king but also the chief queen that Raghunath would share a meal with the king in the chief queen's apartment. The cordial request of the chief queen combined with the king's affectionate persuasion overwhelmed Raghunath: he felt he was a bonded slave, who waited eagerly to act as per the royal couple's wish in order to please them. "Let us go to the inner wing and dine", the king suggested.

"Whatever Your Highness says!", said Raghunath. " Your Highness has not eaten till now on account of me. How can I refuse?"

The king sent orders to the ladies' palace that food should be served. The dishes were served according to the instructions and under the personal supervision of the chief queen. I cannot restrain myself from saying a few things to the readers in this context. The opportunity to have food in the chief queen's own quarters, cooked and served under her special care, was rarely available to the king.The king, mostly, ate his meals in the main dining-hall of the palace, sometimes alone, or sometimes along with his trusted counsellors. There were special and trained cooks who prepared several types of delicious dishes in the main royal kitchen and served them; there were a number of attenders too who waited upon the king while he ate. There were separate kitchens for the chief queen and other royal ladies dwelling in the inner wing of the palace. Besides, the chief queen could not afford to remain present most of the times when the king took his food. I, personally, wouldn't prefer to eat in such an impersonal and formal environment even though the food is divinely delicious and served in a royal style. In my opinion, a man that belongs to a middle class or poor family, enjoys his food better when his loving wife brings him some milk in a bowl and sits by him fanning it. Sometimes while she fans her husband while he eats the wife waves the hand-fan to drive the naughty cat away that keeps mewing and obstinately waits for an opportunate moment to snatch a piece of fish away from its master's plate. She fondly forces her husband to have one or two extra helpings of food. Readers, you must have seen a poor farm-hand who toils in the corn-field from morning till noon. He comes home at mid-day, rubs oil all over his body and takes a bath. After this he sits down to have his meal. His wife carefully puts in a bowl some waterd rice and places it before him. She brings in some salt and fried greens to go with the watered rice. She waits upon her husband while he eats that simple meal with great relish, and lovingly persuades him to have a little more. At that time the poor man must be feeling as happy as Lord Indra, the king of heaven.He forgets that he is a mere labourer. The royal food, though much more rich and delicious, cannot bring so much pleasure and satisfaction. Readers, I don't want to eat in a impersonal and formal environment like the kings do. Let the kings and emperors enjoy their royal food. I don't envy them.

When the dishes were served the chief queen invited the king and his guest to come in. Both entered the room and took their seats. Rasakala, following the chief queen's instruction laid a number of dishes on expensive plates and bowls in front of them. It was customary in the palace that such large quantities of food were served to the royal personages and their guests that they wouldn't feel the need of a second helping. It so happened sometimes that the food that remained uneaten would be sufficient to feed four more people. The chief queen might have sat there attending the king while he ate as it was customary for the host to wait upon the invited guest. But Raghunath was supposed to be her would-be son-in-law. Hence she sat behind the half open door and instructed Rasakala how to serve the food. But Rasakala, who often waited upon the king as he ate, sat a little away from them and fondly slapped the naughty cat that would not leave the place despite several warnings.

The invitation from the king, eating in a royal environment while the princess herself served the food, the cordiality of the chief queen---all these combined made Raghunath feel a little heady. He had left the unconscious Rasakala in the palace and left in a hurry. He did not have an opportunity to take a good look at her. He could not recognize Rasakala who now looked like a princess in rich garments and with valuable ornaments. Raghunath knew that he was the king's guest. He was also aware that it would be indecorous and improper to cast frequent glances at the princess. But her delicate gestures, her stunning beauty and her gorgeous apparel cast a spell over him and he could not desist from stealing a few glances at her. But those few glances were not enough to quench the thirst in his eyes. The more he looked at her the fresher and newer she appeared. His eyes failed to fathom the infinite novelty of her beauty.

As they continued to eat the king asked Raghunath, " You said in the letter that there was a patient at your home. Who was that patient? Is your mother sick?"

"No, no my mother is all right." Raghunath answered hastily. " Another lady was seriously ill."

"Who could be that other lady in your house?" The king expressed his curiosity.

"Your Majesty does not know her", Raghunath replied humbly. "I had brought another lady from Navagram."

Rasakala sat upright; she became alert and guessed from their conversation that the lady that was discussed was Kalavati, her dearest friend. She looked at Raghunath's face with eager expectancy.

"But you haven't told me about the second lady", the king said, a little surprised. "By the way , do you recognize this lady? She is the one you have left in the palace that day. Her name is Rasakala."

Rasakala blushed and pulled the veil over her face. She tried to hide her excitement by hitting the cat softly. "Often Rasakala asked us about a lady called Kalavati whom she said she loved more than her sister. But since we had no idea about Kalavati's whereabouts we tried to calm her anxiety telling her all manner of lies.. The lady at your house must be Kalavati. Is she all right?"

"I thought it wouldn't be wise to keep both of them at one place. So I had taken her to my house. She was more seriously ill than her friend was. But by the grace of God she has been completely cured. A little weakness is there but that will go soon." Raghunath explained.

The news of Kalavati's illness had terribly upset Rasakala, but she felt relieved when she heard that her dear Kalavati had recovered. There rose an irrepressible desire within her to meet Kalavati.

"Rasakala, did you hear that? Your *apa* is all right. Do

you want to see her?" the king asked Rasakala affectionately.

" If Your Majesty will be kind to allow that", Rasakala
replied modestly.

Rasakala's humble reply pleased the king. "Pattanaik,
send Kalavati here next week after she feels a little better. It
is high time the two sisters met each other." He said.

Raghunath kept quiet. The king waited for some time
and continued: "You have now seen Rasakala. She does not
seem to be a creature of this world. She is beautiful like
some nymph of heaven. We are looking after her as our
own daughter. So virtuous and so full of good qualities she
is that she could be compared to goddess Lakshmi. You
have lost your wife. I myself and the chief queen sincerely
wish that you accept her as your wife. Be happy and make
your old mother happy by fulfilling her wish."

Raghunath could not bring himself to say anything
to the king. He was caught in a difficult situation. He had
made up his mind to marry Kalavati. But he could never
dream of hurting the feelings of the king, who seemed to be
very eager to give Rasakala in marriage to him. He decided
that it would make him appear ungrateful if he expressed
his reluctance to the king and the queen. He thought for a
while and said, "I will think about it."

But such a noncommittal reply did not satisfy the
king. "That won't do, Pattanaik", the king persisted. " You
can't escape saying 'I will think about it'; we shall not let
you go unless you promise to marry Rasakala."

What a dilemma!! Man wants something. But God
determines what must happen in this mortal world. Raghunath was in two minds: but he did not have the moral

courage to reject the proposal of the king and the queen, who had been so kind to him. 'May Destiny take its own course', he thought resignedly.

"How can I go against the commands of Your Majesty?" he said finally with a lot of effort.

The ladies in the inner wing of the palace secretly watched the king and his guest through the lattices and small windows. When they heard the conversation between the king and Raghunath they raised a cry --- ' Rasakala's groom' and others joined them instantly to have a look at the groom. The news rapidly spread every the nook and cornor of the palace.

How did Rasakala react to this? Do the readers remember that in one of the earlier chapters Kalavathi teased Rasakala saying that the *Naib* who sat in the palanquin was so handsome that she(Rasakala) would want to marry him. Raghunath was the man who had been sitting in the palanquin on that night, though Rasakala was yet to know this. But she was totally charmed by the handsome appearance of Raghunath. She pretended not to have heard the conversation between the king and Raghunath relating to her marriage with him and gave the cat a couple of blows with a small stick.

After they finished eating the king and Raghunath accepted the *paan* from the queen and came out of the ladies' wing. The auspicious ululations of the ladies that prayed to God for the well-being of Rasakala made the inner wing resound.

***

CHAPTER-34

Kalavati Alone

After Raghunath left for Kujang, Kalavati and Raghunath's old mother were alone in the stone –house on the bank of river Luna. It has been mentioned earlier that, after she rallied a little, Kalavati had set about in looking after Raghunath's mother. Because Raghunath was not at home Kalavati took extra care of the old woman. The old woman found that Kalavati surpassed her son much behind in her sincerity and concern.

She had earlier wished to have Kalavati as her daughter-in-law, and she believed that her marriage with Raghunath would make the life of her son change for the better. Driven by an indomitable curiosity to know Kalavati's past the old lady asked her a number of questions when she found Kalavati alone. But she was utterly disappointed on learning that Kalavati was a widow. "If she had not been a widow!!" The old lady thought wistfully; "Raghunath loves her dearly —probably he does not know that she is a widow. Alas! Why does God Almighty mete out such cruel punishments to virtuous maidens like this one?" Raghunath's mother, with a heavy heart, accused God of injustice and decided to have a detailed discussion with her son after he returned from the king's palace.

The Hindu 'Shashtras' forbid widow-marriage. The old lady would never permit Raghunath to marry a widow in her own lifetime. She wanted to probe at Kalavati's mind, to find out if she desired to marry again.

"I am your daughter, and that makes Raghunath my brother. God had inflicted the punishment of widowhood on me----you need not ask me about remarriage. I have never thought of it." Kalavati replied innocently. The old lady was glad to hear this; she would, of course, have been glad to have Kalavati as her daughter-in-law. But a wise reply of this kind from a girl who suffered the pangs of widowhood at such a tender age, filled her heart with a feeling of deep contentment.

Kalavati had lost her husband; her friendship with Rasakala ,to a certain extent, could mitigate the agony of that loss. She had hoped to derive peace of mind by getting this caring friend of hers married to a suitable young man. But Destiny had willed otherwise; she was once more flung into an ocean of loneliness, drifting aimlessly thrashed by its cruel waves. She found a little respite from the tormenting loneliness in nursing the old woman. But who would want to live in this world without hope, alone and friendless? Her instincts told her that Raghunath was in love with her. But she recoiled from the idea, even though his name, his manners and his voice constantly brought her dead husband back to her mind.

How beautiful the world would have appeared had her dead husband really come back to life!! How the widows unduly punished by God would have thanked Him for getting back their husbands they believed that they had lost forever! Would that have put God in too much of trouble? But this would never happen. Kalavati could have lived her life happily with her husband had he, like the mythical character Satyavan, returned to life. But her husband had not returned. Then how could she accept another man as her husband just because he had the same name, had a voice and behaviour that matched her husband's. Besides, Kalavati believed strongly that a widow should kill herself by drinking poison rather than marry again. She was always trying to invent one way or other to escape the loving glances of Raghunath.

The sincerity with which Raghunath had nursed Kalavati during her illness and saved her life certainly deserved the utmost sacrifice in return. But one must not violate the moral code to fulfill one's duty. If Raghunath wanted to marry her she would rather prefer to drown herself. But she felt restless apprehending that Raghunath might kill himself if she did that. There is nothing more heinous than the crime of being the cause of the death of the one who saved your life. All these disturbing thoughts caused a severe agitation in Kalavati's heart.

On the other hand, Raghunath was planning to marry Kalavati. He knew of Kalavati's past before he set about the burglary. He had no inhibitions about marrying a widow like most of the young men of these days who have come under the influence of the western civilization. Moreover, Raghunath thought, Kalavati was widowed in her childhood. Her nature and conduct appeared to have an ethereal grace about them. Raghunath felt that Kalavati was the gem of a human being and she should be given a place befitting her worth. He had reasoned that to pick up a gem from a place where its value is not recognized or appreciated wouldn't be a crime. He had made up his mind not to marry anyone except this gem of a woman even if the whole world opposed him. Because the Sandha King of Kujang compelled him , Raghunath couldn't find any alternative but to acquiesce reluctantly to the proposal, but he had taken a vow never to touch Rasakala.

He was also worried about his mother's reaction when she would come to know of her son's intention. He knew that the old lady would never give her consent to this marriage as long as she lived. Raghunath was ready to wait till his mother died; he would marry Kalavati after her death. but he was determined never to accept any woman other than Kalavati as his wife.

Alas!! Poor Rasakala had no idea of all this. Or else she would not have fallen in love with Raghunath the moment her eyes fell on him. We need not go into the details of Rasakala's longing for Raghunath. We had better turn our attention to Raghunath and Kalavati. Raghunath returned from Kujanga. He was on the look out for a propitious time to discuss the matter frankly with Kalavati and to find out what she thought. But she kept busy most of the time taking care of his mother. Raghunath hardly got an opportunity to meet her when she was alone.

Kalavati herselff was deeply disturbed. It has been earlier pointed out that she was caught in a dilemma that continued to torment her. At noon one day, after Raghunath's mother went to take her mid-day nap, she walked alone to the small garden near the riverbank. With a heart oppressed by the agony of indecision she sat there, her gaze fixed at the waterline at the far edge of the river and the mirage beyond it. Raghunath arrived there as though at the direction of Destiny and stood behind her. "Kalavati!" He called her softly.

***

CHAPTER-35

Opening Up of the Hearts

Kalavati gave a start when she heard her name uttered and found Raghunath standing so close to her. The sight of him filled her with an unspeakable agony at the sight of him. Why did cruel Destiny make this man a mirror image of her dead husband? Could the pain she experienced at his presence ever be put on paper? How could the agony of a hungry man who is not permitted to eat from the plate of food placed before him be expressed in words? She found herself in a difficult situation and cursed her decision to come to this solitary place all by herself at this lonely hour. Making an effort to appear calm she asked, " Brother, how is it that you are here at this time of the day?" The way she addressed him as "brother" gave Raghunath a jolt. He knew that Kalavati was a calm-tempered, intelligent girl. Until that moment, Raghunath had cherished the fond hope that Kalavati would have no objection to marrying him. But her addressing him as 'brother' smashed his hopes. He had never thought that Kalavati would call him 'brother'; his head whirled at the unexpected turn of events. He let out a deep sigh and sat down by her. "Kalavati, shall I really have to give up all hope?" He asked quietly. Kalavati was happy that her addressing Raghunath as 'brother' had had the desired impact on him. "What hope?" She asked, feigning ignorance.

His eyes cast downward, Raghunath answered haltingly, in a low voice.

"Kalavati you know that I have lost my wife. There is no point in telling things in a round about way. The moment I saw you I had decided to make you my wife and assuage the suffering of my mother who keeps worrying about me. There is no one in this world I could call my own. I have never felt so drawn to anyone since the time my virtuous wife left this world. What more shall I tell you, Kalavati! You resemble my wife in every respect. I was tempted to believe that God has created you for me!!" His voice choked and he broke into tears. Anxiously Kalavati wiped off his tears with the end-border of her sari and said consoling him: "Please, don't cry. The time has arrived to open our hearts to each other. Let us be honest to each other and relieve our hearts of the weight of our unspoken thoughts. The nectar-sweet words of Kalavati calmed Raghunath's agitated mind to some extent. " I had thought that a wife like you would make me forget all my sorrows. But you have addressed me as 'brother'. Kalavati, please tell me honestly what is in your mind." He entreated her.

"I have given it a lot of thought before calling you as my brother." Kalavati replied. "It is strange that God has given me the looks and nature that resemble those of your wife's. You too, remind me of my dead husband. Even you bear the same name. But it is impossible for a widow to marry again. A woman gives away her heart and soul and everything to the man she marries. And she can do that only once in her life. How can I offer you something I have already given to another man long back? You have rescued me from a great disaster; I owe my life to you. Knowing that I could repay a small part of that debt by being your wife,

I would never have declined your proposition but for this reason. Tears rolled down Kalavati's cheeks as she said this. Raghunath wiped her tears and said: " Kalavati, what is the harm if a widow remarries? Though it appears strange Destiny has given me the looks of your husband, and cast you in the same mould as my wife. We have to obey what is ordained by our Destiny."

"How can it be said with certainty that Destiny has ordained our marriage?" Kalavati said calmly. " My husband has abandoned his mortal body; but he exists. Death does not erase one's existence. My husband is not with me at present, but he exists in Heaven. I too shall leave this temporary abode and go back to my permanent Home and will be united with my husband there when my duties here are over. The purpose of my life will not be fulfilled if I marry you. God also would not want it to happen."

Raghunath could not reply to this. One who has faith in God never debates issues like this. He heaved a sigh and said: "It is all right, Kalavati, I shall not mention this ever again. I have not the slightest intention of bringing pain to someone like you. You deserve to live happily after having gone through such a tough time, and I honestly hope for that. If you do not want to accept my proposal I don't want to force my will on you and hurt you."

Raghunatth's words brought immense relief to Kalavati. " Brother, when I saw you for the first time I had wrongly believed that God has brought my husband back to me. But no amount of reasoning or argument can triumph over faith. I would always prefer death to acting against faith. But don't burden your heart. Everything will be well with us if God wills so."

Both fell silent. Both of them experienced the power

and glory of faith flooding into their hearts. The light that illuminated their hearts made their faces glow.

They remained immersed in their thoughts. Neither of them spoke for a while. Kalavati drew lines on the earth with a piece of straw. " Brother," she said after some time, "I have a younger sister named Rasakala. I miss her terribly. Can you tell me where she is now?" She looked expectantly at Raghunath.

Raghunath-	She is in the palace of the king of Kujanga.
Kalavati-	How did you know that she is in the palace? Have you heard this from somebody? Aren't things heard from others usually more false than true?
Raghunath -	I have seen her there.
Kalavati-	Yes, you told me that the king had invited you to his palace. Did you go to the inner wing of the palace? Brother, please tell me the truth. Have you really seen Rasakala there?
Raghunath-	The king himself had taken me to the ladies' wing. We ate together. Rasakasla herself served us food. She sat there and kept driving the cat away.
Kalavati-	Is my Rasakala all right?
Raghunatha-	She is perfectly well. The king is very fond of her.

The news of Rasakala made Kalavati feel relieved and happy. At the same time, she grew suspicious about the kind of work that kept Raghunath occupied. She knew that the Bhuyans were used to launch such raids in Navagram and other villages in the neighbourhood. When the walls of the Choudhury's house were demolished on that fateful fullmoon night of Pausha, they had guessed that the Bhuyan dacoits were carrying out the burglary. But before they realized what had happened both she and Rasakala had lost consciousness. After Kalavati recovered from illness she had discovered herself in Raghunath's home. But she constantly worried about Rasakala and had had many frightful apprehensions concerning the plight of her dear friend. Now she realized that the Bhuyans had given Rasakala as a gift to the king of Kujanga. But how did she herself reach at Raghunath's home? Was Raghunath one among the dacoits? Could it be ever possible that a handsome and generous person like Raghunath was involved in a despicable crime like burglary? Might be! Nothing is impossible in this strange world. Many such conflicting thoughts wrestled with one another in Kalavati's mind. She was brought here by a dacoit, lived in his house and owed her life to him!! And the dacoit was proposing to marry her!! She had to address a dacoit as 'brother' in order to express her gratitude to him. She is a dacoit's sister!! And she looked after him and his house!! The thought filled Kalavati with distaste. The tension and excitement of all these disturbing thoughts seemed to warm Kalavati's blood. She turned to Raghunath and called, "Brother, I shall put a question to you. Will you answer it honestly?"

Raghunath was a clever man. And a guilty mind is always suspicious. He had guessed what Kalavati was going to ask him. He nerved himself to tell her the truth and to see how she would react."Why should I tell you a lie? I have not till now committed the crime of telling lies." Raghunath said.

Kalavati :   Brother, I think you were there in that gang of robbers.

Raghunath: What makes you think so?

Kalavati :   How did I come here if you were not in that gang? Rasakala and I were together. The Bhuyans had taken her away. Why should they have left me alone? And if they had abducted me like her you would not have been able to rescue me from those dangerous dacoits.

Raghunath: Why? Am I not strong enough?

Kalavati: No. You may be very strong. But you are no match for them. In fact, no body is strong enough to fight them. Besides, if you had rescued me from the Bhuyans, wouldn't you have saved Rasakala, too?

Raghunath: It might be that I intended to rescue only one of you!

Kalavati sensed the hint the remark concealed and smiled softly.

"Brother, you are not being honest and trying to evade my question. All right, I shall not ask you anything more." She told him.

Raghunath smiled. "All right, all right, I shall not do this again. But give me your word that you won't tell this to anyone else."

Kalavati: Who is there in this world whom I can call my own and disclose to him any secret? Moreover, I owe my life to you. Could I ever be ungrateful to you?

Raghunath: Yes. I was there with the dacoits.

Kalavati: In whose honour the procession of light was organised? Was it actually to celebrate the occasion of the Naib's coronation that the ceremony took place?

Raghunath: I had impersonated the Naib. The procession of light was oraganised by us.

Kalavati: What was the purpose behind all this?

Raghunath: There were a number of the poor who were dying for want of work. The procession of light and the burglary were organised with the purpose to provide them some monetary help.

Kalavati: But, how could you appear in the guise of the Naib?

Raghunath: Look, it was the duty of the Subadar to enable his subjects to earn their livelihood. It was his duty to look after them, to take steps to ensure their welfare. He did not do this. Therefore, I had to do this even though in a different manner. Didn't that make me the Naib, his representative?

Kalavati: Do you mean to say the Subadar should have organiged a robbery to help his subjects?

Raghunath: He had failed to manage the affairs of the state. We would not have chosen this path had he been a just and a benevolent ruler. You know our people are devastated by a famine. He should have extended help to them at this hour of crisis. Since he did not do so we had to act on his behalf.

Kalavati: The purpose is no doubt a noble one. But in
              the process you have ruined the lives of some
              people. What do you have to say about this?

Raghunath: Those that are ruined were destined to meet
              with this fate. I must tell you that your father
              was a monster. He would not have been of any
              use to the suffering masses had he lived longer.
              He would not have spared a handful of grain
              for saving the lives of thousands and thou-
              sands of famine-stricken people. The riches he
              had amassed will now be used to save people's
              lives.

Kalavati: How can you claim that everything you did
              was predestined?

Raghunath: My dear Kalavati, man has the power to judge
              what is right and what is wrong. The two re-
              vered monks, Hanuman Das and Giridhari
              Das, agreed with us and gave us their bless-
              ings. God speaks through great men like those.
              And you must keep in mind that the dacoits
              never harm the good and the innocent.

Kalavati :   That monk Hanuman Das is our lord and our
              mentor.

              She touched her joined palms to her forehead
              as a token of reverence for the great monk, and
              continued,

Kalavati: No body has the power to disobey him. But can
              you deny that the famine is providential?

Raghunath: Of course it is!

Kalavati: Then you have to accept that God wills the

people to die in large numbers and therefore He has sent this famine to people. You are trying to save them by committing burglary. Are you not going against the will of God? Is it not a sin to disobey God?

Raghunath: You have a point there. We have also deliberated on this matter. No incident occurs without a purpose. Everything happens in this world according to the will of God. He has sent this disaster down to earth to teach a moral lesson to people. The burglary conducted by us is a part of God's design. Those who are destined to survive would be saved in this manner.

Kalavati: I see. And your people have also plundered the home of Rasakala. Haven't they?

Raghunath: Her parents were more inhuman and cruel than the beasts of prey. We have looted the wealth her parents have amassed, killed them, and left her at the king's palace. She belongs in a palace. She lives there looking as beautiful as a nymph and passes her days happily.

Kalavati: I am glad to know that she is well. Her cruel parents really deserved such an end. My father, too, must have died of shock seeing his house lying in ruins.

Raghunath: He is equally inhuman. He had hoarded great wealth using dishonest means working under that corrupt Subadar. He never hesitated to extort money from the poor subjects. He has met his end in the same manner you have just described.

Kalavati: Are you sure?

Raghunath: Yes, I have been informed about it.

Kalavati was a tender-hearted person. She began to shed tears at the news of the death of her father and Rasakala's parents who were in a way close to her family. "Why are you crying?" Raghunath asked as he wiped her tears with the end-border of his cloth. "He had brought me up after all." Kalavati said.

"Why do you think that he had brought you up? Raghunath said, consoling her. It was like some fine God imposed on him which he paid this way. The villain was never very fond of you, nor did you deserve to live in that miser's home. All the way from Cuttack to Navagram the villain had thought of nothing except his wealth. He was not at all worried about you, nor did the thought of what fate might have befallen you cross his mind for once.

Kalavati wanted to avoid any further discussion on the topic. She caught hold of Raghunath's hand and said imploringly: " Brother, please think of me as your own sister, and promise to me that you would not turn down the request I ever make."

"Kalavati, though you are younger than me, I shall regard you as my mentor from this day onwards. I believe that you must have been my sister in some previous life. In this life, too, you have come to me as my sister and taught me lessons on morality. I promise that I shall never refuse to do whatever you ask me to." Raghunath said with great sincerity.

These words of assurance from Raghunath made her extremely glad. "Your kind words have melted my heart." Kalavati said with relief. "Brother, you have no one at home to look after you and mother. It is my sincere wish that you marry Rasakala. Won't you accept this request?" She looked at Raghunath expectantly.

Raghunath had promised to the king that he would accept Rasakala as his wife. His loyalty and respect for the king had compelled him to make that promise. Here, at home, tender-hearted Kalavati brought up the subject again. Raghunath, intending to evade the matter, tried to change the course of the discussion. "Rasakala was worried about you. She became very happy on learning that you are here in my house and are convalescing. Both she and the king have invited you to the palace. You shall leave for Kujanga this week."

"I shall kill myself unless you give me word me that you will marry Rasakala. You promise that you will marry Rasakala and I shall never disobey you." Kalavati said firmly.

Raghunath found himself in a fix. But he knew that no man of flesh and blood could refuse to accept the request that guileless Kalavati made with those nectar-sweet words. He took Kalavati's hand in his own and promised: "Sister, Raghunath will always do as you say."

Kalavati's wish, at last, was fulfilled.

It was late in the afternoon. Thinking that Rahunath's mother might have woken up from her midday sleep, both came out of the garden and headed for the house. In the evening Kalavati came to Raghunath to remind him of the promise he had made to her. When she was reassured that he would not go back on his words, Kalavati handed a tiny, round gold-box to Raghunath. " Brother, keep it carefully under the waist-fold of your cloth." She said, "Ater you are married to Rasakala the two of you will sit together and open it." Raghunath took the gold-box, tucked it in the waist-fold of his cloth and nodded assent.

***

CHAPTER-36

Reunion of Sisters

The Sandha king of Kujanga had allowed the dacoits a respite of fifteen days after the raid at Navagram on the full-moon night of the month of Pausha. That period of rest over, brawny wrestlers like Bahabalindra, Baliarsingh and other dacoits presented themselves at the king's court. The fleet of jaliyas, and a number of boats equipped with arms and ammunitions ready to set out for a new expedition were kept moored in the moat surrounding the palace. The boatmen repaired and readied the oars and other gears for fresh adventure. They twisted one another's arms to test their strength. The king, aware that the dacoits would be setting out on another expedition that day, ordered to keep everything ready for the purpose, and waited for Raghunath.

A few hours before morning, Raghunath left his bed and finished his routine chores. He knew that he would lead the gang on a fresh mission that day. Taking leave of his mother, whom he had told earlier about the king's invitation, Raghunath set off for Kujanga with Kalavati. His mother had allowed Kalavati to accompany her son only after he convinced her that Kalavati would return home quite soon.

The palanquin stopped at the lion's gate of the palace. The air of Paradip resonated with the loud call "Victory to Lord Mahaveer" of the dacoits when Raghunath alighted. At the king's order the palanquin was borne into the inner wing of the palace.

Raghunath bent down to touch the king's feet. He put the dust off the king's feet on his forehead and proceeded along with his associates towards the moat where the boats were moored. As it was getting late, he bade farewell to the king and stepped into one of the big cargo boats. His associates also boarded the boats. When everyone was on board, Raghunath ordered the boatmen to weigh anchor. A loud cry "Hail Lord Mahaveer" that seemed to rend the sky rose from the boats. And before its echo died down the boats were well under way. Pushed forward by the wind, the large boats disappeared from the view in no time.

The king now returned to the palace.

The palanquin carrying Kalavati approached the entrance of the inner wing of the palace. The chief queen along with Rasakala and several royal ladies hastened to receive her. The chief queen and Rasakala, holding the right and left hand of Kalavati, helped her get down. As soon as she descended from the palanquin Kalavati placed her hand affectionately on Rasakala's head and shed tears. Rasakala, for her part, could not hold back her tears. Then she wiped Kalavati's tears and said soothingly: "Apa, why are you shedding tears? By God's grace we have been rescued from a disaster. Please do not cry any more." The surging tides of emotion that rose in Kalavati's heart made uttering words difficult. After a while the raging waves of grief calmed a little. "Rasa, I had lost all hopes of meeting you," she told softly.

The readers are well acquainted with the nature of

the chief queen. She has her own special ways of healing the hearts stricken with even the most intense grief. Her words soaked with affection, the tender look of love in her eyes, and her gentle behaviour could melt the hardest of hearts. How could Kalavati, a softhearted and guileless young girl, resist their magic effect? The chief queen lovingly led her to her chamber. She made her and Rasakala eat delicious dishes, and offered them the *paan* she had herself prepared. Kalavati was greatly touched with such gestures of the chief queen and her kind words. "No one but a mother is capable of giving such love and affection," she said and requested the queen to permit her to address her 'mother'as Rasakala did. The queen gladly allowed her to do so.

The joy of the chief queen who used to shower her motherly love even on birds and animals, knew no bounds when she found a daughter in Kalavati. After this Kalavati, like Rasakala, became quite friendly with the other ladies in the ladies' wing and roamed freely about the palace as if she has been born and brought up there.

Having been united with Rasakala, Kalavati experienced boundless joy. It would be no exaggeration to say that her world revolved around Rasakala. She had no one else in this world whom she could consider truly her own. Kalavati felt as if she had been rendered lifeless by the cruel hands of fate when she had lost that epitome of innocence, Rasakala. Neither of the two wanted to remain away from each other even for a moment after they came together.

The two girls spent the days together happily in the palace in each other's company. They talked of several things. On one such occasion when they were exchanging pleasantries, Rasakala narrated the incident of Raghunath's visit to the palace and of the promise he had made to the king that he would marry Rasakala. Kalavati was greatly happy to hear this. In due course, Rasakala had come to know every detail of the episode of the robbery at Nava-grama and about how Raghunath was seated in the palan-quin in disguise as the *Naib*. Kalavati remarked in jest, " Didn't I tell you that the *Naib* was so handsome that you would want to have him as your groom?" And Rasakala let out a soft, shy giggle.

Kalavati felt happy in the palace. But she could not afford to stay there for many days at a stretch leaving Ra-ghunath's old mother alone at home. Her days were, there-fore, divided between the palace and Raghunath's house. The varied experiences of joy brought a new flavour to her otherwise drab and dreary life.

***

CHAPTER-37

The Famine

Days followed one another. The dacoits in course of time had been able to hoard a large amount of grains and amass a lot of riches. Keeping pace with their success in accumulating the provisions, the shadow of famine, like clouds in the rainy season, spread from all directions and threw a shroud over the land. By the end of the month of Magha, want of work and hunger tortured the wage labourers and other poor people like them. They were compelled to come out to beg.

How precious food is indeed!! And how powerful hunger is!! As long as the stomach is filled with food, the world appears exquisitely beautiful. A man with a hungry stomach has no eyes for the beautiful things around him. An empty stomach renders the world empty of all its loveliness. A hungry man knows no love and affection, and tends to forget his responsibilities even towards his wife and children. It will be enough to say that the man with an empty stomach loses all hope and desperately prays for death.

When such men came out to beg and received alms to quench the burning hunger, they were extremely happy. The handful of alms seemed to bring them heavenly bliss. For some time, after receiving the alms, the love for their wives and children was aroused in their hearts. But it did not last long. The number of beggars grew day by day and alms were not adequate to meet their increasing need. To live became an agony; every village got filled with throngs of skeletal men. Hunger triumphed over the emotions of love and affection and people turned selfish. The husband did not hesitate to snatch food from his wife she had collected with great difficulty, and the hungry mother had no qualms about eating her child's share of food.

There is a saying in the *Hitopadesha* that one should not resort to sinful act on account of a hungry stomach. Perhaps the wise man that wrote this knew nothing at all about a calamity like a famine. And it was but quite natural. He had written this in an era when the kings were ruling judiciously over their kingdoms, and their prime objective was the welfare of the subjects. The kings of those days worked sincerely for the progress of their kingdoms and the welfare of their people and never neglected their responsibilities. Such dedicated and benign kings spread peace over the lands they ruled and made this beautiful world reflect the glory of God. When the king is virtuous his subjects are contented and peace pervades the land. At a time when people live happily under the efficient administration of a virtuous king, and when the environment is peaceful and the kingdom prospers, wise sayings like this sound pleasant to the ear and fill the mind with sacred thoughts. But when anarchy prevails on account of a ruler that is unjust, selfish and sinful, and neglects his moral responsibilities by ignoring the subjects, even God in heaven gets angry. He inflicts punishment in form of natural calamities like famine to teach the world a lesson in morality. When circumstances become harsh and countless people succumb to such calamities wise sayings seem utterly pointless. In troubled times, when these men come under the influence of the devil, they experience no qualms about killing their own beloved children and eating their flesh. What value do such sayings have in a kingdom that writhes under the crushing weight of a famine when parents are tempted to snatch food from their child's hands and devour it themselves? Can anyone afford to follow the path of morality prescribed by these sayings when disasters like famine drive parents to eat their child's flesh? History offers evidence that, in the past, starving people have gone to the extent of eating the flesh of all kinds of animal from horses to human beings. Even today, such incidents may be come across at some places. And who is to be held responsible for this? I can firmly say that the unjust acts of a king bring such peril down upon the kingdom. Our *Shastras* bear testimony to this.

The Subadar was enjoying sound sleep in his villa of Lalbag. The anguished cries of his subjects did not enter his ears. Most of the times, like a woman, he kept himself confined inside the villa. The death of Choudhury, his henchman, seemed to have broken him. It would not be improper to say that a sinner like the Subadar cannot find a place even in hell.

The month of *phalguna* had come to an end. The starving people were forced to consume inedible stuff and this led to the outbreak of an epidemic. The epidemic followed the famine close at its heel just in the manner wind accompanies a fire and claimed thousands and thousands of human lives. Who could be regarded more virtuous than one who stands by suffering people during the troubled times? Orissa had never before experienced so terrible a famine. Who would have come to the rescue of the famine-stricken people of Orissa when the Subadar himself slept snoring loudly in his massive and comfortable palace? However, the ways of Providence are beyond the comprehension of human beings. He has His own inscrutable ways of bringing about events. If He wills to destroy human lives, He adopts certain ways to do that. Similarly, He has His mysterious ways of sparing a few lucky ones if He considers them worth His mercy. Perhaps Raghunath Pattnaik, the chief of the dacoits, was among the few God had chosen to rescue such people. He was the one person that stood by the starving in the villages of Orissa. He should have been regarded the saviour of the people and not the chief of the dacoits. The merciful British Government, after conquering Burma, had coined the term 'dacoit' to specify certain categories of people there. Similarly, the Bhuyans of Orissa may be classified under some such category but by no means could they be looked upon from a negative perspective. It was the selfless and tireless efforts of these Bhuyans that sustained the people of Orissa during the difficult times. Thousands and thousands of people were saved from death only because of them.

Towards the middle of the month of *phalguna* at several places of the kingdom massive sheds were constructed where cooked and uncooked food were distributed to the starving masses. All the foodgrains collected through launching raids at the houses of wealthy men like Choudhury and Dasa, and grain bought subsidized price from generous landowners lay in heaps at these sheds. The dacoits also looted the granaries of those who refused to sell foodgrains at a lower price, though they spared their lives. These foodgrains also were transported to the sheds. Besides, the dacoits had donated their shares of the looted stuff to save the famine-stricken people of Orissa.

The hoard of food grains in the sheds was kept in the charge of the two monks we have spoken about earlier, Hanuman Das and Giridhari Das. The title 'Queen' was bestowed on Kalavati and the work of distributing food was carried on in her name. The work went on in a disciplined manner, and was smooth and unhindered. Kalavati had realized that this was the noblest act of philanthropy, and having accepted with willingness the task allotted to her, performed it assiduously. Both the monks knew her well; in fact it was they who had suggested that the title of 'Queen' be bestowed on her and put her in charge of this noble mission. The king of Kujanga and other royal personnel endorsed the proposal of the monks and requested them to bless Kalavati. She put the dust off feet of the monks on her forehead. They chose her as the one best suited to God's work: to save human lives by offering them food. The monks agreed to extend all possible help to her in fulfilling the noble task.

The food sheds were inaugurated after a sacred fire was lit on altars. The news of the opening of the food-sheds spread with the speed of lightning. Hundreds and hundreds of hungry men, women and children thronged there. The cooks prepared rice, dal and curry and served them to the hungry. This way, the cooks, too, earned their share of virtue through the noble deed of saving a large number of human beings from the clutches of death. When the hunger-worn, emaciated men blessed Queen Kalavati from the bottom of their heart and thanked God for His mercy on them, the sincerity of their emotion might have made His throne tremble.

Not satisfied with distributing food at the food-sheds, Raghunath Pattnaik, Duman Sardar and some others carried rice and other provisions to distant villages affected by the famine. They looked out for people rendered immobile by sickness and age and provided them with food and other amenities. Having received the help they thought they would never get, these old and sick people prayed to God to bless their benefactors.

In this manner, the dacoits exerted themselves to remove the difficulties and supply the wants of the victims of the famine. This way, help in various forms given to the needy was four times what the king might have arranged on his own without the support of the Bhuyans. But the famine had spread to most parts of the state and all this help was not enough to save thousands that succumbed to starvation every day. People died in such large numbers in every village that there was no one available to cremate the dead bodies. The bodies were left to rot. The rotting bodies contaminated the air and fatal diseases spread out that claimed of many more lives. There was no room even in the cremation ground for the bodies. The terrifying screeches and howls of the vultures and the jackals seemed to rend the air. People feared that God Almighty was determined to turn the earth into an enormous cremation ground.

Indeed, a world devoid of hope resembles a cremation ground. To those that had lost all hope in life the earth appeared to be a morbid place; some of them soon quitted this cheerless world and brought joy to vultures and jackals. By the sheer grace of God a few survived and, even though the world had turned into a cremation ground, they were miraculously saved from the jaws of death. It is his faith that sustains man in the hour of crisis. The same object can evoke different responses in different men depending upon the state of their minds. If there is hope in the heart the very same object might arouse a feeling very different from that aroused in a heart that is bereft of all hope. The month of *Baisakha* arrived and the heat of the summer grew intense. The price of grains increased beyond expectation. Even two *seers* of rice were not available at one rupee. It was difficult to keep count of the people that fell victim to starvation and to the epidemic that broke out in the months of *Baisakha* and *Jyestha*.

***

CHAPTER—38

The Subadar

Readers are well aware how inhuman and cruel Subadar Sambhujee Ganesh was. The loss of a trusted employee like Choudhury had affected him terribly. In addition to this the realization that he had caused perpetual woe to two women by sentencing the innocent Khadanga to death filled him with a sense of guilt. He was reluctant to come out of the villa or make a public appearance. The anxiety resulting from a mixed feeling of guilt, fear and shame forced him to keep himself confined to his villa and practically brought an end to his worldly happiness. When a ruthless administrator like the Subadar stopped appearing in his courtroom the employees grew unruly. As it was they were not getting their salaries on time. When they no longer felt the awe the Subadar used to inspire in them they became indisciplined. The court at the villa of Lalbagh remained virtually closed. All matters relating to the administration of the state were dealt with by Duman Sardar at his residence. Shambhujee Ganesh remained Subadar in name and experienced a hellish agony while Raghunath became the de facto ruler of the kingdom. The prophecy of the great Hanuman Das had been fulfilled.

The situation became grimmer as time passed. The subadar had no ears for the tales of woes of his subjects.

When the forbearance of the suffering people crossed all limits they conspired to set fire to the villa of the Subadar. At many places the starving people tried to loot grains from the storehouses of rich people by setting fire to their houses. Sometimes they got nothing except a savage delight but that did not stop them from committing the act. The blaze of fire turned the sun-scorched earth awfully dangerous place to live in. Valuables like gold and silver lost their worth and were considered useless. People wanted food, not ornaments. It is in fact hunger that determines the value of things. A man that knows no hunger may spend money on gems and jewellery but to ,a starving man these have no values. To him a handful of rice appears priceless. The situation appeared unbearable and the indifference of the Subadar had far exceeded the limits of inhumanity. So, some residents of Cuttack swore to avenge the callousness of the Subadar by setting fire to his house.

The readers might not have forgotten uncle Mayadhara, a member of Raghunath's gang, and the shrewdest of the lot. The man had his eyes set on Rasakala. But Raghunatha had left Rasakala at the palace in Kujanga. Mayadhara went to the palace and tried to persuade guards of the queen's wing of the palace to let him abduct the girl. But everyone at the palace including the guards had grown fond of Rasakala and refused to come under the influence of Mayadhara. Soon after the news of the wedding of Rasakala and Raghunath to be held spread about everywhere and the guards could not summon the courage to bring the matter to the notice of the king. Nor did Mayadhara dare seek the king's help to fulfill his desire. The disappointed and vengeful fellow hatched a conspiracy to get Raghunath into some serious trouble. As his mind was preoccupied with evil designs, Mayadhara was not able to pay proper attention to the appointed task of carrying out burglaries. The other dacoits in the gang, sensing something amiss in his behaviour tried to avoid him. There was no alternative for Mayadhar but to inform the Subadar of the involvement of Raghunath in the burglary at Navagram and get him arrested.

It has already been mentioned that the hot month of *Baisakha*, that aggravated the tyranny of the famine reigned over the land. On that fearful new-moon night of *Baisakha* Mayadhara sat before the Subadar in a room in the villa of Lalbagh and gave him details of the burglary that had taken place in Navagram. As he heard the shocking, hair-raising tale of the raid, the Subadar trembled in fury. In a fit of rage he vowed to devour Raghunath alive as soon as the latter came into his clutches.

In the end, the Subadar agreed with Mayadhar that the death of Choudhury could be duly avenged only if Raghunath and Kalavati were captured and put behind the bars, and sent to the scaffold. It must be mentioned here that Mayadhar had not for once spoken about his own involvement in the burglary. He informed the Subadar that one of the dacoits had told him secretly all these things.

Evil men think alike. The Subadar felt satisfied after the plan was made. He asked Mayadhar to spend the night in the villa. Mayadhar agreed gladly, feeling honoured by the Subadar's suggestion. Just then the hall in the front section of the villa burst into flames. The screams of people and the loud crackling of burning bamboos filled the atmosphere and shook even the inner wing of the villa. The panic-stricken Subadar and Mayadhar tried to escape through the main door of the villa but immediately closed the door frightened at the sight of the furious mob that waited outside armed with staves and sticks to attack them.

The loud screams for help that rose from the inner wing of the villa seemed to cleave the sky. The Subadar and Mayadhar escaped through the windows of the apartments of the inner wing along with the ladies. The Subadar and the ladies crossed the river Mahanadi and hid inside the forest of Naraz. But unfortunately Mayadhar was drowned in the river while trying to swim across it. His death proved that anyone that plans to do harm to others is never spared.

**

CHAPTER – 39

Peace At Last

Eventually, the difficult summer months departed and the rains arrived. The torrential showers mitigated the oppressive heat and the fatal forces of the famine too came under control. A large number of people in Orissa had fallen prey to the famine and the few lucky survivors set about tilling their land. They no longer needed help and relief.

"Brother Raghunath, the rains have cooled the earth. You too should rest from the hard work and enjoy some peace." Kalavati said solicitously one day as both of them sat discussing recent incidents. Indeed, after passing through the tough times and after the exhausting work, such words of concern sounded very sweet. Raghunath agreed and taking Kalavati with him set out for the palace in Kujanga the king's advice.

People from several famine-affected regions of the kingdom had sent applications to the residence of Duman Sardar, where he had set up a temporary office after the Subadar's courtroom at the villa of Lalbagh was closed. Duman Sardar had sent the whole bunch of applications to the Bhonsla of Nagpur. An officer was sent to take stock of the situation at Orissa. By the time the officer reached there rhe rainy season had arrived and people had somehow managed to rebuild their lives and make a fresh start.The readers might find it funny that the authorities finally took sought to intervene at time when life was slowly returning to normal. Doesn't it appear ridiculous that a government official pays a visit to a famine-affected region after the calamity is over? To the statesmen at the helm of affairs such matters might appear trifling and funny. How many of those that lie in the cradle of happiness care to sympathise with who suffer?

The officer found that very few people had survived the tyranny of the famine; the villages had come to resemble desolate graveyards. He prepared a report after assessing the situation and suggested that a selfish and heartless man like Sambhujee Ganesh be dismissed immediately from the post of Subadar. We know that the people had already pronounced their judgment on the Subadar; the man was forced out of his palace and was exiled. The report that was sent to the Bhonsla of Nagpur was no more than an official formality.

Raghunath came to the palace in Kujanga accompanied by Kalavati. With the permission of the king he sent for the monks, Hanuman Das and Giridhari Das. Queen Kalavati a ceremonial feast to be thrown. The king and the monks gladly approved of the proposal and it was decided that it should be held on the isle of Nandikeshwari. After the date was fixed the monks, Duman Sardar and Raghunath set about making the necessary arrangements for the feast.

The king, after the discussion was over, paid visit a to the inner wing of the palace. The chief queen, on learning from the king of the grand feast, expressed a desire to attend it. Kalavati listened to the conversation between the king and the chief queen. "Raghunath had given his consent to marry Rasakala. How about solemnizing the marriage on the day of the feast? She suggested.

Everyone heartily approved of the idea. The king, the chief queen and other royal ladies of the palace gladly agreed with Kalavati, and the inner wing of the palace was filled with the auspicious sounds of the ululation and the sound of conches blowing. Kalavatyi was overjoyed at the thought of the wedding of Rasakala whom she loved more than her life. She had little doubt that her marriage with Raghunath would guarantee a happy future for Rasakala. She locked her arms, which were tender and smooth like lotus-stems, around Rasakala's neck and kissed her cheeks in deep affection. Rasakala's soft heart melted at this gesture of love and tears wilted down her lotus-like lovely eyes.

Our existence in this world is surrounded by mystery.. No one can predict what incidents will occur here at what point in our life. Every moment in the duration between our birth and death is controlled by God Almighty, who always wishes us well. One that is spiritually awakened to understand this deep in his heart will enjoy the divine bliss in this world that is otherwise a difficult place to live in.

The isle of Nadikeshwri that we see now was twice its present size in those days, and was therefore the most ideal site for the grand feast. The two monks, Raghunath, Duman Sardar, Bahabalindra and other dacoits occupied themselves with making arrangements for the grand feast while the king, the chief queen, Kalavati and the royal ladies spervised Rasakala's wedding. It was decided that all things required for the wedding would be carried to the isle on the day of the feast.

***

CHAPTER-40

The Wedding and
the Immersion

It was the second of the bright lunar fortnight in the month of Asadha. It was that auspicious day on which the Car Festival of Lord Jagannath is observed at the holy land of Puri. Millions of people from different parts of India, not caring for hunger and thirst, and enduring untold hardship arrived at Puri to witness the Great Lord in the chariot and experience great spiritual bliss. The huge crowd that gathered there felt gratified beyond measure having gained a glimpse of the open round eyes of The Lord that seemed to shower a divine bliss upon them. It is one of the most auspicious days for the Hindus.

The raging flames of famine had died down. A mood of festivity permeated the air. The arrangements for the grand feast at the isle of Nandikeshwari were made for giving respite to people who had worked tirelessly during the famine. The celebration in a way heralded a future that promised peace and happiness.

The isle of Nandikeshwari was transformed beyond recognition. The flowers, festoons and other kinds of decorations made it so beautiful that it seemed to lure people, as if welcoming them to participate in the grand ceremony. The work of cleaning and beautification that went on for the last eight days had so changed its look that the desolate isle appeared lovelier than many well-maintained villages and towns. The work of transporting the provision and other items required for the feast and the wedding ceremony had begun a week before. A gigantic shed, over which gorgeous canopies were hung, was built in the middle of the isle. It was so large and so spacious that ten thousand men could hve sat there comfortably at a time. Besides this huge shed, a number of smaller canopied sheds were built. These lay scattered from one end of the isle to the other. People sat in groups in those sheds and were busy playing various indoor games; they sang and danced, and made merry. There was a row of thatched houses with roofs sloping towards the western border of the isle. Fire burnt in huge cooking-hearths there and cooks prepared several kinds of dishes and sweetmeats.

It was not possible to put an exact figure on people had assembled on that day on the isle of Nandikeshwari. It simply overflowed with people. The monks, Hanuman Das and Giridhari Das, having taken bath and offered worship to Goddess *Annapurna*, supervised the cooking. In the middle of the large shed the king of Kujanga, Raghunath, Duman Sardar and many important persons sat discussing different subject. Colourful flags fluttered merrily on wooden posts.

In the westerly direction of the isle, at a short distance from the sheds separate enclosures with colourful awnings were made for the ladies. The chief queen, Kalavati, and many others sat there exchanging pleasantries. They teased Rasakala talking about her married life and her happy future with Raghunath. The merriment and the jokes seemed to amuse even the sands and stones of the isle.

The arrangements for cooking complete, the two

monks walked towards the place under the big shed where the king was seated. The king got up and received them respectfully. He offered his own seat to the monks and humbly sat down before them. He informed them how peace and normalcy were returning slowly to the land and those that had survived the disaster were now engaged in farming once more. He told the monks that people were gradually coping with the aftermath of the famine. The monks were greatly pleased on learning all this from the king.

It was midday. From the ladies' tent Kalavati came out and walked down to the shed where the king and the monks were busy discussing the affairs of state. She stood, with her palms joined and made her humble submission.

" His Majesty! We are fortunate that God has granted us this great opportunity to get together here on this auspicious day. We are extremely happy that the calamity has retreated. We know how Raghunath has succeeded in saving thousands and thousands of lives risking his own life on many occasions. He is our saviour. Hence we must see to it that not even the slightest trace of dissatisfaction remains in his mind. He had promised to accept Rasakala as his wife. If His Majesty gives us his permission we shall bring Rasakala here and get the marriage solemnized."

Kalavati's proposal was heartily approved. Bahab-alindra and Baliarsingh who stood nearby let out a loud cry of joy "Glory to Lord Mahaveer" which reverberated through the sky and, the next moment, groups of musicians played on different musical instruments. The sound of the beating of drums, the jangle of the cymbals, the music of the pipes that filled the air announced the beginning of the great revelry. The auspicious sound of ululation rising from the ladies' tent and the sound of the conches blowing joined the music. The isle of Nandikeshwari floated as it were in a sea of joy and the hearts of everyone present there were filled with the nectar-sweet emotions of love.

The ladies decked Rasakala in bridal apparel. Raghunath too was made to wear the groom's outfit. The monks walked him to the decorated alter chanting sacred mantras. The ladies led Rasakala there and sat her by Raghunath. Amidst the melodious notes of different musical instruments that were being played by the orchestra, the auspicious ululation of the ladies and blowing of conches, and the chanting of the *slokas* by the monks the marriage of Raghunath and Raskala was solemnized.

The grand feast began. Thousands of people sat from one end of the isle to the other in places of their choice. Leaf-plates were placed in front of them and varieties of delicious dishes and sweetmeats were served. Everyone ate to their hearts' content. The day was about to end by the time the feast was over. Some sat in groups and started singing songs praising Lord Krishna..

Kalavati ate nothing. She had made a religious vow which would be completed that day. She kept a fast and said that she would eat only some fruit in the evening, if necessary. She went to meet Rasakala, and wept bitterly resting her head on Rasakala's shoulder. She advised her to win Raghunath's heart and live happily with him. Before she departed from her, Kalavati fondly kissed Rasakala's forehead. She took leave of the newly-wed bride and came to Raghunath who was sitting alone absorbed in the happy thoughts of his future life with Rasakala. Kalavati took Raghunath's hand in her own and said earnestly: " Dear brother, from now on Rasakala is your responsibility. It was she who always helped to cool the eternally burning flames of grief in my heart. If you fulfill her life with your love and keep her happy, my aching heart will experience eternal peace." Raghunath assured her that he would try his best to fulfill her wish and make Rasakala happy at all costs.

Kalavati felt relieved after listening to the reassuring and kind words of Raghunath. Leaving Raghunath to ponder over the new developments that had taken place in his life she walked towards the river to take her evening bath.

Kalavati stepped into the river. She moved deeper and deeper into the stream till the water reached her waist and finally her throat. Kalavati stood in that neck-deep water for some moments, her eyes travelling in all directions, and finally looked up at the sky. She joined her palms together offering up prayers to God and sank into the water.

Everyone watched anxiously, expecting her to emerge from the water the next moment but she did not come out.

Pandemonium broke out. There was a loud uproar and in no time the news that the queen had drowned in the river spread in all directions.

The tragic incident that occurred even before while they were still in a festive mood had a devastating impact on the minds of the people.

Kalavati was looked upon with great respect and people treated her as a queen. A search team was sent immediately and the rescue operation continued late into the night. Large nets were thrown into the water but Kalavati's body couldn't be traced.

Everyone was left stunned.

The crowd that had gathered there to celebrate the marriage ceremony, returned with heavy hearts.

CHAPTER-41

The Gift of Love

The sorrow that Raghunath and Rasakala experienced at the self-willed death of Kalavathi was beyond words. But Time is a great healer and the wound inflicted by the loss of Kalavathi too healed considerably with the passage of time. One day they sat reminiscing about Kalavathi in the garden adjoing the house. The readers might not have forgotten that it was in this garden that one day in the past Kalavathi and Raghunath had opened their hearts to each other.

"Dear, it was at this place Kalavati had made me promise that I must marry you, and had given me a tiny gold casket. She had asked me to open it only after our marriage. I shall open it if you permit me." Raghunath said fondly. Raghunath took out the gold casket from the waist-fold of his clothes and opened it carefully. There was a large diamond in that casket and under it lay a piece of folded paper. Something was written on it in Kalavathi's own hand. Curiosity urged him to read it, and as he began to read he was surprised to notice that the letter was addressed to him. Raghunath began reading the letter and Rasakala resting her head on Raghunath's shoulder listened.

"Brother,

The world is a strange place. No place could be more pleasant than this world if you conduct yourself with prudence. But one false step and this beautiful world turns into a dangerous forest. In such a precarious place it is only pure love that sustains us and makes our lives worth living. Once you understand what pure and unconditional love means, you can, by the will of God, spread the message of love in this difficult place. But you must have a wife to realize the bliss of pure, unselfish love.

God is the creator of this world; He reigns over it. The divine spirit is immanent in everything that we see here. It is our most important duty to surrender to Him. This absolute surrender will help us redeem our souls. I hope you will make your life a worthy one in this manner.

God has sent our souls to this earth for a temporary stay. I understand that a world ridden with perversion is the most unwholesome place of sojourn for the soul. The soul can return to its permanent abode, which means a total merging in God, only if one is able to drive away all depraved desires while living here, love God and completely give oneself up to His will. Hence, love is the only means of attaining redemption. Everything in this world thrives on love.

I shall put an end to my life once my vow is fulfilled. You won't be able to know when I am going to do that. My heart will find peace if you marry Rasakala and make her happy. May God shower all His blessing on both of you. What else? I had preserved this diamond with the utmost care. This is a 'gift of love' from me to Rasakala on her marriage. You must not grieve my departure from this world. One lives peacefully in the other world if he or she is remembered with love. I shall cite a *sloka* from the sacred *Bhagabat* before I conclude. Ask Rasakala to remember it all her life and act upon it.

"She that sees Lord Hari in her husband

And like Goddess Lakshmi

Worships and serves him

Derives the joys of Heaven on this earth,

Because her husband, too,

Like Hari keeps Lakshmi amused in Heaven

Fills her life with all the love of his heart."

What more is there to say?   Farewell.

Affectionately yours

BIBASINI

Rasakala could not control herself and burst into tears. She cried fitfully entwining her arms around her husband's neck. Raghunath took her in his arms and turned her face to him, lifting her chin. " Dear, please don't cry. No amount of tears could bring her back. She had chosen to leave this world and she had no regrets. Now we must live a worthy life following her advice so that we too should have no regrets when the time to bid farewell to this world arrives."

****

Black Eagle Books

www.blackeaglebooks.org
info@blackeaglebooks.org

Black Eagle Books, an independent publisher, was founded
as a nonprofit organization in April, 2019. It is our mission
to connect and engage the Indian diaspora and the world at
large with the best of works of world literature published on
a collaborative platform, with special emphasis on
foregrounding Contemporary Classics and New Writing.

* 9 7 8 1 6 4 5 6 0 5 1 8 8 *